DESPERATE MEN

FuzionPress

DESPERATE MEN

Paul Vernon Bruce

First Printing: July 2025
First Edition

Paperback ISBN: 978-1-955541-66-4
eBook ISBN: 978-1-955541-68-8
Hardcover ISBN: 978-1-955541-67-1
LCCN: Pending

Interior and cover design by Ann Aubitz

Published by FuzionPress
1250 E 115th Street
Burnsville, MN 55337
Fuzionpress.com
612-781-2815

Chapter 1

CALVIN STEELE TAPPEN IV looked over at his father, Calvin Steele Tappen III, and said,

"What are you saying, dad? We're out of money?"

"Not *we're* out of money. I'm out of money. You never had any."

Calvin Steele Tappen IV, who went by the nickname C4, ignored the pointed slight. The real topic was too interesting to get lost in those weeds.

"How could that happen?"

"Well, I've had a lot of hands in my pockets over many years, including yours. Remember, I lost half of everything when I divorced your mother to marry Susie Floosie, and then when Susie divorced me, I lost half of that remaining half. Then I hit the mandatory retirement age from my law firm, and there wasn't much partnership interest left after the two divorces. So, I hung out my own shingle and have kept the bills paid, but my work is slowing down because my clients are dying off. Besides, I just turned 68 and really don't care to work all that hard anymore. And now that you're pushing 40, I had hoped you'd be on your own by now. You're not exactly helping my finances."

C4 just shrugged. "You know I've had a tough go of it - I had hoped to be running my own business by now, but things just never lined up."

C4 also knew that his dad had been fooling around with an endless line of younger women well before Susie had trapped him into divorcing C4's mother. He also knew that his dad had a long history of pretty shady legal practices that had not warmed the hearts of his old law firm colleagues. Hence, he was left to absorb the full effect of the firm's mandatory, though generally negotiable, retirement age. C4 was interrupted in his thoughts because unfortunately, his dad was still talking.

"Here's what never lined up. You barely got through college but somehow got a decent score on your LSAT. But even at that, only because I was an alum did you get into law school. Then you managed to get thrown out for cheating. Since then, it's been some odd jobs, but mostly my largess that has enabled your lifestyle - ski trips, gambling junkets to Vegas, boating, and all the girls, girls, girls that you seem to collect. In fact, surrounding yourself with clueless women seems to be your only real skill. Don't any of them have any money?"

"Well, you're the one who taught me that. You and Susie Floosie."

"Yes, she was a big part of my downfall. I thought I was making a decent trade. Your mother was sick of me, and Susan was right there in my law office, trying to catch a lawyer. I thought she was from a rich ranching family. Remember, the ranch she took me to for the weekend was just some shirt-tail relative's and while they were rich, she wasn't. Her own family had nothing but 40 acres, a trailer house, a few cows, and a broken-down horse. All about 100 miles southwest of here. I found out later her dad mostly just drank, and her mom waited tables at a small diner in a small town near where they lived. Never met them until after we were married. Their only accomplishment was bearing a cute, manipulative daughter. In fact, I think her brother is still in prison. Great family.

"She knocked me off my feet - late middle-aged guy getting chased by a 20-something chick with a cute smile and big boobs. Turns out even those were fake. Not sure who paid for them. Hardly even got to see them once we were back from our Elvis wedding in Las Vegas."

This was the point in the story where C4 never mentioned the truth. He'd seen Susie's boobs plenty. They had shared a lot of intimate moments. Apparently marrying for money and sleeping with the young, handsome son of the money was always a part of her plan. Susan P. Regent. Old family name, wrong branch of the family. C4 was always amused by the irony. He and his dad had both been screwed by the same woman. She'd always made C4 pick up the check for their amusement time - Vegas, Vail, Virgin Islands, even some places that didn't start with V. She said it would look funny if she had to ask her "husband" for money. After all, Susie was supposed to be independently wealthy. Wanted to make it look like she was off on her own dime with her own friends. So C4 had to beg his dad for money to spend vacation and sack time with his stepmother.

In a few years, Susie was gone, living in Miami with some new guy, and Calvin the third, who went by the nickname CT, was twice broke and C4 was cast to the side, just like his father.

Whenever C4 thought more than a few minutes about the whole situation he got a headache, so he got up and poured himself a shot of single malt scotch. Downed that, then poured another.

CT continued, "So, when are you going to get a job and start pitching in? I've been carrying you on my payroll for years. I honestly can't say where we went wrong. Your mother and I tried to raise you right and your older sisters turned out just fine."

C4 smiled a bit to himself. Instead of listening to his parents, he'd taken on his dad's womanizing and spending habits as his own, and now that lifestyle wasn't helping either of them.

"As a matter of fact, I've got a money-making gig this week. Taking old man Baker to his lake place in Minnesota. Helping him check on things, clear some snow, do some ice fishing. Usual stuff."

"And what does he pay you for that?"

"Couple hundred. Cash. Doesn't last long, but he pays for everything on the trip and he's not bad company. Good story teller. Good food. Good scotch. Good fishing, usually."

"So, if you had 50 of those guys you could almost support yourself?"

C4 smiled to himself again. Poured his third scotch. If this conversation followed the usual pattern, his dad would give up soon and C4 could kill the rest of the afternoon sleeping off the scotch, then go find some entertainment for the night. He would make the rounds of his favorite bars and could usually find an all-night party or poker game, even here in Bismarck. It really was a capital city.

To C4's chagrin, however, CT was now like a dog on a scent. He was not going to quit this time.

"Go easy on the scotch. We need to finish this conversation. I am down to my last few thousand dollars and my next income is my Social Security check, and that's two weeks out."

C4 looked at his dad. Was the well really dry? This was different. C4's thoughts turned desperate. He certainly wasn't a good enough poker player to support himself, either here or in Vegas. And he had burned all the bridges in this town or even the state to get a decent job. He either owed money to or had slept with the wives or girlfriends of every businessman he knew. Sometimes both. Over the past few years, he'd even fooled around with many of their daughters.

More importantly, he actually had no real skills. He had had a couple of sales jobs with car or furniture dealerships, and while he had a bit of a gift for sales, they were looking for people who showed up for work every day and didn't drink between customers. Or feel up the female staff when he got them alone in a hallway.

This was turning into a real problem. And the scotch wasn't helping. Maybe if he went to Minneapolis or Denver or some other city where he wasn't so well known he could try a fresh start.

Somewhere in the back of his mind he realized his dad was still talking.

"So old man Baker only gives you a couple hundred a trip? He's worth millions and I don't mean two or three."

Suddenly a light bulb came on in C4's head. It was dim, but it was a light bulb.

"Dad, you handle old man Baker's estate planning stuff, right?"

"I sure do. Far and away my richest customer."

"Who does he leave all that money to?"

"To his two kids."

"In all the time we've spent together, I've hardly heard him mention any kids."

"Apparently, they went away to college and never came back. I think they're both on the east coast somewhere. I have their contact info in his file."

"And what are the actual assets?"

"Mostly real estate. His house here in Bismarck, his lake cabin in Minnesota…."

C4 interrupted his dad. "That's no cabin, dad. It's a pretty nice home on a really nice lake."

"Hmm… Also quite a bit of dirt."

"Dirt?"

"Yup. Farmland and ranchland all over North Dakota. At least a dozen different locations."

"Is it all paid for?"

"Oh, yeah, it's all debt free. Titles are free and clear."

"Do you think the kids have any idea of the extent of his holdings?"

"I don't know, but I'd guess probably not. Where are you headed with this?"

"In a minute. One more question. Does he have any favorite charities?"

"I know he never misses church. Also, he gives a few dollars to his alma mater, but not that much - the ag school in Fargo, the one that we who were educated at the University in Grand Forks treat with such disdain. Other than that, he has never mentioned any. And I do routinely bring it up in my estate planning work with every client. Most wealthy people like to leave some kind of legacy."

"So, he's going to leave everything to two ungrateful kids, ignoring his favorite charities?"

"That's the way it's structured now. Again, what are you thinking?"

"Ok. If you don't like what I say next, then this conversation never happened. Right?"

"Sure."

"What if you refocused part of his legacy to his church, or NDSU, and then set it up in a way that leaves you in charge of managing it, say to the end of his life. On $5 million your management fee could easily be $50,000, which, when added to your Social Security, would give you enough to live. That part is easy, I would think. In fact, you'd be doing him a service, letting him step down from the active management of at least a part of his empire and having you in charge if he becomes infirm or dies. It's almost your legal duty, with no one else in any position to take that over."

CT offered no objection to that concept, rather just staring thoughtfully at his son, so C4 forged ahead.

"The next item is a little dicier. What if that trust or whatever, allowed you to take it over and manage it solely at your own discretion?"

At that suggestion, CT cringed visibly, so C4 tried to soften his message a bit.

"Just hear me out. You really need some money, given the tough breaks you've had, and your age. You've been a diligent attorney to him for decades. And do you really want large sums to go to the ungrateful, unknowing kids or that cow college in Fargo? Doesn't have to be much, just enough to put us - I mean you - on a cushioned ride out to the great beyond."

CT looked really uncomfortable. But eventually he spoke. C4 was enough of a salesman to stop talking and wait for the response, then, if necessary 'overcome any objections.'

"I have already set up a trust to receive it all, with his daughter as the trustee. And I have done some really tough legal work for him over the years. Helped close some deals some attorneys might call questionable."

C4 waited again, seeing his plan start to soak into his dad's brain. He fought off the urge to pour himself another scotch. This next phase might take some focus. He didn't have to wait long.

CT looked very thoughtful.

"I can certainly make the pitch to set me up as the trustee. Can't imagine his big city daughter has any idea where any of this farmland is or how best to manage or liquidate it. I can readily claim I stand a better chance of managing it well, or unwinding it slowly and profitably."

C4 could hardly control his glee. His dad was clearly getting on board. And once the assets were in his dad's pocket, it was a short trip to his own. He didn't want to push too hard, but he couldn't help asking the next question.

"I mentioned $5 million, what is the total value, in reality?"

CT looked at C4 for a long moment and then apparently decided it was ok to share the info. "As you know, real estate values go up and down, but I'd say it's pretty close to $25 million today."

C4 couldn't help himself. He walked over to the bar in his dad's office and poured himself another scotch. The silence was deafening. Which way was this going to go?

CT spoke next.

"I'm down to about a dozen clients total and Baker is the biggest by far. I make maybe $500 to $1,000 on each of the others per year, at most, unless one of their kids or grandkids gets thrown in jail. Then I can ring the cash register. But you wouldn't know anything about that would you?"

C4 smiled. "Point taken. And you always got me off."

"Sometimes it wasn't easy."

It took some refocusing for CT, since his real reason for going so easy on C4 was that he had endured a few scrapes of his own before he met a woman who convinced him to settle down. His knowledge of the law started from the wrong side, and his own father had let him twist in the wind a lot more than he had let C4.

While that thought revisited CT's aging brain, C4 had decided that he needed to cut off any discussion of his battles with the police and the courts. That path was absolutely counterproductive.

C4 had to control his desire to close the sale, while his dad considered his legal and moral obligations. Knowing CT was borderline destitute might move the bar a bit, but it had to have time to soak in.

Apparently, it was soaking in well because CT changed gears.

"When do you go to Minnesota with Mr. Baker again?"

"Next week. Monday morning, come back Friday."

"Good. Think about this. Very delicately probe him about the Minnesota place. Do his kids ever come to use it? Do they care about it all? Do they even know about it? Tell him how much you love it, and will miss going there when he is gone, God forbid."

"So, kind of head him towards leaving it to me?" C4 thought he was getting the idea.

"Yes, but he has to say it, not you, and you need to be overwhelmed at the suggestion if he does say it."

"Got it."

C4 was ecstatic. His dad was on board. At least for now. That became apparent as his father spoke again.

"If you had that, you could live there, or rent it out and generate some income. That alone would be enough to get you out of my pocket. I'm getting tired of footing all the bills for your condo. The house isn't income-producing for him, but it could be for you."

CT then went on, "And since it is January, I'll call him in for his annual estate review visit. In the meantime, I'll think about your idea of getting control of his trust. I'll make sure my list of his assets is current and ask about his house here and the lake place in Minnesota."

C4 nodded, his dad continued.

"I'll try to meet with him after your fishing trip. That will make him double back on thinking about the Minnesota property."

Again, C4 nodded. This was as much thinking as he had done in a long time, and he was getting tired. The three scotches weren't helping.

Chapter 2

WHEN C4 AWOKE IT WAS FULLY DARK and the clock beside his bed said 6:22. Was that morning or evening? He grabbed the remote and turned on the TV, just in time for the weather forecast. That didn't help. He'd have to pay more attention. Ok. Overnight lows then daytime highs. It must be evening. And he was hungry. Another clue.

He sat up a little too fast. Oh, yeah. The three scotches burned back into his memory, via his stomach. Then he actually started thinking. Was that conversation with his dad real? Think hard. It was, and he had an assignment. Talk to old man Baker about his lake house on this next trip. For the first time in a long time, C4 knew he had to focus on that task and if he did it well, and his dad did his tasks well, they would both be set for life. C4 had to raise his game to get this deal done. Maybe it would take a month, maybe six months, possibly even a year, but it was the only path they had to financial security. He looked at his phone to see if there were any messages or missed calls. The time and date popped up. Friday January 13th, 2023. Lots of winter left, unfortunately. A winter without much money, or any shot at getting any from his usual source, his dad. He needed some sort of short-term plan. He needed some money to impress Baker and some money to live on for as much as the rest of the year.

He looked more carefully at his phone. No missed calls or texts. That was almost always a good thing.

Since it was Friday evening, C4 needed to hit a bar and grab some food to go with his usual Friday evening scotch or three. Then once, for a change, he needed to find a poker game where he could actually win. He needed some cash in his money clip to live on day-to-day, but more importantly, to let old man Baker see that he was anything but destitute. The best way to impress a rich person was with money of your own. In fact, that was the only way C4 could think of to impress anyone, besides his boyish charm, which he used liberally, but it only seemed to work on women.

He'd head over to Mandan and hit one of the cowboy bars. They always drank better than they played poker, and they'd have weekly paychecks all cashed and ready. No scotch over there. Nobody trusted anybody who drank scotch. Just whiskey on the rocks, and the cheaper the better. Then the trick was to get back to Bismarck without getting beaten up. That had only happened once, but that was because C4 had used his winnings to buy drinks for the girlfriend of one of the cowboys, and that proved to be a bad combination. Apparently taking a guy's money at the poker table and then using it to try to seduce his girlfriend was bad form. Who knew?

In fact, as C4 thought some more, he wouldn't do that, partly because he needed the money. In fact, if he cleaned up at the table in Mandan, he'd head out to Dickinson and spend the night, to see if he could take some money in a similar fashion from the oil workers. They made a ton of money and some of them were happy to gamble it away. That would keep him out of sight of the cowboys until he got back to Bismarck on Sunday afternoon. He had a plan.

C4 rolled into the Missouri Breaks Bar and Grill a couple hours later, after a shower and shave, with an overnight bag packed and stowed in the back of his SUV. He parallel parked on a side street in the first spot in a row, so he could drive away quickly if that turned out to be necessary. He even left it in four wheel drive, just in case he had to leave really fast. No sense spinning helplessly if it came to that.

He stepped into the cowboy bar, shook off the cold and the little bit of snow that had fallen on him, and then went directly to the end of the bar.

"Coors tap and a burger and fries, with everything."

The bartender brought the beer and wrote down the order and walked it back to the kitchen.

The beer tasted good, and C4 enjoyed the moment. His eyes moved around the room. The bar ran along the east side of the room, and there were about 20 stools. A row of booths lined the opposite wall with a dozen tables set up diagonally in between. The place was almost full.

Tonight, there were the usual tables and booths of families, now clearing out, some college-aged kids, likely home on break and enjoying reuniting with old friends. And of course, a few tables of cowboys - hats, boots and all, some with girls fawning over them. C4 looked them over carefully, trying to see if he knew any of them from anywhere, including prior poker games. He hadn't played in Mandan for quite a while, but poker players tended to have long memories. No one looked familiar, but C4's memory, on the other hand, due to excessive alcohol consumption, was not great short- or long-term. Tonight would be different. Somewhat sober would have to do.

"Here's your burger. Condiments are right there. Need another beer?"

"Thanks, sure. I'll take one more."

The bartender came back with another Coors, and without looking up, C4 asked his question.

"Poker game upstairs tonight?"

The bartender moved down the bar a bit, and spoke with his back partly turned to C4.

"Yup. 10:00. $50 ante. $25 minimum bets."

"Can I get in?"

"Yup. Just you and one of the family dads over there, who will come back. He plans to forget his gloves. And the three cowboys at that long table over there. At least one or two ranchers will come in in a little bit, too."

C4 just nodded.

While casinos were now prevalent, a lot of serious players still liked the private games. No house share, no risk of IRS oversight. While C4 didn't have the capital to play in the high stakes games that ran in a few spots around town, a good night at a game like this could net him as much as a thousand dollars, and right now that would be enough to get him started.

So, he just sat back and enjoyed his meal, added one more beer, watched the basketball game on the big screen TV and the people. Watched them come and go, eat and interact with each other. Fascinating stuff.

Finally, about a quarter to 10, he went to the restroom, then headed up the stairs in the back of the bar.

The poker table was set for eight. There was a bar on one side of the room, with a sleepy looking bartender, who would walk drinks to the table as they were ordered. By ones and twos, the other players came up the stairs and looked the setting over. C4 ordered and paid for a double Jim Beam. He would have to make it last, as he was getting really low on cash. A guy came in who C4 took to be the dealer, and that proved correct, as he took control of the room and the people in it.

"Good evening gentlemen, I'm your host. Pick a spot at the table unless you want to draw for spots."

"I do,"

Said a big, middle-aged man from the bar. This must be one of the ranchers whom the bartender said was coming in.

"I don't want these young cowhands sitting next to each other. Seen 'em cheat and then share the winnings."

C4 didn't know the man, but he did make a point. If anyone was going to cheat, C4 wanted to be sure it was him.

"Ok. Let's cut cards until we get people in their spots. Before we get any further, you play until you're out of money or 4:00 a.m. Got it?"

They all nodded.

"Oh, and if you do run out of money, any markers are between the players. The house has no financial role in this game. We're just providing the space and me as the dealer. Tips are accepted."

He finished with a smile.

They all nodded again. They all looked serious except for the three young cowhands who seemed to enjoy taking part in such an adult activity.

By 10:15 they were all seated, drinks in hand. The dealer called out the rules again, and then dealt everyone their starting cards. By midnight, two men had left the game, both leaving their contribution on the table. An hour later, another cowboy left, and at that time C4 was up over $500. The cards had been good to him and he'd stayed sober enough to play them well.

He continued to make more than he lost and by 3:00 a.m., he was up almost $1,000. One of the other three remaining players was down to about $200, so C4 decided to see if he could cut him out. For the first time in the game, he looked at his cards and saw nothing, but rather than fold, he stayed in. More cards, more bets, until the guy he had targeted had no way to stay in without borrowing money. There were no takers, so he left, his money staying on the table. Mission accomplished, C4 then had to contemplate whether to fold and take his loss, or keep up the bluff. He decided to stay in. With all the cards for the hand now dealt out, C4 raised $100. One of the other men folded, and now the hand was down to C4 and one other player. The other player, one of the youngest cowboys, who had been as lucky as C4 had ever seen at a poker table in one night, called C4 and raised another $50. C4 called. The cowboy folded. C4 had won his one bluff of the night. And no one would ever know it was a bluff. He was now up about $1,500 and really wanted to end the night. The young cowboy who had just folded, said, "That's it for me. Anybody mind if I walk out with $80? The game is too rich for me now."

C4 and the only other remaining player both nodded. C4 looked over and the other player - the dad who had forgotten his gloves - had about the same amount of money as C4, so he said,

"I can play another hour, or I'm happy to call it a night."

His opponent studied the situation. Looked at C4's stack. Looked at his own. Looked at his watch. Looked at the bartender who was pretty much asleep. Looked at the dealer. C4's eyes followed his opponent's eyes around the room. Finally, he said.

"I'm good. No need to skin the one sheep left."

And he laughed.

"Besides, he's played his one bluff for the night."

And he winked at C4, then stood up.

C4 laughed but said nothing. The two men cashed out and headed down the stairs. C4 desperately wanted to ask him how he knew that last hand was a bluff, but knew better, so left it alone.

Back down through the empty bar, the dealer let them out the side door, right next to C4's SUV, which he started up and drove once around town to be sure he wasn't being followed, then headed to the west I-94 ramp to get to Dickinson. While the $1,500 and change in his pocket wasn't a ton of money, it was a lot to be carrying around at 3:00 a.m. in a deserted town. Especially if one of his earlier tablemates was a sore loser. If someone was lying in wait for him, they'd be expecting him to be headed back to Bismarck. Interesting how self-preservation is front of mind, no matter how you earn a living.

An uneventful hour and a half later, C4 checked into the Holiday Inn Express in Dickinson, and had no trouble falling asleep.

The only problem he'd encountered was that his credit card was declined at check in, forcing him to leave $400 cash with the night clerk in exchange for two nights in a room on the first floor. He liked the first floor in case he needed to make a hasty escape. He wasn't sure why that might be necessary, but you never knew what might happen. Years of a dodgy lifestyle taught one some interesting things.

The next time C4 woke up, there was a sliver of bright daylight creating a white line across the dark motel room. C4 looked at the clock which said 1:12. This time it was obvious that it had to be afternoon, not morning. After a quick, highly necessary trip to the bathroom, C4 laid back down on the bed and turned on the TV. Time for some college basketball. An hour or so later, he woke up again, apparently, he had needed more sleep.

Now he was hungry. And he knew he had to find a poker game. He was less familiar here than in Bismarck and Mandan, so he had to do a little thinking. He had a number of acquaintances in Dickinson, but he was never quite sure which ones he was on good terms with. So many questionable business deals, beautiful wives, girlfriends and/or daughters, poker games where he may have cheated a bit, unpaid sports bets, it all ran together. Maybe he should have kept notes.

C4 jumped into his SUV on that bright brisk day, drove by the McDonald's and over the highway to Wendy's. Even in his cash-strapped situation, a guy had to have some standards. He enjoyed his burger while he sat and contemplated his next move. The place was hopping on this Saturday afternoon, and C4 enjoyed watching the people come and go. Most likely all of them working for a paycheck and enjoying their Saturday off by running errands and spending the money they had spent all week earning. That was not for C4. Life had to be more interesting than that.

He had a couple of favorite night spots in Dickinson, and he tried hard to remember if he had an outstanding tab at either of them, or if his last departure had been at the suggestion of the manager. This much thinking was giving him a headache, so he refilled his Coke and tried to think some more as he walked back out to his SUV, putting on his sunglasses to reduce the bright glare of the sun on the pure white snow. He drove back to his hotel room and tried to plan his night. He knew he had to think before he started drinking.

He'd better avoid both his favorite spots. There was another highly questionable place a few miles out of town, where he knew he could find the game he needed, and where he would not be likely to meet any of the fine upstanding citizens of Dickinson.

After another nap and a shower and shave, C4 was ready to see if he could add to his bankroll. He pulled into the gravel parking lot of the Oilpatch Bar. No pretense of a grill, this was just a bar. It was just after 9:00 p.m. and the parking lot was pretty full, but he was able to find a spot where he could drive straight out with having to back up. Just in case. As always. He once again left the transmission in 4-wheel drive in case he had to take a short cut.

Inside, the place was noisy and even darker than the parking lot outside. He stood inside the door for a moment, figuring out where to start his journey toward a poker game, then worked his way to the end of the bar. There was a small, slightly raised stage in a far corner where two cowboys with guitars and scraggly beards, a drummer who appeared to be high on something, and an overweight keyboard dude were doing their best impression of Merle Haggard. It was good Merle was not here.

As the bartender approached, C4 simply said,

"Coors Light."

"Tap or Bottle?"

"Tap."

The bartender poured the pint and walked it back. C4 put a $5 bill on the bar, and said, "Keep it."

"The Coors is 6. Nice try."

C4 smiled.

"Sorry," and peeled off another 5. "Now, keep it."

The bartender took the other $5 with no expression and turned his back to C4 to tend to his other customers.

In a place like this, C4 always started with a beer, because drinking it slowly took the form of a meal and it allowed him to case the place while he drank it. The customers were almost exclusively male, with the exception of a few middle-aged females. Apparently, this was not a place for a young man to take a date. He worked on his beer and noted a lot of cash on the various tables. That was a good sign. Maybe some of that would be his before he left for the night.

When the bartender came back to check on him, C4 nodded to the wordless question of a refill, and then asked,

"Anybody play poker here?"

"Who's askin'?"

"Just me. A guy who likes to play."

"Let me check."

A few minutes later a huge guy worked his way down the bar. At least six-and-a-half feet tall, well over 300 pounds, with a flannel shirt, a vest, and the greasiest hair C4 had ever seen.

"I'm Oilpatch. You want to play some poker?"

"Yup."

"You a cop or with the IRS or something?"

"No, just looking for a poker game."

Oilpatch stared at him for a few long seconds, then pointed to the corner opposite the stage and said,

"That door at 11 p.m. And if you're a cop they'll never find your body. Got it?"

"Absolutely."

Apparently, this was a place where words were used very sparingly, but with maximum effect.

C4 checked his watch. A little after 10:00. The band took a break, but the noise didn't abate all that much. It was a packed bar, with some pool tables, foosball tables, and a lot of people just sitting at tables, chatting. When the bartender looked his way, C4 signaled for another beer. After this he'd switch to whiskey on the rocks. That should limit his bathroom breaks while playing poker.

When the beer came, C4 ordered some chicken wings from the limited appetizer menu. In fact, that was the entire menu.

C4 was happy to sit at the end of the bar and just watch the people who came, went, drank, danced a little, enjoyed a Saturday evening. In North Dakota. In the dead of winter. Somehow, he and his old man had to turn the Baker fortune their way. Then he could look for poker games in Florida or Texas or someplace warmer than this.

The wings arrived, and he let them cool a bit before he picked one up. As he suspected, they looked and smelled better than they tasted. Oh, well. He slowly ate the half-dozen wings and washed each bite down with a swig of beer. The band had restarted, this time doing some Glen Campbell and other country hits, mixing fast and slow, and as the drinks took their magic effect on the crowd, the dance floor became busier. C4 enjoyed this, especially in these roughneck places. It would just be a matter of time before the crowded dance floor led to some kind of fight. Maybe he should have gone to dental school instead of law school. People seemed to like having teeth and this kind of place generally led to the opposite. He could have just left a card for tooth replacement at every place like this and he'd be set.

On the other hand, that would be a regular job, and C4 knew he wasn't cut out for that. He needed even easier ways to separate people from their money. And that was the Baker Plan. That was how it was taking shape in his oddly clear mind. He and his dad just had to do whatever they could to convince old man Baker to turn control of his fortune over to CT. And from CT it would easily go to C4, first through continual harassment (what his dad called begging), and ultimately inheritance. He knew his dad was too old and tired to put up enough resistance to keep C4's hand out of the cookie jar. Then his dad would die and the Baker fortune, or at least part of it would be his. Then it was Easy Street forever. This was the best plan ever. He just needed a little questionable legal work from his dad and then for a couple of old men to die.

"You going back?"

The bartender was right next to him, nodding toward the mystery door.

"Absolutely. Is there a bartender back there?"

"Yup."

C4 threw a couple of $20s on the bar and smiled.

"That enough this time?"

"It is. Thanks."

C4 finished off his beer and headed back, through the door, for the next phase of funding his retirement plan. Not bad for someone not yet 40 years old.

Chapter 3

THE POKER ROOM WAS OBVIOUSLY a storage room with boxes and crates lining the walls and a poker table and chairs in the middle. The bar was two crates stacked up with an old door stretched across them, and the bartender looked to also be the bouncer. A bottle each of whiskey, vodka, and tequila topped the bar, and C4 wouldn't have bet much that there was any ice available.

There were already four other people in the room, besides the bartender. One of the men was already seated at the table, facing the door, and C4 took him to be the dealer. There were two bushy bearded men in flannel shirts and jeans, who didn't seem to know each other.

The other potential player was a woman, about C4's age, maybe a little younger, but quite attractive. Short dark hair, eyes so brown they were almost black, jeans, and a hoodie. From what C4 could tell she had a nice shape under the winter clothes. He took special attention when she turned to order a drink at the bar. Yup. The jeans fit well. Too bad she was so old.

He was momentarily distracted by the door slamming shut and a young man, cowboy all the way from his hat to his boots, strode in. The dealer gave him a sharp look, which took the grin off his face.

"Get yourselves a drink and let's get started. Oilpatch said there'd be five so we are all here."

The five of them followed directions and everyone took a seat, without any discussion of who sat where. C4 sat next to the dealer, and the woman sat across from him, the two beards sat on his left, the cowboy to the right of the dealer.

Once seated, the dealer spoke.

"This is a friendly game, folks. Every chip is $20. Every ante is $20, every raise after that is in multiples of $20. $1,000 minimum to buy in, so you all start with 50 chips. If you don't have a thousand then either leave, or you've got 15 minutes to go round it up."

He looked directly at the cowboy as he closed his remarks, but the cowboy along with the rest of the players by turn handed the dealer each $1,000.

The opening play was uneventful, like an old-time heavyweight boxing match, everyone trying see if they could discern any patterns or tells in the other players.

The woman was quite affable, as was the cowboy; the two beards just played. The dealer ran the game well. The woman turned her attention to C4.

"So, where you from, new guy? Haven't seen you around here before."

"Montana."

"You don't sound like you're from Montana. You joshin' us?"

"No ma'am."

"Ma'am? How old do you think I am?"

The cowboy laughed. The beards smiled. Just a little bit. C4 decided flattery was his best bet. In fact, it was his only bet. And it was his standard play, for all women.

"Too young to be in this bar, ma'am. Just a country boy expression. Being taught to respect women and all."

C4 tried not to overdo any drawl that he thought his character might need.

"Well, thank you very much. But I plan to sleep alone tonight with all my money. I'm Vicki. You got a name.?

"You can call me Montana."

"Well, isn't that mysterious? Montana it is. You can call me Vicki."

That conversation over, the game fell into a focused pattern as chips moved from player to player. About 1:00 a.m., with the cowboy on the ropes and the rest about even, C4 decided to do his community service and remove the lad from the game. He employed his bluff, and as the bets went round, the pot eased up past $300. The beards folded, but Vicki and the cowboy stayed in. Finally, Vicki called. C4 had to fold, and Vicki and the cowboy had to show. The cowboy had a full house, but Vicki had four eights, so she took the biggest pot of the evening. The cowboy was out, Vicki now had a commanding lead, and C4 was down several hundred. The game went back to its usual ebb and flow, but C4 could see Vicki was slowly increasing her chips. Finally, about 2:00 a.m., the beards were down to a couple hundred dollars each and asked to cash out. Agreement all around, they left.

Then Vicki got really talkative.

"So, Montana, you drift east often, to try to clean out us flatlanders?"

"Not often."

C4 was trying to keep his mind on the game and Vicki out of his business. She was not going to go down easily.

"You staying overnight here or headed west once I've taken all your money?"

C4 tried to ignore the question, staring at his cards.

"Really, I need to know, so I can leave you enough money for gas if you plan to drive home tonight."

Even the dealer smiled a bit. C4 was not used to this. Usually, he was the charming talker. Now he was the victim. He stood, walked over and got a drink. Whiskey on the rocks. There had been ice, but by now, not much was left.

Returning to the table, he decided to match charm for charm.

"I'm at the Holiday Inn Express. Room 117, if you need a place to stay, given your impending lack of funds."

"I can't imagine being that hard up, Montana. I'll try to leave you enough to pay for the room."

From there on the banter never ended. A couple of times the dealer laughed out loud, finally saying,

"This is the most entertaining game I've ever dealt."

Unfortunately for C4, Vicki was winning both the banter and the money. He made one final desperate bet on a decent hand, but couldn't get another six to go with the three he already had, and Vicki's full house cleaned him out. He'd lost his chance to add to his Baker Plan stake. This was bad.

"Sorry, Montana. Let me buy you a drink. You'll want to sleep this night off for a while anyway."

C4 realized he had probably had too much already, so declined. His first good choice of the evening. Even the chicken wings were causing him some distress by now. He smiled the best smile he could muster.

"You won, fair and square."

Then he turned to the dealer.

"It was fair and square, wasn't it?"

"Absolutely."

Vicki stood.

"Then I gotta run, guys. I teach Sunday School in a few hours. Probably should freshen up a bit."

With that, she was out the door.

"She doesn't cheat, does she?"

The dealer smiled.

"Not that I've ever seen. She lives out on a ranch somewhere. She plays a lot, and she almost always wins. She's a good card player and a good people reader. And she can hold her own in any conversation."

C4 nodded, cashed in his few chips and headed out. He could tally the damage tomorrow. Gambling loss on top of two hotel nights, drinks, burger, wings. Not a profitable trip at all. And on Monday, he had to drive old man Baker to Minnesota.

The drive back to the hotel was cold, lonely, and dark. He parked, went into his room and collapsed on his bed, only partially undressed and was soon asleep.

Somewhere in his dream he heard a rap on a door and a voice.

"Montana? You in there? You alive?"

He looked at the clock. 5:00 a.m. Only a couple of hours after he'd hit the bed, and he would have been happy to sleep a lot longer. Or maybe he could. Dreams were funny that way. But then there was another rap on the door. And again,

"Montana. Let me in."

C4 got up and went to the door. It was Vicki, which he should have known, given she called him Montana. He let her in.

Sleepily, C4 said, "Don't tell me you blew all that money already."

"No, but the beard brothers followed me when I left the bar, so I didn't dare drive out into the country alone. Apparently, they're sore losers. Or just like my looks. You never know with those guys."

She pushed the door open enough to slide in.

"Glad you gave me your room number. It's good for a girl to have a safe place to go."

C4 still wasn't sure this was all a dream. He let the door shut and followed her with his eyes as she set her purse down next to the TV, then pulled off her hoodie, temporarily exposing some surprisingly firm midriff while she did. He remained mesmerized.

"Want to use the bathroom before I take my shower? A girl can't go to bed dirty, can she?"

Again, C4 was uncharacteristically speechless. This woman was like the energizer bunny.

"Come on, Montana, snap out of it. You were more fun when you were losing at poker. This your first time alone with a girl?"

Finally, he found his voice.

"No, just kind of a surprise to see you again. Don't you have a husband or something? Or a sister in town?"

"Would it bother you if I was married? You don't seem the type to let that get in the way."

C4 tried hard to get his brain to help him get up to speed with the situation. Vicki continued.

"Look, Montana. I'm sorry to barge in like this. I do have a good friend in town, but I didn't want to lead the beard brothers to her house any more than I wanted to lead them to my house. A well-lit motel parking lot and an unknown room inside was as safe as I could come up with. Now, again, do you need to use the bathroom before I…oh never mind. If you need to go, just come on in. Just don't peek behind the curtain."

With that, she stepped into the bathroom and closed the door. C4 heard the shower start, then sat back down on the bed. He was used to being in complete control, especially when it came to women. Now he was anything but. Vicki was singing a bit in the shower.

Unable to help himself, he walked over and looked in her purse. The wad of cash tucked into an inside pocket had to be close to $10,000. That was more than her winnings from the Oilpatch. Maybe the beard brothers were on to something. The shower stopped, so C4 put the purse down and sat back down on the bed. A few moments later Vicki came out of the bathroom holding a towel up in front of her. She dropped the towel.

"Guess who can't pay the rent. Is that bed big enough for both of us?"

C4 awoke again a few hours later. It was now light enough to see around the room. Yup, Vicki was still there. Another personal best, kind of. The oldest woman he'd ever slept with. Now he did need the bathroom, so he went in and took full advantage of the room, showering and shaving before he came back out. Vicki was still sound asleep.

He felt no remorse over sleeping with her, any more than he had with any other woman he'd slept with, married or not. In fact, in this case she had come to him and needed a place, and it was the only bed after all. What he was processing in his now fully awake mind was all that cash in her purse. Money he desperately needed. While he thought, he quietly got dressed. Then he sat awhile and looked at her. She was a better-looking meal ticket than his dad. And she certainly knew how to get her hands on money. Maybe it was time for a change of plans. He stared at her and contemplated his options.

Unfortunately, it was not likely she would allow him to attach himself to her. And he had no way of knowing if there was a husband or boyfriend or if that cash in her purse was really all she owned. He hadn't even seen her car. And the Oilpatch wasn't exactly an upscale supper club. No, he needed to stick with the Baker Plan. But he still needed some cash to show old man Baker that he was a man of means, and to live on, at least for a month or so.

Vicki stirred, opened her eyes and looked around, a bit confused by her surroundings, but like most predators, she quickly got caught up, and smiled at him.

"You might have guessed this wasn't my first time in bed with a guy. But I must say it couldn't have been yours either. I found our time together quite enjoyable."

C4 had to smile a bit but said nothing. Vicki continued.

"Look at you all chipper and cleaned up. Why don't you run down the hall and get us each a coffee while I sneak out of bed and dress. I'm actually much more shy than I let on last night."

C4 nodded and replied.

"Good idea. Black? Or all full of cream and sugar?"

"Looks like you got some of your wits back. Black is fine. See you in five."

C4 now had a plan. He went out the door, and let it latch loudly, then counted to 10, and quietly snuck back in, making sure the bathroom door was closed, grabbed his coat and keys and then slid his hand into her purse and took a handful of bills out of the middle of the stack of bills he'd seen last night. There might be a chance she didn't notice the money he'd lifted, at least not until he was well away. Then she could start looking for him in Montana. Big state, Montana.

He went quickly out the door, letting it close quietly, out the back door and to his SUV, which started right off and within a minute he was on I-94 headed east. Only when he was on the road did he count his "winnings."

He almost drove off the road. It was all hundreds, and there were at least 30 of them.

The Baker Plan was now in full effect.

Chapter 4

WHEN C4 WHEELED into his heated parking garage it was still Sunday morning. He parked and took the elevator up to his top floor condo. He sometimes told people he was trying to impress that it was a penthouse, though it was just a standard condo unit that happened to be on the top floor. Two bedrooms, two bathrooms, a laundry area and a nice enough kitchen, dining nook, and living room. A picture window looked out over the front door of the building with a view of both downtown Bismarck and the capitol building. It was modest, but had been listed as a luxury condo, a lot of the luxury being the heated indoor garage and an elevator right to his door.

He needed to sleep and then get ready for his trip to Minnesota with old man Baker. He undressed, carefully counting his money and putting it into his gold-plated money clip. Just over $3,600 in total. It was good to have, and when at some point on this trip east, whether it was a gas stop or a restaurant or bar, he could pull out his money clip and make a show of extracting a fifty or a hundred and insist on paying for something to show Baker his healthy financial status. He wouldn't take it all with him, of course, but a thousand or so would be sure to impress. He couldn't make the pitch for the lake place, or set in motion the wheels his dad needed rolling to take over the Baker estate if he didn't look like he was independently wealthy. Rich old people don't trust paupers or leeches.

C4 dropped into bed and the next time he woke up it was mid-afternoon. Time for some food. He had to be careful not to flash any real money anywhere in Bismarck, or word would get around and any number of people to whom he owed money would come calling, trying to collect. Yet he had to make Baker believe he was wealthy. If the Baker Plan worked, by the end of the year he might not be wealthy, but he could at least have a steady stream of income that would provide a nice base for his less reliable money-making schemes. If nothing else, he could use the steady income to travel a bit and expand his markets to where he was less well known. Then once Baker was dead, the stream would increase and once his dad died, it would all be his. Patience is supposed to be a virtue, he thought, but it sure doesn't feel that way.

As he stepped into the shower he was still thinking. Once his dad had everything in Baker's estate locked down, then there was no reason for Baker to stay alive. C4 wondered how old he actually was. Maybe that was his line of questioning over the next week - ages for Baker and his kids, grandkids, or anyone else who might be in the potential line of heirs.

Clean and dressed, he headed out to his favorite diner, where he usually ordered a BLT and a salad. He hated exercising, and his health club membership, paid for by his dad, was essentially for appearances and a place to meet up with people. And of course, occasionally find a healthy local girl to date. Watching his diet was his one and only form of self-discipline.

As he pulled out of the garage, he called his dad, who answered on the second ring.

"You're alive!" exclaimed CT.

"Yup. Just been playing some poker. Won big."

C4 figured he'd better leave it at that simply to head off the usual line of questioning which always started with 'How much did you lose?'

"Really? Did you cheat?"

"Thanks for the vote of confidence, dad. Just hit the right tables and the right cards. I'm headed out to Archie's for a bite. Care to join me?"

After a brief pause, CT replied,

"Sure.I had brunch with some friends late this morning, so an early dinner will work. Puts me firmly in the senior citizen camp. See you in a few minutes."

Both men were soon seated in a booth toward the back at Archie's, and CT asked all about C4's winning poker weekend. C4 had to be very creative to avoid any talk of Vicki or the fact he'd actually stolen the money he had on him.

"Just some cowboys and oil field guys who were easy to part from their paychecks. Got enough winning hands along with a bluff or two to come out well ahead. Don't think I'm ready for the big time, I just had a good weekend."

C4 also wanted to head off any questions about why he couldn't support himself by playing poker. CT looked up toward the door behind C4 and redirected the conversation.

"Good looking woman just walked in, about your age, headed our way. Maybe you could score some more money off her."

Just then Vicki used her hip to slide C4 across the vinyl booth seat and make a spot for herself.

"Hi, Montana, fancy meeting you here. This your brother? Good looking family!"

CT smiled.

"I'm his dad, actually. Just call me CT. He was just telling me what a great weekend he had playing poker. Were you part of that great weekend?"

"I sure was. He cleaned me out of about $3,000 and tried to seduce me after that."

She looked sideways over at C4.

"Or was the seduction first? It all blurs together for me."

"It was you who tried to seduce me. That much I remember clearly. It's so good to see you again!"

"I was hoping you'd remember me fondly. I never did get my coffee this morning. What happened? Were they out?"

CT was clearly enjoying Vicki and the conversation. He couldn't decide whether to stare at Vicki's dark brown eyes or C4's somewhat bewildered brow.

"I'm so sorry. They were brewing a new pot, and rather than wait, I was going to run across the street for coffee, then, you know, traffic and all that."

"I'm pretty sure I know the 'all that.' By the way, there was some extra room in my purse, so I brought your shaving kit. You forgot that in your rush to get me a cup of coffee."

CT looked them both over closely and had to wonder what all had gone on between them.

The waitress came just then and dropped off C4's BLT and his dad's soup and sandwich.

"Looks like you've added to the looks of the booth. Can I get you something, miss?"

"Yes, thank you. I'll have what he's having," Vicki replied, nodding toward C4's BLT. "But with fries. And a Diet Coke. And check back for dessert. My boyfriend is buying so the sky's the limit!"

"I'll get that started. Glad to see he's got a girlfriend. Maybe the rest of us are a little safer now."

As the waitress walked back toward the kitchen Vicki turned to C4 and said,

"Do the two of you have some history? Or is there lot of history I need to catch up on?"

Turning to CT she asked, "Is he a bit of a ladies' man?"

CT laughed.

"You could say that. He gets around a bit. Where you from, Vicki?"

"Out west, kind of by Dickinson. Just a ranch girl who likes to play cards a bit. You both live here in Bismarck?"

C4 slowly, almost imperceptibly shook his head but CT replied.

"Yes, we do. He didn't share that with you?"

"Not yet. We're just getting acquainted. Learning about each other. Usual process."

"Here's your Diet. BLT will be right up."

"Thanks, honey. Lucky for you, my boyfriend's a big tipper."

The waitress looked at Vicki for a moment, then turned and walked away.

"That's news," she muttered, just loud enough to hear.

Vicki laughed.

"I swear, it's almost like she knows you better than I do. Did you used to date and then you ran out on her?"

Turning to CT she said, "Does he tend to run out on girls?"

CT laughed. "I really don't know. He's had to run from a few husbands."

Vicki tried her best to look shocked. "Husbands! Really, Montana? How could you?"

C4 knew he had to get this cut off.

"Come on, dad. That's just an old rumor around town. Vicki, I'm surprised to see you so soon. I thought we had another date next weekend."

C4 put a lot of emphasis on the word 'next.'

"Oh, did we? I guess I forgot. Lucky for me, when I checked out of the motel, the clerk let me see your address. You left so quickly I was worried about you."

"No need to worry."

"Oh, I was. I just couldn't wait to see you again. You probably have that effect on a lot of people."

C4 tried for a change in direction.

"Well, I'm just glad you found me. After we eat, I can show you around Bismarck, kind of a private tour."

"That sounds great. And if you leave anything out, I'm sure if I circle back to your dad, he can fill me in."

"No need. My tours are quite complete."

"Good. I wouldn't want to come up light."

Vicki put special emphasis on the word 'light.'

"Here's your BLT, ma'am."

"Ma'am? How old do your think I am?"

"So sorry. Just trying to be polite."

From that point, the three of them enjoyed their meals, with a little casual banter. When the waitress came back to check their progress and ask about dessert, CT said,

"Nothing more for me. Montana, sounds like you're picking this one up, so thanks."

"Oh, he will. Nice to meet you CT. You must be real proud of your son."

"At times, yes. You look like a real catch, Vicki. I think he's got his hands full."

CT stood and walked out just as the waitress returned.

"Dessert for anyone?"

Vicki wasted no time.

"We'll split a piece of apple pie."

The waitress made the note and walked away. Vicki looked right at C4 and in a stage whisper said,

"What the hell, stealing from me? After all I did for you?"

C4 knew he had to stay as far from the truth as he could. There was no way he wanted her in on the Baker Plan and he needed her out of Bismarck as soon as possible. He also knew he had very few cards to play. First some deflection.

"All you did for me? You took all my money at a poker game and then took advantage of my motel room."

"Took advantage? I provided you some desperately needed female companionship. I kept your bed warm. I shared my time and myself. In every way."

C4 knew that was almost true, so let it drop and took another tack.

"Look. I really needed some cash. I just grabbed. I didn't know I'd taken that much. Can I give you two thousand back and we can treat the rest as a loan? Just for a week or so. I have to go out of town tomorrow on business and I need to have a little spending money."

"What kind of business?"

"Perfectly legal business."

"That's not much of an answer. Lots of businesses are legal and I doubt you're involved in any of them."

"Doing some work for my dad. He's an attorney. I need to take a look at some property for one of his clients, and the people I'm dealing with need to believe I'm far from broke. And I'm not broke, just a little short on cash right now."

"Well, so am I, as you well know. Tell you what. I know you won't have any money to repay me in a week. So let's get a little more real. I'll loan you the thousand and you repay me two thousand in 30 days. Right here in this restaurant. 3:00 p.m. It's January 15th, so I'll even throw in an extra day and make it 31. Same date in February. Unless you want to pay me back a day early. Kind of a Valentine's Day date?"

C4 knew one of the options involved the police and there weren't many other options available so he said,

"Deal. I'll go with the 15th. That should be no problem."

Knowing full-well it was a big problem.

"That's too bad. I was really hoping for a Valentine's date."

Just then the pie came with two forks, so Vicki took a bite and said,

"I'm going to change the nature of our relationship and tell you the truth. I didn't get your address from the motel clerk. I did get your license plate number and had a friend on the Dickinson Police run the plate. Got your address from her. Also, you have an interesting record. Not all good. But besides the police, I know people on the other side of the law, as well. They work on oil rigs and on ranches, but are also willing and quite able to help with things like collections on the side. Know what I mean?"

C4 did, so he took a bite of the pie and nodded.

Vicki went on.

"I need one more thing. Maybe two or three. I'll lay them out and you can count them afterwards."

C4 just looked at her.

"I need a better name than Montana. And I need to see your apartment. I know where it is, because I waited there half the morning and all afternoon until you came out. Once again, I need a shower. I have some more appointments this afternoon and I need to be clean. I think I get dirty just being around you. Then I'll get out of your hair. For exactly 31 days. And the two thousand, right now. Before you forget or run out on me again."

Just then the waitress walked up with the check.

"You'd be lucky to let him run out on you."

Vicki laughed.

"I don't doubt that, but I need him for a little while yet. Pay the girl, Montana. Give her a nice tip. Take it out of your share, though."

"Oh, and a real name, or at least something better than Montana. Or should I ask your friend, the waitress?"

"Just call me Cal. Old family name. You need to move first."

"Money first."

C4 thought for a moment then offered,

"It's back in my condo. I'll pay you when you leave."

C4 pulled out his money clip and put a hundred on the table.

"I didn't mean that much of a tip. We'll have to wait while she makes change. More of a chance to get to know each other. It's ok if the fine upstanding people of Bismarck see us together, isn't it? Or do you have a wife back at your condo with a .38 special?"

"No wife. Can't comment on the gun."

C4 figured leaving Vicki guessing about a gun gave him some kind of control.

"Then as soon as we get your change, we'll head over. Get me my shower and my money and I'll be out of your hair before you know it."

C4 decided to push the envelope a bit, saying,

"How do you know I won't rob or even kill you in my apartment?"

"You're not that stupid. And it's not your style. You're more sleazy than threatening. Your record looks like a wildly extended juvie record, not like a career criminal."

C4 had no response. Vicki apparently knew how to judge people, just like the dealer at the Oilpatch had said. He was going to have to get rid of her somehow. She was too smart to keep around.

She followed him to his condo, trailing him right into the garage.

He got out of his SUV and pointed her to an empty spot across from his.

"That belongs to the Washburns. They're in Arizona for the winter. I hope you plan to be gone before spring."

"Definitely. Just a shower, some cash, and I'll be on my way. As I said, I'm a busy girl, on a tight schedule."

They walked to the elevator, and rode up to his condo. Just walking and being with her he couldn't help notice her classic beauty and her bearing. She exuded beauty and confidence in a bit of a hard-bitten way. He could be attracted to her if she wasn't so darned smart and hard on him.Unfortunately, a half-hour later when she came out of his shower, she was fully dressed. He handed her the two thousand which she thumbed through and then stuffed into her purse.

As she walked to the door, she turned back and said,

"Our next date is in 31 days, honey, but you never know when I may pop up in the meantime, checking on the guy who owes me money. I may have others keeping an eye on you, also. Have a nice trip."

Chapter 5

MONDAY DAWNED, DIMLY, WITH CLOUDY SKIES and light snow. From his top floor condo, C4 looked out over downtown Bismarck and it looked like a snow globe. He focused on getting ready to pick up old man Baker, which he was supposed to do at 9:00 a.m. He thought how rare it was to sleep overnight and get up in the morning, but that would be his life for the next week.

First, he had to get showered and packed, and gas up his SUV for the trip. In the winter they used his SUV for the trip, and Baker always gave him an extra $50 to wash and gas it when they were back in Bismarck. In the warmer months, they drove Baker's cream-colored Sedan DeVille. Made for a nice trip.

As he showered, he racked his brain. What was old man Baker's first name? He always called him Mr. Baker. That seemed to work ok, but to make the sale he now needed to make, a first name would be helpful. Maybe he could call his dad. No, wait. He'd ask Baker himself, as a way to foster a deeper relationship. That should work.

C4 pulled up in front of the Baker home on Avenue B right at 9:00 a.m. He walked to the front door, rang the bell, and in a few moments Bella answered. C4 always thought that was a bit funny. A maid named Bella answering the bell. Bella had been with Baker for many years. There was plenty of room for her in the stately old home.

"Good morning, Bella. Is Mr. Baker ready?"

"I'm here," replied Baker as he came down the front stairs.

Bella seemed pleased that she didn't need to answer. Her disdain for C4 was hard to miss. That would make it even more fun when the Baker Plan left her homeless and unemployed. C4 stepped in and picked up Mr. Baker's roller bag. He carried it to the running SUV to avoid rolling it through the fresh snow. Baker followed him down the sidewalk as Bella closed the front door behind the two of them. C4 opened the passenger door for Baker before he put the roller bag in the back next to his own duffle.

With C4 back in the driver's seat, the two headed east out of Bismarck. Once on the freeway, the roads were good, so C4 set the cruise control at a speed at about five miles per hour over the speed limit and they started burning up the miles. Time for some casual conversation.

"So, Mr. Baker, how long have we been making these trips?"

Baker looked out the window, thoughtfully. "Oh, gee, it must be close to four or five years now. I do appreciate your company and your driving. I enjoy these trips a great deal."

"So do I. I hope the fishing is good. I know the food and liquor will be."

"Yeah, nothing like fresh caught fish from the cold water under the ice. And you clean them well. No bones."

"Thanks, it's one of my handful of skills. My dad taught me when I was a kid."

"Good for him. He's a really good guy."

C4 paused. The conversation was definitely positive all around. How to keep it that way?

"He sure is. How long have you owned your lake place?"

"This one, about 25 years. Had one on a smaller lake and then sold that and bought this one, and then remodeled it to be just what I wanted. My wife loved coming to the old one, and after she passed away, I bought this, partly because the old one reminded me too much of her, and partly to have a really nice place for the kids to come back to."

"And did that work for your kids?"

"No, once they moved east for college, it just got to be too hard for them to come back and forth much. My son bought a sailboat, so that's what he does all summer. My daughter had a series of boyfriends who took up her time. She was married for about 20 minutes a couple of decades ago."

"Grandkids?"

"None from her, and my son never married."

C4 just took that in. Baker took advantage of the conversational lull and went on.

"He's a bit of womanizer. The sailboat works well for that. Something to show off, someplace to take a woman he's trying to impress."

"So, they never come back to North Dakota or Minnesota?"

"Every year or two I twist their arms to make the trip back, usually late summer. My daughter just moved to Florida, so maybe she'll come up a little more now, to escape that summer heat."

"And your son is where?"

"New York. Connecticut, actually. Keeps his boat on Long Island Sound."

"Do you ever get out there?"

"Not much. I just find the traffic and all the people a bit overwhelming. I could make a trip to Florida, though. Maybe take in a little spring training baseball. End my winter early."

C4 smiled. As much as letting Baker out of his sight was contrary to the plan, it did sound nice. So he tried to make light of it.

"Well, if you need a travel companion for that trip, just let me know. I wouldn't mind seeing some spring training baseball either."

"That might just work. We could take your dad, too. Make it a guy's week. Watch some baseball, play some golf. Maybe a little fishing on the Gulf?"

This was now going much better than C4 had ever anticipated. Getting closer to the Baker family had to be a good thing. Maybe he could feel out the daughter as well, and not need to wait until late summer. The son remained a mystery, at least for now.

"That sounds great. You don't have to sell me on Florida when we're in the middle of a North Dakota winter!"

With that, the two men fell into a period of silence. C4 was a little surprised at how much he'd learned in such a short period. Maybe he could learn more about people if he asked a few questions. Baker seemed perfectly willing to share. Who knew?

After a bit, old man Baker fell asleep. C4 liked that. He could just drive and stay engrossed in his own thoughts. C4 wondered how old the man was. His dad would have to have that in his records. He had to live long enough to get their plan in place, but not too long after that.

Right now, his tasks consisted of getting them both to the lake, turning the heat up, getting a fire started in the fireplace, and getting the luggage in. Then he would hopefully get a nap before they went out for dinner. Baker had agreed a couple of years ago to have a local guy clear the driveway and sidewalk of snow before they got there. A phone call beat the heck out of an hour or two with a snowblower, shovel, and broom, with Baker sitting in the SUV, burning gas. Baker paid the guy, but C4 always left him a tip as well.

With the driveway and sidewalks pre-cleared, C4 always took some time to walk around the property, checking to make sure everything was wintering well. Once in a while, he had to use a snow rake to drag some snow off the roof, and he always checked the rodent traps in the garage and in the cabinets in the house. It was no mystery why all types of animals in this climate spent the fall and winter looking for a warmer place to live. He knew Baker could pay some local guy to do the same through the winter, but making these trips provided C4 with a little spending money and filled some of his time in the winter. Doing these odd little chores, while beneath his dignity, gave him a chance to poke around a bit in Baker's property. Now, with the Baker Plan under way, any way to ingratiate himself to Baker was clearly of value.

Winter, that was his bane. In the sun-drenched Bismarck summers, he could fill hours at the golf course, honing his decent enough golf game, and hustling the local golfers a bit to make a little money on side bets. Nothing big, just enough to pay for his golf and a few drinks, with maybe a little left over. The country club was one of the few places he knew he couldn't afford to wear out his welcome.

He also enjoyed the outdoor cafes where he could watch and sometimes pick up a pretty girl. Usually some out-of-town girl who didn't know him, and Bismarck had a steady supply of those.

The rest of the drive to the Minnesota lake home and the evening followed the normal pattern. C4 was careful not to keep prying into Baker's family or favorite charities. He had several days to get it all covered and didn't want to set off any alarms for the old man. He did, however, express his appreciation for the lake home.

"This place is just great. Every time I'm here I enjoy it so much. Even in winter like this. The quiet, the view of the lake. The fireplace. It's all so nice."

"Glad you do, Calvin. I enjoy it too. I'm glad you can help me make the trips we do. I wish my kids enjoyed it more. It's a hard sell for most people in the winter. But the summers are spectacular."

C4 nodded.

They enjoyed their time together, following a pretty solid routine. Baker used a local guide to rent a fish-house for ice fishing, just for the mornings. When they got back from fishing, Cal cleaned whatever fish they had caught, and fixed a quick lunch, and after that, both he and Baker napped. Both of them enjoyed a drink before dinner out at one of the handful of restaurants that remained open all winter. If they had caught an abundance of fish, C4 cooked up another meal of fried or baked fish, using recipes he remembered from his mom, along with some garlic toast, all accompanied by a bottle of wine from Baker's decent enough wine collection.

C4 had his own bedroom and each evening used a cell phone call to update his dad on the day's discussions. The old man slept in the master suite, of course, and once they finished their fish dinner, or came back from a restaurant, they had one more nightcap and then headed off to their respective rooms. C4 had never seen more than a glimpse of the master suite and figured he didn't need to see any more of it. His room was nice enough, in the loft, with a view of the lake. The days were so peaceful, the week always went quickly.

On this trip at each quiet opportunity, either in the early evening or when fishing, C4 gently prodded Baker on his kids to learn more about them, reminding him how much he enjoyed the lake home, too bad the

Baker kids didn't make more use of it. All in all, he thought he had completed his assignment admirably.

They began their drive back to Bismarck Friday mid-morning and quickly found they were driving into the increasing force of an Alberta Clipper. The wind driven snow made visibility poor, but with the SUV and limited traffic, they made it to Jamestown with no real difficulty.

Baker awoke as C4 worked his way down the freeway ramp for their usual gas and restroom break.

"Are we stopping?"

"Yup. Usual break. We're at Jamestown. I've been listening to the radio and it looks like this will blow over in the next couple of hours. How about I buy us lunch somewhere halfway decent, and we can take a short break? Hopefully, we should still be home before dark."

"You're the driver. I'm good with what you decide."

"Great. Let's cross over the highway to Applebee's and see if they can find us a quiet booth."

With that C4 worked his way over the somewhat slippery overpass and into the Applebee's parking lot. He found a place as close to the door as he could and helped his passenger out of the SUV and into the warmth of the restaurant.

Greeted and seated almost immediately, C4 was happy to have a good window view where he could keep a close eye on the freeway and the weather. He knew he could tell a lot from the traffic - how heavy, how slow, any crashes or other problems.

He also knew that as the wind subsided the temperature would drop, and he wanted to be sure to deliver his passenger happy and healthy back to Bella. Now that the Baker Plan was his only pathway to lifetime financial security, having the old man die now, under any circumstances would be extremely unfortunate.

The conversation was limited to mundane topics until their food came, which they both ate in relative silence until C4 offered up what he thought was something safe.

"I can see why your kids don't come back here in the winter. This is kind of beautiful, but not exactly relaxing if you have to travel."

Baker looked up from his food to C4 and was apparently thinking hard. This went on so long C4 was desperately hoping the old gent wasn't having a stroke.

"It isn't just the weather. Like a lot of other poor farming kids I met at NDSU, then called NDAC, or Agricultural College, many years ago, we were all there with the goal of improving our lives. Better farming skills, better jobs, better wives, any and all of that. I met my wife there and after graduation I got a job with an ag services company in Fargo. All was good for almost a year, then my dad had a stroke and died, and I had to go home to run the farm. Right in the middle of spring planting. My mom was completely dependent on me. My older sisters and brothers were long gone, with jobs and families in cities far away. They had left and never looked back. They're all dead now.

"It wasn't my plan, but it was what I knew I had to do. I knew I was tied up for the summer. My wife wasn't happy to be out on a farm in the middle of North Dakota, having grown up in Fargo, but she went along.

"Our plan was to do all the summer work, sell the cattle off and find a renter for the future. Unfortunately, the cattle market was so bad, and I already had the hay baled, and my mom seemed so lost that I knew I had to stay at least through the winter. My wife, of course, stayed as well and we made it through that winter, all the while exploring opportunities to get out of the farming business.

"As the winter went on, however, a couple of my dad's friends approached me about renting their land and another neighbor wanted to retire and sell me his small farm. With all that land, both rented and owned, we'd have a pretty good-sized operation for that time and place. And my wife was pregnant, and not doing well, so we had to stay put. So, I took on the extra land, borrowed some money and bought a bigger tractor and the bare minimum of additional equipment I needed. The next spring I went into farming full time. In April my wife had our first baby, a girl we named Kelly, and from there, I kept borrowing and buying more land, renting some out and farming most of it. Branched out into cattle west of the river, and crops east of the river and over many years, built a bit of an agricultural empire. It all came together because my college degree and my knowledge of farming and finance made the local bank willing to lend me whatever money I needed. And my willingness to work really hard."

The old man paused, ate a bit of his food and took a couple of sips of coffee. This was entirely new for C4. No one had ever shared that much with him in his whole life. Or if they had he hadn't listened. He really wasn't sure what to do. No need, as Baker looked up and continued.

"A few years after our daughter, Kelly, was born, our son Kevin followed, and for several years after that everything seemed to be going fine. But I was so caught up in my success that I hadn't noticed my wife's health slowly deteriorating. By the time Kelly started college, my wife was pretty sick and died a year or so later. Kelly and Kevin had raised each other while I had worked and traveled from property to property. I guess I was just escaping from the whole situation.

"So, the kids hardly knew me at all, and left as soon as they could. I paid for good colleges out east, and they thankfully took advantage of that, rather than getting into trouble. Since then, they have forged their own successful lives without me. You can see, then, that it's not just the winter that they're avoiding."

C4 was really at a loss. It was like he was listening to someone speak to him in a foreign language. The silence this time was way too long so he asked the only question he could think of.

"What was your wife's name?"

"Kathryn, or Katie. Wonderful woman. Beautiful woman. We were Kendall and Kathryn, but mostly people called us Ken and Katie. She was just too frail and too lonely for the life I dragged her into."

Chapter 6

THE CONVERSATION FELL AWAY AFTER THAT. Their plates cleared, they each had a refill of coffee and as they sipped, C4 stared out the window. It looked like the snow had stopped falling and the wind was dropping.

C4 felt he should say something but had no idea what to say, what to ask, or how to take part in a conversation like this. It was clear that Baker's two kids had no interest in his empire and almost certainly never would. It also appeared that Baker's relationship with his alma mater was over. He'd paid for an education, which had been provided, and that was the sum total of the deal. That would all be good news for his dad.

C4 looked up and Baker was staring out the window as well.

"Well, Calvin, can we make it to Bismarck?"

"I think so. It's definitely clearing up. The traffic is moving along pretty well and I've seen one snowplow go by. By the time we gas up, we should be fine."

C4 stood up, took a fifty out of his money clip and dropped it on the table, making sure Baker saw the full extent of his cash supply. He supplemented the fifty with a comment.

"I can sure pick this one up. I'll pay for the delay."

With that they both got back in C4's SUV and headed to the gas station across the way. Baker sat in the comfort of the warming vehicle while S4 pumped some gas, and then they were off.

The rest of the trip went fairly well, and with the roads better, C4 used the time to think. By probing Baker's past a bit, the old man had opened up and revealed considerably more than C4 could have imagined possible. He now knew Baker's name and the names of his wife and kids. He knew a lot more than he had previously known about his family and his college and his agricultural empire. The old geezer would prove an easier mark than he had dreamed possible. The old man's fortune was as good as in the Tappen family coffers. It was just a matter of a little legal work and the passage of time.

By the time they approached Bismarck the roads were clear, and while the temperatures were dropping, they were traveling at speeds near the speed limit. C4 drove directly to Baker's house, carried the old man's bag to the door where they were greeted by Bella, who had a big smile for Baker and a smirk for C4. For the first time C4 actually enjoyed the smirk. She'd get hers, soon enough.

"Glad you're back. The weather had me a bit worried."

"No problem, Bella. Calvin took good care of me."

Bella looked at C4 and shook her head. C4 waited for a comment but none was forthcoming, so he smiled at her and left. She shut the door behind him, and he heard the bolt lock as he walked down the steps to the sidewalk to get back in his SUV.

He drove straight to his father's law office. His assistant, a middle-aged woman named Taylor, was not there, as usual for this time of day.

His dad was at his desk, looking over some documents.

"Figured you'd show up. How was your week?"

"Great. I asked the old man some heartfelt questions about his kids and he really opened up. Both his wallet and his heart. The wallet part wasn't much, just an extra hundred, and I spent fifty of that on lunch on the way home. But the conversation was priceless."

C4 recounted the conversation as fully and accurately as he could, focusing on the lack of interest Baker's kids had in him or his real estate empire. And no special love expressed for NDSU. It looked like the path to Baker's fortune, just like the weather outside, was clearing.

"That does all sound good. And Baker never suspected why you were probing?"

"I sure don't think so. The fact that he opened up as much as he did, I think, indicated he was happy to be having a heartfelt discussion."

CT nodded and looked thoughtful.

"So, no real love for NDSU and his kids had no real love for him. I suppose I need to find out if there are any other potential heirs or any other organization dear to his heart. I can probe that when we do our annual visit. Right now, his will says his kids get it all."

C4 looked a bit perplexed, so CT continued.

"We don't need some niece or nephew showing up and claiming the old man wanted them to have all or some of it. Like the Minnesota lake home, or some other particular piece of property. The will needs to be iron clad, as do the revised trusts I set up."

C4 nodded. This was bit over his head, but he figured his dad was most likely right.

"You did your part, Cal, now I have to do mine. This will take some time and a great deal of finesse, so just be patient and let me guide Mr. Baker to get his will and trusts to a position where we can serve his interests best."

C4 was a bit confused by his father's obviously careful choice of words, and his thoughts must have shown, because the next thing his dad did was wink at him and say.

"Go buy yourself a drink, son. I'll take it from here."

Exhausted from all this positive human interaction, C4 bid his father farewell and headed for his condo.

As he drove into the condo garage, he thought he caught a glimpse of one of the beard brothers from his Oilfield poker game sitting in a parked pickup at the end of the visitor's lot outside the garage. As the garage door closed behind him, he convinced himself it had to be some-one else. But that did bring to mind… he now had less than four weeks until he had to pay Vicki $2,000. His choices were limited. He could come up with the money and pay her, getting her out of his life, hope-fully forever. That seemed out of reach, however. He currently had about $1,200 in cash, and he'd need most of that to live on for the next month. Fortunately, he was facing a cold winter weekend with lots of time to spend at home, thinking, or maybe drinking. C4 was pretty sure he'd think better after a good night's sleep and that started with a few rounds of scotch. Everything went better with scotch. He opened the bottle and poured himself a double or maybe even a triple, into a glass of ice. He'd figure out how to get rid of Vicki later. One scotch led directly to another, and the evening passed quickly.

C4 awoke to the beginnings of the sun lighting up his condo. He turned on the TV to KFYR. The scroll at the bottom of the screen showed a temperature of -17 and a wind chill close to -30. Good day to stay in.

He rolled out of bed, took a shower and dried off, got dressed in some sweats, and headed to the kitchen to see if he could find any food. In the fridge he found one egg left in a carton, with an expiration date of yesterday. Close enough. In the freezer he found a bread wrapper with the heels of bread. No butter anywhere, but he did have peanut butter and jelly, so breakfast was quickly cooked and eaten. His first meal since Applebee's in Jamestown, it felt pretty good.

After the sun came up a bit more, he'd walk over to the grocery storeand get some more food. He didn't need much. He was low on scotch though, and there was a liquor store next door to the grocery store. He'd really have to bundle up.

Why did he even live here where it was so cold for so many months? Oh, yeah. The condo was paid for (by his dad, years ago). His dad paid for everything else, and he had no way to earn a living for himself. Now, with his dad broke, everything kept coming back to the Baker Plan, so it had to work. He couldn't see any other options. Perhaps he could figure out how to get rid of Vicki before he started drinking. He hated to drink before noon, anyway. People thought poorly of you if you were a morning drinker. He couldn't have that.

What to do about Vicki. Obviously, coming up with the money and paying her off was the slickest. He had to give that some real thought. How could he come up with a couple of thousand dollars? Even if he got a job, it would be hard to clear two grand inside of four weeks. Or even enough to hold her off. The problem was, no one was hiring in January. The Christmas rush was over.

Another alternative was just to stay out of sight, but unless he had a plan to have two grand in another few weeks, he couldn't hide forever. He had to work the Baker Plan. Having the one thousand Vicki lent him had helped him start his part of the Baker Plan, by showing the old man that he had money of his own. He knew that Baker had seen his full money clip the couple of times he'd pulled it out and paid for a meal or gas. That was necessary for Baker to trust him. He again thought to himself that having money was the only way to have someone else trust you.

The next likely option was to get two thousand from his dad, and given their last conversation about his dad's financial situation, that seemed unlikely. Especially since there was no way he could come clean about Vicki. He'd have to create some other reason to need the money. Car repairs? No, his dad would just offer to take the bill. Taxes? No, he had no income. Even the condo property taxes were paid directly from his dad's account. Hopefully that didn't stop.

Maybe he could get Vicki to fall in love with him so thoroughly that she'd forgive the loan or at least give him more time. He didn't even know how to find her. Or her full name, or if Vicki was even her real name. She sure had no trouble finding him. Besides, the waitress at Archie's might have ruined that. Who the heck was she anyway? C4 sure didn't remember her from anyplace else. Maybe he'd somehow offended her mom, or sister, or just a friend. Women were really hard to figure out.

None of that moved him any closer to having $2,000 to give to Vicki in just a few weeks.

A really bad thought kept lingering away in the back of his mind, something Vicki had said. His record was like a wildly extended juvenile record. No real crimes, just a lot of bad judgment situations and questionable dealings. Maybe it was time to do one slick crime, pocket a few thousand dollars, pay off Vicki and make the rest of it last until the Baker Plan came in. As soon as his dad had put himself in charge of the Baker empire, the fees would start rolling in and then C4 would get his hand back in the cookie jar. It had been his idea, after all. He'd have to net at least $10,000 on this one-shot crime. No violence. Vicki was right. That was not in his DNA.

What crime would work? Knock off a bank? No, too many cameras, marked cash. It was like they were waiting to trap some unsuspecting robber. Who else had lots of cash, all in small to medium bills? Think, C4, think.

Liquor stores had a lot of cash and unfortunately, especially in the smaller towns, a shotgun under the counter. Could he raid a poker game just before everyone cashed out? All that cash just sitting on the table. No real incentive to call the police.

The problem was, as Vicki had said, those poker players are often better connected with arm busters and hitmen than the police. That was a different, but very real, risk. Besides, almost all the poker players within driving distance knew him. Vicki, Vicki, Vicki. It was like she was living in his head. Unfortunately, it wasn't rent free.

Then the solution came to him. Was there a way to lift ten thousand from old man Baker himself? Then it's not even really a crime, just an advance on the ultimate takeover of the property. Clear cash, clear conscience. Now he had something to work on. And a celebration. He bundled up and headed out into the cold to buy some groceries and a bottle of scotch. He had a plan. Money to live on and money to pay Vicki back. Not sure which made him happier.

45 minutes later, C4 stepped back inside his condo, relieved to be out of the cold. He set down a bag of groceries and the smaller brown paper bag holding a full liter of scotch. It was not his favorite single malt, but he went down a rung to get the volume. He had a lot of thinking to do and in the meantime needed to manage his money.

He turned on the gas fireplace and continued to warm up as he put the groceries away. He placed the scotch on the end of the kitchen counter that served as his bar. He had no real use for mixes, just scotch and ice. He forced himself to turn away from the scotch and think about his plan. The short-term plan, his bridge plan to the Baker Plan. That's what he'd call it, the bridge plan. Maybe he did have some marketing genius. He was good at branding things.

Right now, more than a drink he needed a warm meal, so he opened a can of soup, poured it into a bowl and placed it in the microwave. As that heated up, he cut off a few slices of the loaf of the artisan wheat bread he'd also purchased. Within a few minutes, he had his meal ready.

As he sat at the small dining table and ate, he went back to noodling on his bridge plan. Unfortunately, another nagging thought kept replacing his planning thoughts. He felt like he was being watched. There were a number of people in the grocery store, but no one seemed out of place. He had been one of just a handful of people in the liquor store, but again, no one stood out. It must just be his imagination. C4 shook off the thought and focused on his meal.

Back to the bridge plan. Baker was, by local standards, very wealthy and all of it was self-earned. He had inherited very little. In fact, as Baker had told him, after his dad had died, he had had to support his mother and his own young family, and then later share the inheritance of the farm with his now deceased older siblings. He had built his farming empire piece by piece, through financial acumen and hard, hard work.

What kind of person does that take, and more importantly, C4 wondered, what kind of person does that build? Clearly someone who values hard work and honesty. Someone who'd likely be a conservative. Or maybe not. Did Baker ever mention his political leanings? C4 tried to remember but maybe it didn't matter. What did people do who are self-made multi-millionaires? They worked hard to keep the money they earned.

Baker could be living in Florida, but he stayed here. His home was nice but not ostentatious. He retained Bella but with her live-in arrangements he probably wasn't paying her much. Did he even pay anyone to actively manage the real estate and collect the rents or did he do all that himself? C4 was amazed at how little he knew about the Baker Empire despite the hours he'd spent with the old man.

Then just as his spoon picked up the last of the soup, it struck him. People like that were usually not all that trusting, and Baker was sure to have money stored away outside of his real estate, with its clear titles held by some government entity or another, and outside of banks and brokerage companies. Baker had to have some stash of cash, gold, and maybe fine art; in other words, physical wealth, all outside of the purview of the tax collectors and other government watchdogs.

C4's thoughts went to Baker's Bismarck home. There is almost certainly a safe and perhaps even some really expensive sculptures or other art work inside that home. The problem was twofold. He'd never been in the home past the foyer and more importantly, with Bella in charge of the house, he was unlikely to ever get past the foyer.

What about the Minnesota lake home? How likely was it that Baker had a safe or even some really nice art work there? Pretty likely. C4 racked his brain, forcing himself to mentally work his way room by room through the house. There were some nice paintings on the walls and a few small glassworks on the mantel. Chances are there was a safe that would have some gold or silver, and maybe some cash? In fact, he had heard Baker in his bedroom closing something that had sounded like a safe just before they left one time. Putting more money in? Hopefully so.

That had to be his opportunity. He didn't know enough about art to know if he was taking a priceless masterpiece or one of Baker's kids' fingerpainting projects. It had to be cash or bullion. No need for a fence, then, either. How to get back to the lake? What if people asked questions? He'd say Baker had sent him for something he had forgotten on their last trip. He knew how to get into the house, using the spare key all lake homes had. C4 actually knew where it was stashed, since they'd had to use it once to get in after Baker forgot his key in Bismarck.

The bridge plan was definitely coming together. He'd head to the lake first thing tomorrow morning, and be in and out in an hour or so. He would formulate the details of his plan as he drove. Time now for some scotch. Maybe even dinner out, letting people see him in Bismarck. Life was good if you just let the right things happen.

The bridge plan was beginning to unfold nicely. A few rounds of scotch, a little college basketball on television, a late afternoon nap and this time when C4 awoke he knew it must be evening, closing in on 7:00

p.m. Just to be sure he turned on the TV. Yup, just in time to see the final puzzle on Wheel of Fortune.

He allowed himself to lie quietly on the sofa for a while, enjoying his impending wealth. Maybe he could find some female companionship for this cold winter night. That would beat an all-night party or a poker game. Time for some fine dining. He knew his best odds were a late dinner at The Riverview Supper Club. One of the waitresses would likely be lonely enough to enjoy a few free drinks and some company.

With that he drifted back to sleep.

He awoke a half hour later to a full bladder, and stayed in the bathroom until he'd cleaned up, including a shave and some cologne. Dressing in a nice pair of wool slacks, oxford shirt, and sweater, he was ready to go. Down the elevator to his SUV, then out the garage door into the cold, dark outside world.

Riverview here we come. Dinner, a few drinks and if he found the right target, a few drinks for his intended companion and then, if it all went according to his plan (maybe he really was a planning genius) a night of love.

Chapter 7

C4 AWOKE TO THE SLIGHTEST SLIVER OF LIGHT coming through his bedroom window. It must be morning. He then realized he was not alone. But it wasn't the same 'being watched' sensation he'd had yesterday. He cautiously looked over. It was a somewhat familiar face. Not Vicki. It was the hostess from the Riverview Supper Club. She was still sound asleep.

He climbed out of bed as quietly as he could and headed to the bathroom. When he returned the girl, (what was her name?) was awake and watching him.

"Close your eyes, so I can get out of bed, unless you're getting back in."

"I'd love to, but I have things to do today and need to get going."

"Well, that's a new brush off. Did you not enjoy our time together?"

C4 thought hard.

"I sure did, and we should enjoy each other's company again some time."

She smiled.

"We sure should. I'll leave you my phone number."

"That would be great."

C4 fought back the urge to ask her to leave her name on it as well.

"Can I take a shower before I go? I think I smell of expensive men's cologne."

What was it with women and showers? He hadn't noticed until Vicki had said it, but all women wanted to shower once they'd been with him. Oh, well. He had a few minutes and could have a coffee and make one for the road while she showered.

"Sure, no problem. Coffee?"

"No thanks. Once I'm ready I really need to get going. Can you drop me at a friend's house?"

"Depends. Where is it?"

"East side of town, just off Rosser. Not far."

"Sure, then."

A half hour later they were both in his SUV headed out of the underground garage. She wore her work uniform, and a pair of oversized sunglasses. It was a ten minute drive to the address she gave him, all in silence, with no reference to a phone number.

"This is it. Thanks."

"No phone number?"

"No need. You know where to find me. And I know where to find you."

C4 thought that sounded a bit ominous but said nothing.

As she walked away toward the house, C4 noticed she paused, put a ring on her left hand, then went around to the back door. He drove away quickly, hoping no one had noticed his SUV stopped in front of the house. Not that it mattered to him that she was married. But it might matter to her husband and C4 didn't need any complications in his life right now.

He went straight to the freeway and headed east. A half hour later, he took the exit for Steele and headed to one of the dozen or so gas pumps at the gas station just off the road. He sat in his SUV for a few minutes checking in all directions to see if anyone had pulled off behind him. Seeing no one, he stepped out, went inside, purchased a breakfast burrito and a coffee, and left another $20 to prepay for his gas. Life would be easier with a credit card, but for now this would have to do.

Every time C4 made this stop he had to wonder. A whole town with his middle name. Why was there no Steele family fortune to go with it? He'd asked his dad a few times over the years, and there was some convoluted story about farmland and politics and the Great Depression, but C4 always lost interest before he heard anything that would qualify as a real answer. All he knew was he still had no money.

Back outside he pumped his gas and watched the freeway, the gas station activity, and the surrounding streets in all directions. Nothing suspicious. Was he getting paranoid now that he was so close to enjoying life on easy street? Or was it the husband of the hostess he was fearing, or Vicki or someone she might have tailing him? Keeping a close eye on someone who owes you just two grand seems hardly cost effective, but Vicki seemed to have her own way of doing things.

All his surveillance and ruminations abandoned him when the gas pump clicked off, signaling the end of his $20. Time to move on.

He watched his mirrors carefully when he pulled back on to the freeway. If he was being tailed, whoever it might be was good about not showing it. He drove in relative peace and comfort for the next hundred miles, cruising through Jamestown, purposely skipping his usual stop. He headed instead for a roadside rest stop where he dumped out the last of his coffee, used the restroom and got back on the highway as quickly as he could. Still no sign of a tail. That put the hostess out of his purview. No husband would follow him this far. That left only Vicki. C4 put that thought aside as he now focused on his task for the day.

Approaching Fargo, he decided to kill some time there, so he could arrive at Baker's lake place mid-afternoon, when the people who were in the area for the weekend to snowmobile or ski or ice fish would be pulling out. That would leave him enough daylight to search the house and get his hands on something that he could use to meet his short-term cash needs. Maybe he'd even be able to find the safe and figure out how to get in. He just knew there had to be something there that would help him out. Couldn't stay too long, in order to have his time match his story that Baker had sent him back to locate and procure some forgotten object.

C4 pulled off at the I-29 exit and headed south to Fleet Farm. He could walk around there for a bit, top off his gas tank and head to Baker's lake place with a full tank and via back roads. Just making a day trip out of it.

Fleet Farm was hopping on a Sunday afternoon, and C4 saw all kinds of things he wouldn't mind having. Everyone familiar with the giant store called it 'The Man's Mall.' Everything from clothes to farm and ranch gear, fishing and hunting gear, furniture, flooring, you name it. Before the Baker Plan, he would have indulged. But not now. His future was almost secure, and he couldn't risk screwing that up. He needed to hoard his cash and keep his head down. He knew the crux of it all was to score something at Baker's lake home this afternoon that gave him the cash he needed to get through the next several months. The C4 austerity plan to accompany the C4 bridge plan, which was all necessary to ultimately put in place the Baker Plan. This was getting complicated.

C4 pulled into the drive at the Baker lake home, plowing through an inch or two of new snow. He parked as far in as he could. He wanted to be out of sight as much as possible. He pulled on a pair of thin gloves so that his fingerprints wouldn't show up in inappropriate places. He walked to the house briskly and opened the garden tool bin next to the door. Sure enough, deep inside he found the spare key. He then stood up and looked about. He knew the homes directly on either side were empty through the winter, with the summer occupants far enough south that there was no risk of them showing up this time of year. He then had a terrible thought. What if someone told Baker he'd come back? He'd have to say that he had forgotten something of his own and needed to come back without bothering Baker. That would work. He hoped. On the way back to Bismarck he'd have to think of an item important enough for him to make that trip.

He opened the door and went in. Even with the curtains closed, the late afternoon sunlight lit the home up. C4 knew the longer he was here, the more suspicious his presence would be. He was here to grab a for-gotten item for himself or Baker, depending on who asked.

He kicked off his boots and moved into the house, heading directly to the master bedroom suite. If Baker had a stash of cash or gold or anything valuable, it would most likely be in this suite. He had also had access to all the rest of the house through his many prior visits and as hard as he had thought over the course of his journey to get here, he hadn't pictured anything that was of great value and/or wouldn't be immediately noticed and missed.

He pulled open the bathroom window curtains, not directly visible from either the lake or the road, and the room flooded with the additional light. He looked carefully at these unfamiliar surroundings. He searched the bathroom cabinets quickly, then moved to the closet, and within moments found a trap door in the floor. He moved a few pairs of shoes, trying to be careful to note their location in order to be able to put them back exactly where they had been. He lifted the trap door and there it was. A floor safe with a combination dial. He now needed to find the combination.

He was giddy with his success thus far, but knew he had to control himself if he was to get his hand on the contents of the safe. A thorough search was in order.

He went one by one through Baker's bureau drawers, moving clothing carefully and feeling around the edges, but with no success. He searched the kitchen cupboards, again no success. Finally, he sat down on the bed, afraid of the defeat that was sadly at hand. Such a good plan, such an early success, then nothing. Now he'd have to look for a piece of art. That he'd need to fence. With little or no knowledge of its value. Much riskier both in terms of process and value.

He remained on the edge of the bed and contemplated how close he'd come to a successful trip. He had found the safe. He just couldn't find the combination. Maybe it wasn't here at all. Maybe Baker kept that in Bismarck and only brought it with him when he needed it. Maybe he just had it memorized. He might, but most likely it was written down and stashed somewhere in case one of the kids needed it after the old man was dead. It had to be somewhere, hopefully here in this house. He stood and re-searched all the places he could think of one more time. He sat down on the bed again. The clock was ticking. Really. He could hear it. He wanted to smash it. Then he saw one little cabinet he'd not noticed before, deep in the corner next to the closet.

He rose pensively and walked over to it. It was overall about four feet high, unusually ornate compared to the other décor. The top was only about 12 inches by 12 inches, underneath that were four small drawers and the entire thing stood on four curved legs. Very out of place. Maybe it was worth something. But Baker would certainly miss it if it were gone.

On the top of that small cabinet was an equally ornate lamp and a small, gold framed photograph of the most beautiful woman C4 had ever seen. And he fancied himself an expert on beautiful women. She was blonde, with shoulder length hair, somewhat wavy. A style clearly out of date today. The photo had been colorized, and with that touch-up, her eyes were brown, and her facial features were classic, and the makeup she was wearing was perfect. He couldn't help himself. He picked up the picture and gazed at her image, then for some reason he'd never know, he turned it over. On the back was a handwritten note - "To Kendall, Love Kathryn. NDAC 1958."

So, this was Baker's wife. She was indeed stunning. It made C4 wonder what their daughter looked like. He put the picture back just as he had found it. Then he opened the top drawer and found a selection of scarves, earrings and an old pocketbook style purse. He opened the purse and there he found his fortune. The combination to the safe, and the instructions. Right three times to 14. Left twice to 40, then back right once past 0 to 22. Squirreled away in what was apparently a shrine to Baker's late wife. The one who was too frail for the life fate chose for Baker. Made ultimate sense. The one place Baker could easily tell either of his kids to find the safe combination. In mom's purse.

C4 couldn't help himself. He looked in the other two drawers and found more memorabilia. Pictures, and an old dried-up lipstick. Some more earrings, other jewelry and a bathing suit. A jeweled hand mirror. Some programs from shows and other events in and around Fargo. Even a brochure for a hotel in Chicago, of that same vintage. For a crusty old guy, this revealed a much softer side of old man Baker.

C4 jarred himself back to reality. He needed to open the safe and see if his luck continued. He got down on his knees on the floor and tried the combination. No luck.

"Get yourself under control, man, and try it again."

He looked around for no reason. He'd actually said that out loud.

He focused again on the safe, steadying his hand carefully and following the instructions as perfectly as he could. He turned the dial right three times around to clear it, stopping on the first number, then left twice, carefully stopping on the second number. Then back right to the third and final number. He felt the resistance on the dial and carefully turned the handle to open the safe. He was in! Now what would he find that was important enough to be carefully hidden and secured in a floor safe? Hopefully not just another tribute to Katie.

There were some papers - a copy of Baker's will and some other documents C4 put out of the way quickly. Then some cash. Bundles each of fives, tens, and twenties, and under that, two bundles of hundred-dollar bills. C4 was beyond ecstatic. But not because of the cash, which he did not stop to count but because under the cash were a solid coat of gold coins. One ounce rounds, no denomination, no serial numbers. Completely untraceable. These C4 did count. He set them up on the floor in stacks of ten, and had ten such stacks, and another eight. A hundred and eight ounces of gold. He resisted the urge to use his phone to price them, but he knew they were worth at least $2,000 each.

Now the dilemma occurred to him. If he emptied the safe, he'd probably have a quarter of a million dollars, all untraceable. But then he really had to disappear. He had to be long gone before Baker looked in this safe. He realized he was shaking. If he took this and bailed out, he'd end his dad's chances to take over the Baker trusts. This would replace the original Baker Plan and his dad would be left high and dry. There was a chance he might not get caught, but if he did, he'd go to prison, and his dad would be ruined. He wished he had more time to think.

This was a huge decision. C4 wasn't good at making big decisions. His whole life was a testament to that. He was still down on his knees, weighing his decision, well aware of the ticking of the clock on Baker's bureau. It would be dark soon, and he knew he couldn't stay long given his story for making the trip. A quarter of a million dollars now or a nice long-term income stream that left him fixed for the rest of his life. His natural inclination was to take the money and run. But if he got caught there is no way his dad could or would bail him out. He realized his knees were starting to hurt. His back also hurt. He wasn't used to being on his knees and he could feel it. He was so tense he feared he'd leave a drop of sweat on the floor. It wasn't that he was working from a well-formed conscience, but just figuring the odds. Baker would almost certainly look in the safe again, sometime, and C4 had to be on the short list of suspects, given his past and his known access to the house.

If he took just a few of the gold pieces, Baker may overlook that, but certainly not all of them. Stick with the plan were the words emblazoned in his mind. *Stick with the plan.*

So, there it was. He had to stick to the Baker Plan devised by him and for him and his dad. To execute that plan was still the goal. If that worked, he'd have this much money every single year. Besides, this was all part of the plan. If he just took enough gold to live on until his dad could get the full Baker Plan in effect, it really wouldn't matter. It was just an advance on his lifetime income stream. His focus cleared again. Now on to how to best execute the bridge plan that helped him get to the ultimate plan. How often did Baker look in this safe? How often did he count everything? Hard to believe it was very often for either. It was down under the floor and Baker was a lot older than C4. Getting on his hands and knees to open and dig through the safe couldn't be all that easy. Maybe he hadn't opened it in years. *How best to execute the bridge plan?*

C4 zoned out the clock and thought as hard as he'd thought in a long time. He'd take five of the gold coins and nothing else. That was at least $10,000, he told himself, and that would be enough to pay off Vicki and then support him until the real Baker Plan took effect. If he took more, he'd show the money somewhere, sometime and then get caught. If Baker could look in the safe and see the difference between 103 and 108 gold rounds, he was some type of savant. The only risk was that he counted them. C4 prayed that was a really low risk. He would stick to the plan. He had never had to work harder to control his natural instincts. Right now, that meant he also really needed a drink, and he knew there was a bottle of really good scotch a few steps away. *No!*

Ignore the scotch, take the five coins, put everything else back and get away. C4 realized he was talking to himself.

"You got what you wanted. Now escape. This is the best long-term outcome you could hope for. This is exactly what you came for."

C4 had also never done so much self-talk. Mostly because he'd never had or exercised any type of self-control. This, like listening to Baker talk about his life and family, was completely new territory.

C4 kept himself physically controlled. He put five of the coins in his pants pocket and then put the remaining gold coins back in the safe, then the cash, then the documents. He made everything look exactly like he'd found it. He closed the safe and spun the dial twice to the left. He put the trap door back and put the shoes back where they had been. He put the combination back into the purse and closed the drawer. He smoothed the bed where he had been sitting. He walked to the side door where he had come in and then almost panicked. He retraced his steps and went back to close the bathroom curtains. Then he went back to the door, put on his boots, walked outside, replaced the house key exactly where he had found it, walked to his SUV and drove away. He felt freer with every mile.

He'd driven for about a half hour when his phone rang. C4 was startled back to reality. He picked it up carefully. It was his dad. He had to answer, and make it sound like nothing at all was going on.

"Hey, dad. What's up?"

"Where are you?"

"Driving."

"Where?"

"Out of town."

"Why?"

C4's head was spinning. What story would his dad believe?

"I need to stay out of town for a day or two."

"Why?"

"It's kind of embarrassing."

"It usually is. Anything I need to do or be aware of?"

"I don't think so. I picked up a girl at a bar on Saturday night and we spent the night together. Now it appears that she's married."

"That's never bothered you."

"Thanks. But she had me drive her to what she said was a friend's house and I think it was actually her house."

"Does she know where you live?"

"Yes, we spent the night there."

"That's kind of careless."

"I know but it's a result of my new austerity plan. Until something comes along."

"So, you need to stay out of town for a few days in case her husband is looking for you?"

"Exactly."

"And this is cost effective because…"

"Good one. Maybe I can find a friend in Fargo or Grand Forks where I can bunk for a night or two. Should only cost me a meal or two or some beer."

"Good luck. Let me know when you are back in town."

"Will do."

With that the call ended. C4 was very much relieved. He hadn't given up a clue. Now, however, his mind had cleared enough to know he had another problem. He couldn't just stroll into the only gold dealer in Fargo tomorrow morning and cash in five ounces. Someone at the gold dealer would easily remember that if it turned into an investigation. No, that wouldn't work. So as soon as his route took him into North Dakota, he turned north. Grand Forks it was. He'd cash in one there, another in Fargo, and then one each in Sioux Falls and Rapid City before heading home to Bismarck. No, he'd skip Fargo entirely. Safer that way. He'd keep one for later. He'd stay on the move for a few days, and hopefully come home to domestic bliss. In other words, an empty condo. Until then, sleeping on couches of old friends was back in vogue. Like being in college again.

Chapter 8

"TOMMY! HOW HAVE YOU BEEN? Cal Tappen here."

"We're fine. What's up?"

"I need to be in Grand Forks tonight. I've got a little business to take care of tomorrow morning. Are you open for dinner and a drink?"

"Let me check and get back to you. Connie is out at the mall with our youngest daughter. They should be back any time."

"Ok. Just give me a call."

The call ended, C4 checked his watch. He was about 45 minutes from Grand Forks and it was now 4:00 p.m. The sun was getting lower in the sky. He knew he'd have no trouble getting a room at a motel on a Sunday night in January but would rather save the money. Besides, it would be nice to catch up with Tommy and his wife. He had met them both in college, and he and Tommy had continued on to law school, Tommy graduating on time, while C4 had been thrown out for cheating. He knew from sporadic contact with Tommy that Connie was a nurse, and they had three children and had built a nice life in Grand Forks.

C4 thought about a plan B for the night. Was there anyone else in Grand Forks he could ask to bunk with? Only one name came to mind. An old roommate who had not quite gotten through college, so had gone to work, and been married at least twice. Now he was, as far as C4 knew, still in Grand Forks, working construction and leaching off his parents for what he couldn't afford.

Did C4 still have his number? He carefully scrolled through his phone and found it. Steve answered after a few rings.

"C4, is that you? I thought you'd died or something. Where you been?"

"Bismarck as always. How you doing, Steve?"

"Good, good."

"Are you home?"

"No, I'm at work."

"Work? I thought you were doing construction."

"I am, in the summer. Through the winter I do some bartending. College towns are thirsty towns. I tend bar a few shifts a week. Doesn't screw with my unemployment and keeps me in the bar. Get it? Instead of out of the bars?"

"I got it. I'm on my way to Grand Forks, and wouldn't mind seeing you. Where you working?"

"Trixie's. Downtown. Stop in when you get here. I can probably manage a free drink. It's slowing down. Even college kids quit drinking early on Sunday night."

"Sounds good. See you in a half hour or so."

C4 figured that he'd have a drink at Trixie's and even if Tommy called back, he'd work something out and between the two old friends he should be able to land a place to stay.

A few minutes later his phone rang.

"Hey, Cal. It's Tommy."

"Hello. Thanks for the quick return call."

"No problem. I talked to Connie, and tonight isn't good for us. We're having her sister and family over for dinner and we tend to visit awhile, so it's just not going to work out tonight. Sorry about that. Maybe next time you're in town."

"I understand. Enjoy your evening."

The call ended, C4 knew his only hope now for a free room was with Steve, so he'd better behave and be nice. Then he reflected on Tommy and Connie. Tommy was a really good guy, and they had gotten together a handful of times since C4 had left law school. Usually when Tommy's work had taken him to Bismarck. Dinner, a drink or two and that was it. It was nice to catch up. Now, as C4 recollected, he hadn't seen Connie since their wedding. C4 wasn't part of the wedding party, but he was invited. Took a really hot plus one. Had a great time.

It was odd to have a good friend and not have even seen his wife since their wedding. As he drove, C4 worked his way back through his many memories. He smiled a bit as he remembered that once, at a frat party, still undergrads, he and Connie had hooked up in an upstairs bedroom, whose he didn't know. He had caught her coming out of a bathroom and all but carried her to the bedroom, locked the door and "enjoyed her company." He had always thought of it as consensual. Good word, consensual. Maybe she didn't see it that way. He did have to drag her into the room and lock the door and hold her down to get started. A few times she did get noisy, and he had to cover her mouth, but he was used to that. Maybe she didn't think it had been consensual. Women were funny that way. But if she was still mad about that, wow that had to have been almost 20 years ago. That's a long time to hold a grudge. Oh well.

Exiting the freeway, he worked his way down Demers Avenue and toward downtown. After a few passes down the narrow streets, he found Trixie's. He vaguely remembered it from college but didn't think the name had been Trixie's. He parked on the street and walked in. He saw Steve immediately. He had to be 50 pounds heavier and had a puffy looking face. C4 was glad he was taking better care of himself than Steve.

"Steve!"

"C4, you old dog! Glad you made it."

"Me too. Where's my free drink?"

"Not so loud. Trixie is in the office, with the door open."

"There actually is a Trixie?"

"Sure is. Scotch? On the rocks?"

"Absolutely."

Steve poured a rail scotch and set it in front of C4 who just couldn't help himself.

"So why are you on the wrong side of the bar?"

"Long story. My last marriage ended just like the first one, in divorce. No kids this time, so we just split. Found myself with some free time during the winter, so decided why not get paid to be in a bar, instead of the other way around?"

"Makes sense. And your parents?"

C4 remembered Steve's parents with some affection, as they had bailed the two of them out of various scrapes more than once.

"My dad passed away a couple of years ago. My mom is in an assisted living facility. Doing well, enjoys the place better than the empty house after my dad died."

So that was the reason Steve was bartending. Getting his side support from his parents had dried up, as had any chance for an accommodating wife. Now this made sense. Looking him over as he walked down to refresh the tap beer for another customer, C4 wondered how long he could even work construction. Steve returned and sat down on a barstool he had dragged behind the bar.

"Sorry about your dad, Steve. He was a good guy."

"Yeah, he was. Cigarettes and beer took their toll. My mom took better care of herself. She could last another decade or two. Now she wants to be careful with the money she has left."

"How old is she?"

"Seventy-nine. I was the youngest of the kids, so she was already a little on the old side when I was born."

C4 thought for a moment. Parents running out of money. It was like an epidemic.

The two reminisced a bit about college days, and how much the world had changed. Steve poured C4 another scotch and said,

"That's all I can do. The rest you have to buy." Steve went on.

"What brings you to Grand Forks?"

C4 stared into his drink and thought, *I should have seen that coming.*

"Just exchanging some legal materials for my dad. He has a client who has properties in various places and I'm helping out by being his courier. I do what I can for him."

C4 took another sip of his scotch. *Wow, that was almost the truth.*

"Good for you. Wish I had my dad back. How is your dad doing?"

"He's doing fine, thanks. He's not with my mom anymore. They split about 10 years ago."

C4 stopped there. There was no need for any of the lurid details about Susie. Or being broke now. Steve interrupted the silence.

"That's too bad. Happens a lot. My mom and dad managed to stay together but part of that was my dad's failing health. My mom just stood by him until the end."

"Good for her. She was always so nice. To us, to everyone."

"Thanks, she really is still the best. Although a few times we got in enough trouble where we actually needed a lawyer. Then your dad jumped in, and was a real savior."

"He sure was. And your parents helped us out too, when they could. We had a hard time behaving for those few years."

"We sure did. At least you got a degree. I got a football injury and two years of credits over three years. Glad I got a good job in construction. I had a good first marriage and ended up with a couple of really good kids. They're both in the Cities now and doing well. I try to see them a few times a year. Got a grandkid on the way. Their mom is down there now too. I just never took well to married life. Too much partying."

"And the second marriage."

"Thought I'd found true happiness, since we were both partiers. Then she found a guy she liked better. Younger, better looking, more money."

"Sorry to hear that."

"And you?"

"Never married. Enjoy my freedom too much. Worked at a variety of jobs, kind of between things right now, so helping my dad out when he needs me."

"Sounds good. Where are you staying?"

"Probably just a motel. Any recommendations?

"Why not just stay with me? I've got an empty sofa. Not deluxe but we can catch up some more."

"So, who's this, Steve?"

Trixie had come out of her office. She looked older than Steve and Cal, maybe by 10 or 15 years, but still a good-looking woman. Medium height, bleached blond hair, hard blue eyes. Cat-eye glasses hanging on a chain over her ample breasts.

"This is Calvin Steele Tappen the Fourth. Goes by C4. Old college buddy. His dad's a big shot lawyer in Bismarck."

"Nice to meet you, Calvin. I didn't even know Steve had gone to college. What brings you to Grand Forks on a Sunday afternoon in the dead of winter?"

"Just doing some courier business for my dad."

"You must work cheap."

"I do. He runs his own private practice law office and I help out where I can."

"Good for you."

"Steve, pour your friend another scotch. On the house. It's nice to see kids helping their parents."

Trixie pulled a light beer tap for herself and went back into her office. C4 looked at his watch. Exactly 5:00. It's good to have some personal standards, he thought.

A small group poured into the bar, then another. Steve and Trixie were both busy for the next half hour pulling tap beers, mixing drinks, pouring wine, refilling the snack bowls. C4 sat at the end of the bar, taking it all in. Slowly unwinding from what had been a day that was both nerve-racking and exhilarating. He played the whole day over and over in his head. Should he have just taken all the money and made a run for it? But to where? And he knew that if he got caught, he'd be in more trouble than his dad could possibly get him out of. And why would he? He would have poisoned his dad's only remaining well.

"Well, C4. House rules. Buy one drink, get three free. You've gotten your three free, so you need to buy one."

"Absolutely."

C4 pulled out a $20 and put it on the bar. Steve came back with a fresh scotch.

"Nice little rush there. You and Trixie look like a good team."

Steve nodded.

"She's easy to work for. And with. Knows this business inside and out."

Just then another group of six came into the bar.

"Got to run. Be right back."

Again, Steve was busy getting everyone served. This group of three couples took a table and looked to settle in. All were about C4's age, but he didn't recognize any of them. Once they were all served, Steve came back to C4's end of the bar.

"Here's my apartment key. Address is on this napkin. Go ahead and make yourself at home. We'll close at midnight, and I should be home right after that, unless Trixie lets me off early. Depends on how busy we stay. Hope you remember how to run a TV. There should be a frozen pizza in the fridge. Make yourself at home."

C4 nodded, took the key and the address and headed out. He would have said more, but Steve had gone back to checking on the other customers.

C4 walked out the door into the light of the streetlights and headed to Steve's apartment. He would have driven around a bit, but he was tired, a little drunk, and really cold. He certainly didn't want to get picked up with five ounces of gold in his pocket.

He found the apartment easily, and walked up the half flight of stairs, unlocked the door and let himself in. From inside the apartment, he could hear a stereo from a neighbor thumping out the bass line to some song or another and above him a baby cried.

He turned on a light, found his way around, and put his small duffel in the bathroom. One advantage to his lifestyle is that he always had an overnight bag in his SUV. You never knew when you might have to hit the road for a day or two. Today's events were not the usual reason, but it was good to have been prepared. He put the gold coins in a pocket inside the duffel, making sure they were secure. Didn't want those to slide out of his pocket and end up in Steve's couch cushions.

He found the pizza Steve had promised, set the oven to 400 and put the pizza in. He'd never been a fan of preheating. He sat down on the couch and turned on the TV, easily finding an NBA game.

Chapter 9

WHAT WAS THAT NOISE? Piercing, annoying. C4 struggled to wake up. Smoke everywhere. Alarms going off. The pizza!

He made his way to the oven, grabbed the pizza, burned his hand. Turned the oven off. Grabbed an oven mitt, slid the pizza out onto a plate and ran out the door, down the stairs, and threw the pizza into the snow. Panic almost over, he went back in, got up on a chair and pulled down the smoke detector, removing the battery. Then he turned on the kitchen stove vent fan and went around opening windows. Now another sound. A knock on the door.

He went to the door.

"You ok?"

"Yes, just burned a pizza in the oven."

"Who are you?"

"A friend of Steve's. Name's Cal. He gave me a key. He gets off work at midnight."

C4 paused, but his visitor apparently expected more detail, so he kept going.

"I'm visiting Steve from out of town. We met at Trixie's, he gave me a key and told me to come over. He doesn't get off work until midnight. I put a pizza in the oven and fell asleep."

"Do you need any help?"

"No, I've got the fan on and opened some windows. Hope it blows out quickly."

C4 was still getting a grip on the situation, so only then did he notice that his proposed rescuer was a male, maybe 20 to 25 years old.

"Who are you, if I may ask?"

"I'm Ross. I live upstairs. The smoke alarm was loud in our apartment. Thankfully, it didn't wake the baby."

"I'm glad for that too. Thanks for your offer of help. Now I owe Steve some dinner."

"Just call Mickey's. They'll deliver. No smoke, no fire,"Ross smiled as he replied. "The number is probably on the refrigerator. We all use them. Good pizza, too. They'll even deliver beer with it, if you ask nice."

"That sounds like a good idea."

"Well, if there's anything else I can do, I'm right upstairs. Knock gently. As I said, the baby is sleeping."

"Thanks for your help."

"No problem. The building manager is pretty much AWOL, so we all look out for each other. Steve's a good neighbor. He's been here the longest, so we all rely on him to know the ropes. If we can help him or a guest, we'll do that."

"Thanks. I've known Steve a long time. He is a good guy. I'd better get back in and close the windows before the water pipes freeze. And reassemble the smoke alarm. Thanks again."

The door closed and C4 looked around. No real damage and with the fan on and the window open, the smoke was clearing quickly. He put the battery back in the smoke detector and nothing happened, so he got back up on the chair and put it back in its place. Then he looked at the refrigerator and sure enough, there was Mickey's number. He dialed it and in a quick minute he had ordered a pizza and a six pack of the same brand of beer that Steve had stocked in the fridge.

Should have done that the first time. Better pizza and no risk of damage.

Pulling on his boots and jacket, he went out into the front yard, grabbed the shovel from the back of his SUV, scraped the pizza up out of the snow and carried it to the dumpster in the back.

Back inside, he took off his outerwear and closed the window, leaving the fan running. He knew Steve would smell smoke when he got home, so he'd have to come clean about burning the pizza.

He immersed himself in the local news, weather, and sports and planned his next steps. Another visit with Steve when he got home, a decent night's sleep on the couch, hopefully, a trip to the local gold dealer, and then a trip to Sioux Falls to cash in two more gold pieces, then on to Rapid City, then home. Lots of driving. There was a knock on the door.

C4 got up and went to the door.

"Pizza for Steve. Six pack of Coors Light."

The delivery guy looked directly at C4 and went on.

"You're not Steve. And somebody burned a pizza. What's the deal?"

As much as C4 wanted to put this smartass in his place, he knew he was already on thin ice, so was as nice as he could be.

"I'm a friend of Steve's, staying overnight. And yes, I did burn the original pizza, so you're the backup plan. What do I owe you?"

"$22."

C4 peeled off a 10 and a 20 from his money clip.

"Here you go. Have a good night."

"Thanks, you, too."

C4 let the door swing shut and carried the pizza to the coffee table. He pulled off one beer and put the rest in the fridge. With a slice of pizza and a beer, things began to look better. That could have been a real disaster. Thank God for the smoke detector. He had really been sleeping.

He enjoyed a second slice of pizza and another beer, then peeled off a third beer before he moved both to the fridge and sat down to refocus on some late night TV.

The door swung open, and Steve walked in.

"What the heck happened here? Do I smell burned pizza?"

"You do. I put it in the oven then fell asleep. It burned, I cleaned it out and called for delivery. Should have just done that to start with."

Steve just nodded, so C4 continued.

"Steve, is this the beginning of old age? Unable to heat up a frozen pizza without creating a mess?"

"Let's say no. Let's say it was four scotches on an empty stomach after a long day."

"That's very gracious. I'm glad I didn't wreck your apartment."

"Me too. Can I have some of your pizza?"

C4 laughed.

"Of course. The pizza and the beer are both in the fridge. But then you knew that."

Steve microwaved a couple of slices of pizza, then the two men settled in with their pizza and beer and left the TV on for some background noise.

"By the way, the smoke alarm went off and a neighbor came and offered to help. Said you were the de facto caretaker of the building."

"Complex, actually. There are three four-plexes here, and the firm that owns them is in Denver. The manager is in Bismarck, so we never see him here. Except for one trip in the spring and again in the fall to see if there is any maintenance work. Other than that, we're on our own. I'd just call myself the dean of the tenants."

"Good for you."

"Thanks, C4. I have been here the longest, so can generally figure out how to get things taken care of. It's comfortable enough for me, and as the dean, I can help keep things under control. Once in a while, I even give the manager a heads up on some required maintenance or even a bad tenant. Sometimes before their rent checks start to bounce."

"You should negotiate some kind of a rent discount."

"I could, but I just want to be one of the tenants. Not have any special status. This all works better than if I were perceived to be part of the ruling class."

"Got it."

"How about you, C4. Still in that nice condo in Bismarck?"

"Yes, I am. I like it. Especially the heated garage. Saves a lot of wear and tear on me and my car."

"I bet. How's your dad?"

"Still working."

C4 figured the less he said about his dad's situation the better, so he took a swig of beer before he continued.

"In his own practice now. Kind of winding down but doing well. He loves what he does, so hopefully his health holds up so he can keep going awhile longer."

There was a long pause as both men ate and drank and looked at the TV for inspiration. C4 broke that silence.

"We sure did some stupid stuff in college."

"We sure did. We were just lucky we never got into any real trouble. Or got hurt. We drove drunk a lot."

"Yes, we did. And your parents and my dad bailed us out frequently. We were lucky to have that."

Another pause, then C4 went on.

"So, Steve, you dropped out after your junior year?"

"After my third year. I just wasn't 'making academic progress,' or so I was told. I ended up with about half of enough credits to graduate. But then another friend got me hooked up with a big construction crew, and that made it easy to move on. Met my wife, started a family. Problem was, I still hadn't grown up and kept on drinking like I was a frat boy."

C4 nodded.

"I'm glad we kept in touch through the years. I know I went to your wedding."

"Yes, thanks for coming, despite the fact it was rather sudden. Despite that, she was a good woman, but I wasn't ready to settle down, so she kept the ship sailing as long as she could. Now we're all doing well, in our own ways, her, the kids and me."

"Glad you recognize all that, Steve. And by the way, thanks for putting me up for the night. It's nice to have some extra time to catch up."

Again, some silence. Then Steve reopened the conversation.

"So, you're delivering some papers tomorrow morning?"

"Yup. Just a drop off and pick up and then I'll be on my way."

"How about you, C4. Did you ever get close to getting married?"

"No, I never did settle down enough. Never found anyone I wanted to marry, I guess. I missed out on that, but I've had a good life. Stayed close to my dad, especially after my mom left him."

While that wasn't quite accurate, C4 figured that was a better story than what had actually happened. Wanting to move on, he changed the subject a bit.

"Do you ever see Tommy and Connie anymore?"

"Not really. I'm here in the low rent district and they're way out on the south side in a big house with a big yard. He just made partner in a law firm here in town and she's still working as a nurse. I'm sure they're doing quite well financially. They have three kids - girl, boy, girl - and are living the dream. Why do you ask?"

"Just curious. I was kind of close to them in college. Connie was a sophomore when we were seniors. I was invited to their wedding, but not much contact after that."

"I heard Tommy just quit partying during your senior year and that she was part of it. In fact, I heard she had some bad experience at a frat party when she was a sophomore and they were first dating. She quit the party scene entirely after that and he went along with it. Guess he was serious enough about her and law school to turn the page and grow up."

C4 thought a bit trying to remember anything about any bad experiences she may have had, but nothing came to mind.

"Interesting. He's a good guy. Glad he's doing well."

Chapter 10

WHEN C4 AWOKE THE NEXT MORNING, it didn't take long to figure out where he was. The couch was ok, but not exactly a suite at the Waldorf. He rolled to a sitting position and then headed to the bathroom. He went ahead and showered and shaved and was fully dressed and back on the couch when Steve rolled out of the bedroom.

"Sleep ok?"

"Not bad. Can I buy you some breakfast?"

"Sure. I'll get dressed and we can head toward the mall. I've been walking in the mornings since Christmas. Trying to stay in some kind of shape to go back to work in the spring. It may not look like it, but I've actually lost a few pounds."

"Good for you. If we drive separately, I can just get to my stop and you can walk or head for home or whatever."

"Great. Just follow me. McDonald's is right on my way."

The breakfast conversation followed the same pattern, some updating and some reminiscing. It was a comfortable, friendly conversation. C4 was glad that despite some bad choices and some bad breaks, Steve seemed to have created a solid life for himself.

"Thanks for breakfast."

"Thanks for the place to stay. Sorry about the burned pizza."

"No problem. The complex has seen worse."

With that they each got into their cars and while Steve drove towards Columbia Mall, C4 sat in his car and used his phone to locate the local gold and coin dealer. It was down Washington Avenue a handful of blocks and had just opened for the day.

Once Steve was out of sight, C4 made the short drive and parked in the strip mall parking lot. He got out, dug through his bag and pulled out one gold ounce, kept it carefully in his left hand, closed and locked his SUV and walked to the door. He took off his cap and waited to be buzzed in.

He knew he had to have a story about how he got the gold piece, since he had not bought it at this dealer, so was ready for the question.

"Yup, simple gold round. Today I can give you $2,375 for it. Can I ask where you got it?"

"Denver, I think. Don't remember the dealer. I'd been working and traveling and had some cash and checks and bit by bit I converted some of it to gold pieces. Easier to travel with and keep track of."

The proprietor just nodded.

"So, you're just cashing in one?"

"Yup. Just cashing them in as I need the cash."

"So you want to be paid in cash?"

"That would be just fine."

C4 followed closely as the dealer counted out the cash and except for a twenty, put it in his money clip, then went out the door. Step two of the bridge plan was underway.

He pulled back out onto Washington and stopped at the first gas station, used the $20 to buy gas and then headed south, then over to I-29 and started his trip to Sioux Falls.

The weather was in his favor, cold but clear with a little ground drifting. He was through Fargo well before noon and with a couple of stops for gas, snacks, and a restroom, he rolled into Sioux Falls around midafternoon. Driving straight to the gold dealer he knew there, he used the same story to cash in two more gold pieces. This time he got $2,410 per gold ounce. His cash stash was growing nicely. Even with his travel expenses, and with the thousand he borrowed from Vicki, he now had about $7,000.

No stress or suspicion so far. Back on the road, he headed west on I-90 and made it to Chamberlain before he decided to call it a night. He had no problem getting a room in the motel right off the freeway and was able to find a place to buy a fifth of scotch to go with his Dairy Queen chicken strips. He took a quick swig of the scotch straight from the bottle, then enjoyed the chicken strips along with more of the scotch. That, along with the ice machine at the end of the hall and a bed and a TV, and C4 was well into his own personal comfort zone. Everybody has one. Steve, Tommy, old man Baker, his dad. His was just a little different. Doing nothing and having money come in. The Baker Plan would keep him in his comfort zone the rest of his life. He was looking forward to completing his circuit at Rapid City, as he nursed scotch after scotch into his system, getting more comfortable all the time.

C4 awoke with a start. He sat up and the room swirled. Composing himself, he checked his surroundings, and it all came back to him. Motel room, South Dakota. Scotch. He looked at his watch, having learned to never completely rely on a motel room clock. Almost 9:00 a.m. He had to get moving, if he was going to get to Rapid City and home to Bismarck yet today.

He went to the bathroom, washed up, brushed his teeth, grabbed his bag including what was left of the scotch and headed downstairs. He checked out, grabbed a coffee and muffin and headed across the street where he topped off his gas tank, then rolled on to the freeway and pointed his SUV west again. It was normally just a few hours to Rapid City. He made good time and gained an hour, shifting to Mountain Time, so he was at the gold dealer before noon.

Using the same story, he was talked into a slight shift of plans. He sold one gold coin and traded the other for 100 ounces of silver. Not only did he now have a nice sum of cash, but he had none of the gold ounces that could be traced to Baker in any way.

Completely satisfied, he headed out of town toward Bismarck. It would be a five hour drive and he'd lose an hour going back to Central time, but he should still be back home in time for a nap and dinner and a return to his normal lifestyle. Unless the Riverview hostess's husband had gotten wind of the situation. He'd have to keep an eye out for that. As for Vicki, she could watch him all she wanted. He had the money he needed to pay her back and he would do so right on time. Just as she had dictated. It would be so nice to get rid of her.

His only enemy right now was the weather. As he drove north, the snow started, the wind picked up and by the time he was halfway to Bismarck, the driving was getting tough. He stopped for gas, took a short break, and watched the weather on the TV in the truck stop. It was not going to get better, but it wasn't going to get worse either. He pondered his options. He was giving some serious thought to just spending the night at the truck stop when he overheard a couple of truckers saying they were going to 'pound it out to Bismarck.'

C4 waited until they were out and rolling and then decided to follow them. If he could keep up with them, he'd make it. Turns out they had more sense than he did and once they rolled out onto the highway, they seemed to lock in at a speed of about 40 miles per hour, sometimes slowing when the visibility decreased. C4 stayed within sight of their taillights, and after a while he noticed there were a few cars piling up behind him. Luckily, everyone had enough sense to stay in their lane and not try to pass this convoy. Mile by mile, up and down hills, through small towns, they just kept rolling and it was already dark when they crossed into North Dakota. C4 hadn't felt a sense of community like this since his frat days in college. He did have to pee into a coffee cup and then carefully dump it out the window to avoid spraying the car behind him. At about 8:00 p.m. they all rolled into Mandan. C4 took the first main street turning east and drove through town to get to his condo, facing some snow but avoiding any more highway time. As he felt himself relax, he determined that he had never needed a drink more in his life.

To celebrate he opened his bag and took a swig of scotch. He still had a maybe a 15-minute drive in these conditions to get to his condo, but needed the drink sooner than that. He had just put the bottle down on the seat next to him when he met a Mandan police car. He watched in his mirror and the squad car kept moving to the west. That was a break. An open bottle and almost $10,000 in cash might raise some legal eyebrows. In 4-wheel drive, C4 made it through the mostly unplowed streets and drove into his garage and parked. He was completely exhausted. The heat would melt the snow and ice off his SUV and he would finish off the bottle of scotch in the comfort of his own home. He had just run an entirely successful bridge plan operation. All that was left was to turn his attention, and his dad's, to the ultimate goal - the Baker Plan.

Then he realized he had a new problem. A car had followed him into the garage, one he didn't recognize. That was not supposed to happen, and he wondered if he should confront them, as much as he hated doing that. Was it the hostess's husband? That would be bad. He was contemplating his options but before he had to make any decision, the other car parked in the first empty spot, and a woman stepped out. She was all bundled up for the weather, and before he could react, she literally ran to him throwing herself into his arms. He gently pushed her back and got a look. It was the hostess from the Riverview Supper Club.

"Where have you been? I have been hiding for days. My husband says he's going to kill us both."

Only then, as he gently pushed her back and the dim lights of the garage showed her face did he see the badly blackened left eye. This was real. Not some girly fantasy. Her husband was on the warpath.

"How have you avoided him? How are you sure he didn't follow you here?"

"When I got home Sunday morning, he was asleep, but when he woke up, he started asking questions about where I was all night. I said I stayed with a friend because I knew he was drinking. He started calling the friends he knew, and I tried to get him to stop, saying I didn't want to get anybody else in trouble. Then he started smacking me around. At one point he started choking me. I was able to get away and get to the bathroom and lock the door, Then, it got really quiet. I stayed in the bathroom for an hour or so. When I came out, he was passed out again, and I packed an overnight bag and left. I took our car and left town so he couldn't follow me. I went to Minot and stayed with my aunt and uncle for that night, but when my uncle found out why I was there, he threw me out. He didn't want their family exposed to Trevor given his reputation for violence. So, I spent one night in a motel in Minot, then came back here and stayed with different friends, always moving, and then I kept trying to come back here, but you weren't here. I wanted to warn you, and didn't have your phone number. So far, he doesn't know who you are or where you live."

C4 was overwhelmed by all those words coming at him, and was already well beyond exhausted. He had been looking forward to a few more belts of scotch and the comfort of his bed. Now this. What a mess! There was no way he wanted to get into the line of sight of this woman's husband. C4 was a lot of things but a fighter was not one of them. He began to compose himself. First, he needed a short-term plan. But she had started talking again.

"Please let me stay with you. He can't get in here and if we hide my car, he won't even know I'm here. Just for a couple of days."

This piqued his interest.

"What happens in a couple of days?"

"He gets on the company bus and heads out to the oilfields for a 10-day shift. He works 12-hour shifts for 10 days."

C4 was trying hard to catch up.

"And after that he comes back and won't want to kill us?"

"He usually settles down after a week or so."

"Usually?"

There was no answer as she had started sobbing and C4 felt compelled to hug her again to keep her from collapsing. With no clear thought on how to get rid of her, he said,

"Leave your car in stall number 7. They're in Arizona for the winter so we all use that one as an extra. I'll wait until you do that then we can go upstairs."

She silently nodded and went back to her car. C4 kept thinking how much easier this would be if he knew her name.

He had gone from emotional exuberance from getting his bridge plan to work, to exhaustion from the hard winter drive back to his condo, and now to some other emotion he couldn't figure out. Now he had to take in a woman being beaten and pursued by her irate husband. Who also wanted to kill him.

She parked her car and came back with a small duffle. He grabbed his bag, then opened the door to the elevator lobby for her, and once the elevator came, they rode silently up to his condo. With his key, he let her in and then turned on a light. She looked much worse in full light and when she took off her coat, he could also see black and blue marks around her neck. Apparently, her husband had some real anger issues. And to think, C4 reminisced, that he had told his dad he had to stay out of town for a few days to avoid a jealous husband. Turns out that was actually the case.

But C4, being C4, wanted to probe the issue. There was a chance that this girl had fallen in love with his condo and apparent wealthy lifestyle and was just attempting to worm her way into his life, jealous husband or not. The house where he had dropped her a few days ago was nice but not exactly grand, and she was working at a pretty low-paying job.

The problem was, C4 wasn't that good at asking probing questions or developing well-formed insights into someone's personality. Again, he was in new territory, and it was starting to wear him out. He started with his only known tactic.

"Drink?"

She had collapsed on his couch and now turned her face up enough so he could see her bruises and her teary eyes, and she simply nodded.

"Scotch ok?"

C4 felt a need to lighten the mood a bit. Mostly for himself.

"And before you answer, that's pretty much all I have."

She smiled a bit and nodded again.

C4 asked, "rocks or neat?"

"Rocks would be fine. Thanks."

He took his time digging out a couple of clean glasses and using the refrigerator ice maker to put some cubes in each glass. He grabbed his scotch bottle out of his travel bag and poured a couple of ounces into each glass.

He handed her one of the glasses and then sat down in the recliner at the end of the sofa.

"Ok. I think I have the big picture. Take your time and fill me in. We've got time to talk through things and figure out what we need to do."

Again, she just nodded and took a sip of her scotch and shuddered just a bit. Apparently, scotch wasn't her drink of choice. C4 decided to let the silence work. She had to talk at some point. She did.

"I think I told you most of what I know. But what you do need to know is that he is insanely jealous and has done this before, even when he just thought I was with another guy, and I wasn't. As I said, he leaves for work tomorrow evening and won't be back for 10 days."

C4 let that soak in. So, she had to stay out of sight for another 24 hours. The big question is what happened after that.

"Have you called the police?"

"Not this time. I did once and it all got worse."

"Why don't you divorce him?"

"Same reason. He just goes insane. Unless he would be locked away, I am never safe."

C4 could see she had a real problem and now he was in the middle of it. So, the next question popped readily into his head.

"If you knew this about him, why did you come back here and sleep with me?"

"I didn't mean to drag you into this."

She was now sobbing as she tried to answer the question. C4 went to the bathroom and brought her a box of tissues.

"I was just desperate for normal male companionship. I wanted to see if I could remember what that was like."

She paused to breathe and to wipe her nose and eyes.

"Since he was so jealous all the time, I thought cheating on him for real would be no different. But he saw through my usual innocent protests and figured out I'd actually been with someone. I just wanted a normal night in bed with a normal man. And you were in the right place at the right time."

C4 knew it was none of his business but asked his next question anyway.

"Why did you marry this guy?"

"We were both very young and hadn't dated long. We snuck away, flew to Las Vegas and got married. He had never acted like this before that. Now he wants to have kids and I won't do that with him, so he's getting worse and worse."

C4 hated the next question, but knew he had to ask.

"Does he have a gun?"

"Several and he's a good shot. He's in the National Guard and has his marksmanship certificate proudly displayed on our bedroom wall."

That was not what C4 wanted to hear.

"How will you be sure he gets on that work bus tomorrow evening?"

"A friend will text me and let me know. She works out there, too, so she'll be on the same bus."

"And he knows you actually slept with someone?"

"I think he figured it out. He was worse than usual."

"So, he may not settle down this time? He may go to work for 10 days and just make a better plan to kill us?"

C4 regretted his choice of words immediately. She fell back on his couch and sobbed openly and seemed to be unable to quit. He tried a more reassuring tack.

"Do you have parents or a brother or someone to protect you?"

"Not really. I ran away from home to marry Trevor and they all just turned their backs on me. They tried to warn me, but I was too stubborn and too much in love to listen."

"Would they help you now if you admitted you were wrong and were really sorry?"

"I don't know. They were pretty mad."

C4 thought hard. His dad had stood by him through some tough situations, often caused by some stupid decisions. That's what parents were supposed to do.

"Are they near here?"

"Not really. Trevor is from the Jamestown area, I'm from Wahpeton. We met while he was at Science School in Wahpeton, and I was still in high school. We eloped the day after I graduated. I did get that much right – finishing high school."

C4 thought it hard to believe that her parents wouldn't take her back and protect her. If only he could get her to Wahpeton. Or even pointed in that direction. Then maybe he could stay completely out of her husband's sights. Literally.

"Can you call them?"

"I guess. They were really mad, and we didn't talk for a long time. We've made up a bit since then, but we're still not on any kind of decent relationship footing."

He gave that some thought. You'd think her parents would help her no matter what. Regardless, she was in no position to have a telephone conversation until she composed herself.

"Why don't you do that in the morning. Right now, let's fix a bite to eat and just relax and make a little longer-term plan."

"Thank you so much. Can I use your bathroom?"

"Of course. I'll dig out some food."

Twenty minutes later, C4 had some eggs scrambled and bread in the toaster when she came out of the bathroom, having showered and changed into a pair of his sweatpants and one of his t-shirts.

"I helped myself to some of your clothes. I'd been wearing mine a long time."

"No problem. Washer and dryer are next to the bathroom. Help yourself."

C4 nodded toward the table, and they sat down to eat. He topped off their drinks and they both dug in. Nothing like scrambled eggs, toast, and scotch to top off a tough day.

C4 couldn't think of any other way to get at it so he said, "I have an embarrassing question to ask."

"And that is?"

"What's your name?"

She smiled.

"I didn't think you remembered. I was waiting for you to ask. Jolene."

"Thanks."

Even with his natural lack of empathy, C4 knew the best bet was to try to normalize the situation, so once the dishes were cleared, they sat on the sofa and he turned on the TV. Just like a normal couple. Again, new territory for him. One more scotch and C4 turned to her.

"I'm going to bed. What can I do for you?"

"Take me with you. I really don't want to be alone."

And she stood and followed him into the bedroom, taking off the clothes she'd borrowed as she walked along.

C4 looked her over and thought, *if I'm going to get killed by her husband I might as well get my money's worth.*

Chapter 11

THE WINTER SUN WAS BURNING through and around the curtains in the bedroom when C4 awoke. He cautiously looked over and she was there in his bed sleeping soundly. Crap, it wasn't just a dream or a hallucination and the whole fear of her violent, well-armed, well-trained husband gunning for both of them was also likely just as real. He hadn't made a habit of pursuing married women but when one landed in his lap from time to time, he hadn't turned her away. He'd just never come across this situation before.

He got up and went to the bathroom, closing the door quietly. He took a shower, shaved, and picked out some sweats from his closet as he worked his way back through the bedroom. Only then did he look at the clock. It was almost 9:00 a.m. Apparently both he and Jolene needed some serious sleep. He looked over at her and smiled a bit. She was good to have in his bed. He should ask her how old she was. Maybe she could be good company as he embarked on the Baker Plan. She would certainly fill the bill of arm candy, once she healed up a bit. He just had to find out if she was good company in other ways. Maybe it was time to settle down like all his old friends, whatever that turned out to mean.

He wandered into the kitchen and did a quick assessment of the food situation. Clearly Jolene couldn't leave the condo, but he might need to make his usual grocery and liquor store run. Then he had a weird thought. Maybe before he went, he'd ask her what she wanted to eat. Wow, it was almost like he was already domesticated.

He made a pot of coffee and sat down, turning on the TV. He was glued to ESPN when an hour later, he heard Jolene get up, use the bathroom and make a quick phone call, come into the living room, again wearing his t-shirt and sweats.

"Good morning. I take it you slept well."

"I sure did. My first good night's sleep since the last time I was here. Seems like a long time ago."

C4 thought about all that had happened since their initial night together and he had to agree. He'd sure been busy. They'd both been on the run, for different reasons, and now were finally settled in somewhere. Together. He decided to pull them both back to reality.

"I'm thinking you need to stay right here for the rest of the day, until you get the text from your friend that Trevor is on that bus, but I did a quick look around, and we have just enough eggs and bread for one more light meal, then it's over. And we're almost out of scotch. So, I need to go out."

He stopped there, waiting for some kind of reply, and waiting to see if his suppositions were accurate.

"I guess you're right. I need to stay right here. I wish you didn't have to go out, but some food would be nice."

"At some point we're going to get hungry, so I do need to get us something. I can walk to both a grocery store and a liquor store, so no need to move either car. What do you like to eat? Within reason, of course."

"Just some bread and sandwich meat, maybe chips and a few snack foods?"

"Ok. By the way, who did you call this morning?"

"My school. I am a teacher's aide so I called in sick again today. I can't risk Trevor showing up at school and killing me or dragging me out by the hair. Way too risky for the kids and other teachers."

C4 had to admit to himself that he was shocked at that thought. This guy was a real demon if he'd do that.

"I'll bundle up and head out. While I'm gone feel free to wash your clothes or find some more of mine. I'm cold just looking at you. And the t-shirt is a bit sheer, if you get my drift."

Jolene laughed.

"I was trying to tempt you back into bed. Or are you too old for that?"

"I'm not too old. Just too hungry and since you brought it up, how old are you?"

"Don't worry, I'm quite legal. I'm 21, in fact, or else I couldn't work at the Riverview."

C4 zipped up his jacket and walked out the door. Twenty one? That may be another record, at least in recent years. Vicki the oldest, now Jolene the youngest. Setting records all over the place. If only someone wasn't tailing him to collect a debt and another person trying to kill him. Life was way too interesting, just not all in a good way.

C4 was almost done in the grocery store, staring at a package of chicken breasts when someone bumped into him. Not hard, but enough to notice. He looked over, and there she was, Vicki.

C4 immediately asked, "what are you doing here?"

"Protecting an asset. And you? Eating awfully healthy all of a sudden, aren't you?"

"Just stocking up on some food to have in my freezer. Why are you so interested?"

"I just like shopping here. Can I stop up to your place?"

"I'd rather you didn't. I need some private time. Been traveling as you well know."

"I do know. Who's the girl?"

"What?"

"The girl, and I do mean girl. Who is she?"

"Don't know what you're talking about."

"Really hot, about five foot five, a bit buxom, shoulder length blonde hair. Works at the Riverview. Am I getting warm? Or are you the only one getting warm?"

She nudged C4 a bit as she finished her question. How could she possibly know so much?

"She's in a bit of bind. I'm kind of helping her out, like a friend."

"I bet you are. I hear her husband's quite the hot head."

"We shouldn't be talking here."

"You are right. Take good care of her. And yourself."

With that, she walked away. C4 watched her pay for a couple of items at the express lane and then she was gone, dropping her oversized sunglasses over her eyes as she walked into the snow-brightened sunshine.

C4 was so shaken by his interaction with Vicki that he almost forgot to stop at the liquor store. He picked up his bottle of scotch and added a bottle of decent red wine for dinner. Might as well go out with a little class.

He had his arms full making his way home. He dropped all of his purchases on the kitchen table and turned back to the foyer to hang up his parka. Jolene came out of the bedroom.

"I was straightening up a bit, where do you want your duffel? Any dirty clothes to wash? Our clothes might as well be together, too."

C4 thought about the cash and the silver in his duffel, and tried hard not to look shocked. He spoke, trying to remain calm.

"Just leave the duffel. I'll get it later."

He must have sounded more gruff than he intended, because her reaction was a bit more shocked than he had intended or anticipated.

"I'm sorry. I was trying to be helpful. I should have respected your privacy, especially since you live alone. I certainly don't want you to throw me out."

C4 had to smile at that. If only she knew what he had going on and why he needed some privacy.

"Let's have some eggs and toast. We can throw in some cheese this time, and some pepper and onion if you want. Pretend we're eating healthy?"

"Let's do that. I'll cook. I need something to do. And it looks like you bought the stuff to make a salad. Should I do that too?"

"Absolutely. I'll put everything else away."

Jolene did a nice job with brunch, prepping, cooking, and cleaning up, and the rest of the day turned into what C4 thought must be normal for a couple spending a day together. Some conversation, a little napping, lots of TV. He tried to take advantage of any conversation to learn more about Trevor, his background, friends, anything that would help C4 do his best to avoid him or at least minimize the danger he and Jolene were both in.

He also got to know a lot more about Jolene. Besides being a good companion in bed, her most endearing quality seemed to be that she could stand some level of silence. The conversation was not nonstop, rather ebbing and flowing, following a very relaxed, casual pace. He found he actually liked her. Another new experience. He could not, however, forget his conversation with Vicki. How did Vicki know about Jolene and Trevor? It was like she was the CIA and James Bond all rolled into one. She was getting scary.

Jolene had just put the chicken breasts in a pan in the oven and Cal was opening the wine to breathe before pouring when Jolene's phone pinged. She turned from the oven to her phone on the counter and smiled.

Jolene read aloud, "He's on the bus, and we are headed west. P.S. He's snoring."

C4 let go of tension he didn't realize he had been holding.

"I'll drink to that."

He poured two glasses of wine, and they toasted. Then they headed for the bedroom to release more tension.

C4 was relaxing in bed, Jolene was in the bathroom when he heard another ding. He realized it was the oven timer. The chicken was done. He jumped out of bed and headed to the kitchen, not wanting a repeat of the pizza fiasco at Steve's.

He had put the chicken on top of the stove and was about to get a fork to check it when he felt a slap on his butt.

Jolene laughed and said,

"I'll do that. You should probably put some clothes on. I'm getting hot just looking at you."

"Good one. I wasn't sure how long you'd be in the bathroom."

C4 went back to get his clothes. This was actually kind of fun. Better than being alone, that was for sure.

Dinner was great. Good wine, good food, and good conversation. They discussed Jolene going back to her house to live for the next week or so, and normalize her life as much as possible. Back to work, both at the school and at her job at the Riverview.

Over dinner Jolene said,

"I have an important issue."

C4 was at a loss to figure out what that was, so he simply said,

"And that is?"

"We should have each other's phone numbers. Don't worry I won't put your full name and address in my phone."

As she said that she smiled and winked at him, with her one good eye. Apparently, this girl had some guts and a sense of humor.

"We should. Just put down Carlene or something like that. Make sure it looks like a female name."

They both laughed a bit. C4 was happy to have anything relieve the tension they were living with. They exchanged numbers and while it wasn't exactly an intimate moment, it surprised C4 how nice it was to have that handy way to reach out to her. It was all essential because they'd have to stay in touch, of course, to keep each other safe and apprised of Trevor's whereabouts. Jolene's friend would keep her posted.

The evening passed almost sadly, though C4 was ready for some alone time after the past few days. He really did enjoy Jolene's company in bed, and the next morning, Jolene was up early, by C4's standards, to head off to her school job. He spent the day doing his own laundry and doing a little cleaning. He carefully put the cash in his top dresser drawer, hidden among his socks, and he put the silver pieces in an old cowboy boot he never wore any more. He had actually nodded off about 3:00 p.m., and within minutes his phone rang. It was Jolene.

"After school I went home. Trevor trashed the house before he left for the oilfield. It's unlive-able. You should see it. Furniture broken. Food smeared all over. Holes punched in the wall, cupboards torn off the wall, broken glass all over the kitchen. I don't know what to do. There's no way I can get it all cleaned up. He soaked our bed with something. The couch is destroyed…"

C4 cut her off.

"I'm getting the picture. Just get what you need to live for the next few days and come back here. I'll let you in at the garage door."

C4 waited a few minutes then went down to the garage. He kept an eye through the window in the man door and when he saw Jolene's car he opened the garage door for her. She rolled in and he pointed her to spot number seven where she had parked before.

She parked carefully, then got out with her purse, and opened the back hatch. C4 reached in and took the roller bag, pulling out the handle.

"Thank you for taking me back in. You've been a savior!"

She then walked up and put her head on his shoulder. He tried to make the situation a little lighter.

"You're pretty good company. It's no hardship. Besides, it's almost time for someone to cook supper and you're a much better cook than I am."

"You're so sweet. Let's go up. I need a drink."

Chapter 12

BACK IN HIS CONDO, he poured a couple of scotches on the rocks for them and when he sat down next to her, she had her phone out.

"Here are the pictures I took. He wrecked almost every room. And artfully applied ketchup in an attempt to look like blood splatter."

C4 looked over the pictures.

"I think you need to call the police. Even if they don't do anything you will want a police report on file. And it should help you get a restraining order. My dad can help with that."

"But I did cheat on him."

"That doesn't give him the right to beat you and threaten to kill you and wreck your home. What that should get you is a trip to a marriage counselor, or a divorce attorney like civilized people, not death threats."

Jolene nodded like she kind of understood, but wasn't quite buying it.

"Please just call the police now and meet them there. I was just kidding about supper. We'll eat when you get done doing what you have to do."

She nodded again. This was going to be hard for her.

"Can you call a friend and have them meet you there? A witness and some support wouldn't hurt."

C4 was somehow being remarkably helpful and supportive and realized it.

"In the meantime, I'll call my dad and see if there is anything else you need to do. He's a lawyer with years of experience."

He looked at her carefully. Despite the healing of her bruises, partly covered by makeup, she still looked stricken. He hugged her and said,

"I wish I could go with you, but that may only make things worse, especially with the police. Kind of nervy of me to show up there to help you out. Besides, I'm sorry to be so selfish, but I'd rather remain the 'mystery man.'"

"I understand."

She took her phone out of her purse and pushed a predial, and another button to put the phone on speaker.

"Terry? Is that you? Can I have your help?"

She explained the situation and a young sounding woman replied,

"Absolutely! Carson and I will meet you there to see if there is anything we can do. Don't worry. We'll help you."

Jolene hung up then typed out a text.

"What was that?"

"I texted my friend who went to the oilfield with Trevor to let her know what he did. So she can keep an extra eye on him. We don't want him coming back early. He is clearly out of control and may be willing to sacrifice his job to finish hurting me."

C4 walked her back down to her car and let her out the garage door, noting the time she left.

Then he walked back up and sat down on his couch, and dialed up his dad.

"Cal, long time no call. Have you adequately dodged the irate husband?"

"Actually no, and it's worse than that."

His dad simply replied,

"Fill me in."

C4 gave his dad the whole story, about visiting friends in Grand Forks, traveling south and then working his way back to Bismarck, obviously leaving out any mention of the gold he had to convert to cash. His description of the current situation clearly showed his genuine concern for Jolene. When he stopped talking his dad offered his thoughts. "She definitely needs a restraining order. I can draft that for her. And she can file it tomorrow morning. I can even go to court with her. I'll need her full name."

"She'll be back here when she's done with the police."

"She's living with you?"

"Staying. I have a secure building where we can hide her car. This is the safest place she has. She can't let him catch up to her at either of her workplaces. Both are too public."

"You're right, Cal. Sounds like you are doing the right thing. How old is this girl?"

"Twenty-one."

"Wow. Nasty place to be at that age."

"It sure is. Thanks for your help. We'll call when she gets back."

"Ok. I'll be available. By the way, I have my annual estate planning meeting with Mr. Baker on Thursday morning."

"Good. I'd almost forgotten about that in the middle of this other situation."

C4 hung up. This was a real mess. For everyone. The moral of the story seems to be don't cheat with the wife of an insanely jealous husband. For all of his womanizing he had never envisioned this scenario. Maybe in a movie. Now he was living it.

Jolene was gone for a couple of hours. She texted him a little after 6:00 p.m.

"Coming back. 10 min."

C4 walked down to the garage and watched for her car, opening the door to let her in. This time she had a larger roller bag that he pulled up to his condo. She didn't say a word until they were inside and she had collapsed on his couch.

"This is a real mess, and I'm so sorry I dragged you into my train-wreck of a life."

He sat down next to her.

"I was quite complicit. Tell me everything. What did the police say?"

"They took a lot of pictures. Asked me a lot of questions. Took a lot of notes. Told me I needed a restraining order. Said that tomorrow they'd have someone contact Trevor and question him. And just so you know, I gave them Terry's address as my temporary location."

C4 nodded and said,

"Sounds about right. Do you want to eat something? I called my dad and he said he'd write you a restraining order and file it with the court. Tomorrow if you want."

"I don't know if I'm hungry or not. Not sure I'm up to talking to your dad either. Just give me a minute, ok?"

"How about this. Why don't you go freshen up? It would be better if you met my dad personally. He can add some comfort with his experience."

"Ok. I may just stretch out for a bit and process my day."

Jolene went to the bathroom and as soon as the door closed, Cal dialed his dad.

"Jolene is back and is really devastated. Can you come over here and meet with her in person? I think she needs some positive interaction and some reassurance you can help her, more than just a phone call."

"Absolutely. I'll be there in ten. Door code still the same?"

"Yes. Thanks."

C4 sat and waited for a few minutes, then went in to check on Jolene.

"My dad will be over in a few minutes and the chicken from last night is warming in the oven. It can be to be ready to eat whenever you want some."

"I'll be out in two minutes."

C4 walked back out to the kitchen just in time to answer the knock on his door and let in his dad.

"Thanks for coming over. That was a quick ten minutes. Jolene will be out in a minute."

He said it loudly enough that she could hear him and know they were not alone.

"Want a drink, or something to eat?"

"No thanks, I already had something."

Jolene made her entrance.

CT stood up and said,

"You must be Jolene. Sorry you're having to go through this."

"Thank you. You look just like Cal. And I should let you know I don't have a lot of money for legal fees. But I really do need help."

"Don't worry about the fees. This is a pretty straightforward process for me. I have my standard legal pad. You just talk, I'll take notes, maybe ask a few questions, and then tailor a restraining order designed to protect you from your husband. That sound ok?"

Jolene nodded, and she reluctantly started her story.

"I was a senior in high school when I met Trevor at a party. He was a college guy, and I was so impressed. We hit it off right away, and by the time I was ready to graduate we were madly in love. My parents were against it of course. I am the oldest of three, and had really good grades. I'd been accepted to college and they thought that was the plan. They would not help us get married, so we eloped. They were so mad. Still are. They could never stand him. I guess they were right.

"When we got married, we moved to Bismarck, and I tried so hard to be a good wife. To prove to my parents that I was a grown-up and had done the right thing, and to make Trevor glad he had married me. He got work in the oilfields pretty easily, and we always had enough money to live, buying our little house on the east side of town after less than a year of marriage. I got a couple of part time jobs so I never had to ask him for spending money. I started to furnish and decorate our little house. The more I did, the angrier he got. He beat me, a little at first and then it just kept getting worse."

She started to cry, and C4 handed her some tissues. He'd have to buy some tissues the next time he went out. Composed, Jolene continued.

"I hate to even have to mention this, but even the sex got rougher and rougher. I was glad when he went off to work for days at a time. He always accused me of cheating on him, otherwise I'd want sex more. But I didn't, not like that."

She smiled at C4, who felt compelled to ask her what had been on his mind for days.

"Why did you come back here with me, if you aren't in the habit of doing that?"

"Because you were handsome and sophisticated and instead of acting like you were trying to pick me up, like the other jerks who come to the Riverview, you were just nice to me. It had been a long time since I'd been with a man who was just nice to me."

She started to cry a little bit again and the two men looked at each other. The lawyer in the room took over.

"I really appreciate that background. I do need to ask you some hopefully pretty easy questions in order to draft the restraining order."

Jolene nodded and that part of the interaction was pretty straightforward. Legal name, address, all those details, and then more on locations where Trevor would not be allowed, such as Jolene's school and the Riverview Supper Club. Then he followed up with one last question.

"Why do you think he trashed your house?"

"I can't say for sure, but I think he saw it as a sign that I was my own person. That house was the home I was trying to create. It was just too much 'me'".

"Thank you very much. I know this was hard. I'll file this in the morning and let you know if I need anything more, or if you need to make an appearance. We'll have the order served on Trevor once it is in place. Just to warn you, that may trigger another outburst."

"I can't imagine a positive reaction. Thank you and I will pay you, I promise."

The two men stood.

"I'll walk you down, dad. Jolene, I'll be right back. You should really eat something. If you want, I can help you when I come back up. I'll only be gone a minute."

There was silence until the two men were in the elevator and the door closed, then CT said,

"I have a few comments. One, wow! She is a knockout. If I were her husband, I might be insanely jealous, too. Two, lucky you, picking up the wife of a pure psychotic. Number three is actually a question. When did you get so warm and helpful and domestic? Where has that been the past 30 or so years?"

C4 smiled.

"Points taken. I'm also a bit surprised at how helpful I've been, but she is literally running for her life. Even I couldn't abandon her to that. And he did threaten to kill me as well. There's more than a little bit of self-preservation at play."

The elevator door opened. When CT walked out, he turned and said,

"We'll be in touch."

When C4 went back into the condo, Jolene had the chicken out of the oven and was setting the table for two. He took that as a good sign.

Chapter 13

IT WAS STILL FULLY DARK on Friday morning when C4's phone rang. He grabbed it as quickly as he could, trying not to awaken Jolene. The prior evening with his dad had been a somewhat comforting end to a very trying day and he was glad she was asleep. He checked the bedside clock. 6:15. He was alert enough to know it was a.m.

He walked out into the living room before he spoke.

"Hello?"

"Hi. Sorry to wake you but wanted to give you a heads up."

"Who is this?"

"Never mind who this is. Listen carefully. The police are going to stop by to see Jolene. Let them in and be ready to be supportive."

The caller hung up. C4 stared at the phone. That was more than weird. Would this whole situation ever stop getting weirder?

He sat down on the couch and started replaying the last week in his head. For a guy who liked to sleep, drink, and put very little effort into getting the money he needed to live, this had been an extremely busy week or so. Thinking back to the poker game he won in Mandan, to the game he lost in Dickinson, and Vicki. There he stopped. Somehow this all seemed to be connected to Vicki.

He dozed off a bit, but then his intercom buzzer rang. He answered.

"Hello."

"This is officer Ray Crosby of the Bismarck Police. We're here to see Jolene Buchanan."

"Come on up."

C4 pushed the admittance buzzer and went to wake Jolene.

She was sitting up in bed, oblivious to her lack of clothing. He smiled just a little bit.

"You should probably put some clothes on. You're getting visitors."

She covered up.

"I heard something going on. What time is it?"

"About 6:30."

There was knock on the door.

"I'll get that. You come out when you're ready."

C4 opened the door. One of the cops he recognized immediately from prior interactions. The other he did not. Older, carrying a Bible. That was odd.

"Good morning. Thanks for buzzing us in. I'm officer Crosby. I believe we've met before. This is Officer Arnegard."

"Jolene will be right out. Coffee?"

"That sounds good. Can we just sit at the table?"

"Absolutely."

The two policemen sat down, and C4 started a pot of coffee. Once it was starting to brew, he set out cream and sugar and four cups. Except for the coffee maker the silence was deafening. C4 tried to lighten the tension. Another new experience for him.

"Usually, I'm the one you're looking for, though I think I have settled down a bit."

The older cop had the decency to smile.

"Don't worry, you're still on our radar. I actually wish we were here to talk to you."

That did not bode well, C4 thought. Was this about the trashed house? Couldn't be about the missing gold coins or they'd be there to talk to him.

Just then Jolene walked into the room, dressed nicely, even wearing shoes.

Both policemen stood when she approached. The older policeman indicated the one empty chair and said,

"Please sit down."

Jolene looked confused, but sat as directed.

"What is this? Am I in trouble?"

"No, you're not. But I need to ask, you are Jolene Buchanan, is that correct?"

"Yes."

The older policeman looked from Jolene to C4 then back to Jolene and continued.

"I am a Bismarck police chaplain and I am sorry to have to tell you that your husband, Trevor, was killed in a work accident last night."

Jolene looked truly stunned.

"Are you sure?"

"Yes. We always make sure before we deliver news like this. He was driving from the oil rig he was working on to get some parts they needed to make a repair when he drove off the road. His truck rolled several times. He was dead at the scene. There will be an OSHA investigation, of course, but it looks by all accounts to be accidental."

This was the weirdest thing C4 had ever heard, especially given his 'heads up' phone call. The timing of this was just too strange to be a coincidence. Or was there a god who could reach down and fix things that really needed fixing?

"May I pray with you?"

Jolene just sat there for several long moments, expressionless. She had come out of the bedroom without any makeup on so both policemen had certainly noticed the bruises. Once again, they looked from Jolene to C4 and then back to Jolene. Given all the tears she had shed in the hours C4 had known her, right now she seemed to be too stunned to cry. Or maybe she just couldn't cry any more. Or maybe she was relieved, or even happy. She showed no emotion whatsoever.

The chaplain broke the silence, again.

"May I pray with you?"

Jolene looked directly at him like she was seeing him for the first time.

"Of course. Please do."

The chaplain led a brief prayer followed by the Lord's Prayer.

The prayers completed, the chaplain lifted his head up and turned back to Jolene.

"Is there anything else I can do for you? Contact a pastor? A friend? Your parents? So, you know, we will have to contact Trevor's parents. He also had them listed as emergency contacts."

Jolene still looked stunned. No response forthcoming, the chaplain put a business card in front of her and said,

"Please call me if you think of anything at all."

The two uniformed men rose, and C4 walked them to the door. The door closed, C4 turned back toward Jolene who still sat slumped in her chair, staring at the card on the table. He walked over behind her and put his hands on her shoulders. The only sound in the condo was that of the coffee pot finishing brewing. His life was now completely out of control. All because he had brought a girl home from the Riverview. The Baker Plan, the bridge plan, all faded into the background. He just kept finding himself in one new situation after another. And they weren't getting any better or more normal.

Or were they? He had never known Trevor, thankfully, and now he was gone and Jolene no longer had to live in mortal fear. He had a hard time feeling bad. And he felt bad that he didn't feel bad.

Jolene stood up.

"I'd better get ready for work."

C4 hugged her as gently as he could, being sure to position himself between her and the bedroom.

"No, no, no, no, and no."

"Cal, what are you doing. I have a job to get to."

"Jolene, listen to me. I don't know what you're feeling right now, and you may be numb. But you can't go to work a half-hour after you learn that your husband is dead. Even if you're not devastated by the news, and I wouldn't blame you if you weren't as sad as a new widow would typically be, you still can't go to work. You do need to call your parents and reach out to Trevor's parents, but first, I'd call your friend who worked with Trevor to see if she knows more than we were just told."

Jolene collapsed on the couch. This was getting to be the new normal. Jolene collapsing on his couch. C4 sat down in his recliner, facing her at an angle.

"I'm going to call my dad. No need to file that order."

No response. C4 dialed up his dad.

"Good morning! What are you doing up at this early hour?"

"The police were just here. With a chaplain."

"What's going on?"

"Jolene's husband was killed in a work accident last night out in the oilfields."

C4 let the silence soak in, for all three of them. He knew his dad knew what this meant, but he was waiting to see if saying it out loud jolted Jolene out of her stupor.

"I'm so sorry for her. I won't file the order, obviously. Is there anything else I can do?"

"Not sure yet. I'm guessing some probate stuff, but that doesn't need to start today."

"Right. Let me know if you need any help, personal or professional."

The call ended, C4 turned his attention back to Jolene. He wished she would cry or laugh or talk or anything. Once again, a whole new experience. He wished he could quit having new experiences, at least for a while.

He moved over next to her and put his arm around her. They just sat there for a few minutes, then she spoke, still staring at the coffee table.

"I should be sad, but I'm not. But I'm not happy either. I guess I'm just relieved. I'm glad we had no kids. This is not what I wanted, but yet I am feeling mostly relief. I feel bad that I feel relieved. I just don't know what to do next."

"You should call work and tell them you won't be in. Then I'd like for you to call your friend who rode the bus out to the oilfields with Trevor. Maybe she knows more about what happened and you can get some closure. And you really should call a pastor or a funeral director or somebody. And your parents and Trevor's parents."

She started to cry, and C4 knew he'd way overdone his helpfulness.

"Or maybe just call your best friend and have her come over."

At that, Jolene nodded and handed Cal her phone.

"Terry. Top of the recent calls."

C4 pushed the button Jolene indicated and a voice answered after several rings.

"Hello, Jolene?"

"Hi, Terry. You don't know me; my name is Cal Tappen. I'm with Jolene and she just found out that Trevor was killed in a work accident last night. She'd really like you to come over and help her with calling people and all the other arrangements that she has to take care of."

Silence, then,

"Oh my God! I'll be right over."

C4 gave her the address and less than 15 minutes later, buzzed her in.

After the most basic of introductions, Terry and Jolene sat down at the kitchen table and Terry started making notes of things to do, mostly people to call.

The rest of the morning was a whirlwind of telephone calls in and out – family, friends, the pastor at a church in Bismarck that Trevor and Jolene had attended with Terry and her husband once or twice. The pastor came over and with him, they called a funeral director. C4 once again couldn't fathom how much his life had changed, all because he'd picked up a girl at a club. It was something he'd done countless times over his life. But this time it had all turned out differently. He was amazed at how kind and helpful everyone was. A swath of humanity he had not experienced before.

He tried to stay out of the way, but also found himself listening in. In particular, to a call to Jolene's friend, Mary. The one who worked in the oilfields and had been keeping an eye on Trevor. He said nothing to Jolene or Terry about his early morning call, but was very interested in hearing more from Mary, to see if there was any suspicion that Trevor's death was anything but accidental.

Jolene finally agreed to call her, so they all three sat at the kitchen table. Jolene found her number in her phone, then handed the phone to Terry, unable to talk. Clutching her tissues. Terry put it on the kitchen table, on speaker.

"Mary, this is Terry, Jolene's friend. How are you doing?"

"Stunned, I guess. Is Jolene there?"

"Yes, I'm helping her with some calls and arrangements."

"Thank you for doing that. I would sure need some help if it were me. Is there some way I can help?"

Terry looked over at Jolene, who nodded. Terry continued,

"Yes please, can you tell us any more about the accident? What happened?"

"Well, like all of us, Trevor started his shift at 9:00 p.m., and a few hours later, he was sent from the drilling rig he was working on to a supply shed for some replacement parts for the rig. He took a company truck, an old one-ton flatbed and took off. He was probably in a hurry since the rig was shut down while he was gone. It should have only been a fifteen-to-twenty-minute round trip. He hadn't come back after a half-hour, so one of the guys on his rig called the supply shed and found out he'd never gotten there. A couple of guys from the rig took another truck and drove the route he would have followed and saw tracks going off the road. Apparently, he'd swerved sharply, and gone down a steep em-bankment. His truck was upside down on the bottom. It was dark, of course, and they saw it only because the lights were still on. They called 911 before they even went down there to check on him, but he was non-responsive. The EMTs arrived within 15 minutes, and they pronounced him dead."

Mary took a break to breathe or cry or something and that was the first C4 noticed that Jolene was holding his hand and also holding Terry's hand. Jolene composed herself enough to speak.

"Thank you, Mary. It must be hard for all of you out there."

"We're all in shock to some degree or another. We know we are in a dangerous business with all this equipment and the long hours and all that. This happens from time to time, but it's still painful when it does. It reminds all of us to be more careful. What we don't know is what caused Trevor to swerve off the road. There were no other tracks, so it may have been a deer or a wild horse, or anything. We may never know."

Terry looked at her two companions, and then asked,

"Is there anything else we should know?"

"Well, the only other thing is that the rumor we're hearing out here is that his seatbelt broke. That's why he took the brunt of his injuries when the truck rolled several times down into the ravine. Some of us don't even fasten our seatbelt when we jump in a truck to run an urgent errand. If you get caught that's an automatic fine and if they catch you again you can be fired for it. It looks like he had fastened his, but it still didn't help him. The broken seatbelt will likely be key point in the OSHA investigation."

Mary had apparently run out of things to say, so Jolene spoke again.

"Thanks so much, Mary, for talking with us. It helps to have some picture of what happened."

Then Terry said,

"Mary, tell everyone out there how sorry we are for your loss. That has to be hard to lose a coworker in an accident that could have happened to anyone."

"Thank you."

C4, however, sat and wondered. *Could it really? Why the swerve? Could a seatbelt just break? Did the person who called him just before the police know what really happened?*

Mary was speaking again.

"Please let me know about funeral arrangements. I'd like to come and if there are enough of us who can get away, the company will provide a bus or arrange other transportation."

That was more reality than Jolene was ready for. She was silently crying, so Terry replied.

"We will do that, Mary. I'll put your number in my phone, so I can reach out. We really appreciate the information. You take care of yourself."

"I will. We all will. Jolene, you take care, too."

Jolene managed to rasp out a 'thank you.' The three of them looked at each other and Terry ended the call.

Terry looked at C4, not unlike the way Bella looked at him during their brief interactions at Mr. Baker's place, but her words did not match the look.

"Thank you, Cal, for being here for Jolene and for giving her a safe place when I couldn't and nobody else would. You may have saved her life. And you are being wonderful right now, letting us camp in your kitchen doing these unenviable tasks."

C4 was a bit taken aback, both by the difference between her look and her words, but also by her profound thanks. He stifled his standard hip shot reply of 'my pleasure' figuring that could be too easily misconstrued.

"I'm glad I could be here for her, and I am glad for all the help you have been to her."

Jolene managed a little laugh.

"That's quite the little lovefest. I don't want you two running off together and abandoning me now. Terry, you should go to work. I can manage from here."

"No, Jolene, you and I are going to my house to continue these calls and arrangements so that Cal can have some peace."

After some back and forth, Terry had talked Jolene into going home with her, and C4 was actually relieved. Now it was his turn to collapse on the couch.

While Jolene went into the bedroom to pack some things to take to Terry's house, C4 quietly asked Terry,

"Jolene said she gave the police your address when you left her house last night, right?"

"Yes, she did. Why?"

"Did the police call you this morning to track her down?"

"No, why?"

"Because they knew to come here, and I would have thought they'd have contacted you first. How did they know she was here?"

Just then Jolene came back out of the bedroom.

"What are you two whispering about?"

Terry replied.

"Nothing really, just making sure we are both doing all we can to help you."

Jolene smiled and said,

"I know I can count on both of you."

She gave C4 a quick kiss on the cheek and then took Terry's hand. C4 held the door for them while they walked out and to the elevator. Once the elevator doors closed, he let his door shut. He sat down at the table and finished his coffee. *How did the police know to track Jolene down here?*

Chapter 14

HE WAS OUT OF THE LOOP on moving Trevor's body back to Bismarck and then on to Jamestown, the interaction with the state coroner, who had informed Jolene on an early call that a few tests were routine, and making funeral arrangements. And the sheer volume of phone calls - Jolene's family, Trevor's family, the funeral home, pastors, and churches.

He just knew his job for the next few days was to stay completely out of the way and see if Jolene chose to reappear in his life. He enjoyed, in a sad way, the solitude. He easily fell back into his old lifestyle, sleeping until noon, drinking all afternoon and evening until he fell asleep either in bed or on the couch. Not even taking a shower. The only difference is that he didn't go out looking for fun or trouble. He just hibernated. His condo, the grocery store, and the liquor store became his universe. Friday afternoon blended into Friday night and then Saturday.

His dad came over and brought him some dinner on Saturday evening. C4 cleaned up enough to be presentable. Even CT was worried. Sunday, he fell back into his bad habits, drinking before noon. That had been a stupid rule anyway, when you live alone.

On Monday, he thought of Jolene all day, knowing that was the day of Trevor's funeral, which was back in Trevor's hometown in the Jamestown area. He'd texted Jolene a couple of times and Terry had responded, filling him in so he knew the burial would also be back in Trevor's home church cemetery outside Jamestown in the spring. He had enough information to know Jolene was in Jamestown Sunday and Monday, even if he'd wanted to see her, or she him.

In fact, he wondered if he wanted to see her, feeling somewhat responsible for what had happened to her. Her husband was dead and while it was apparently a work accident, the call he had received just before the police came had been very strange. Who was it and how did they know and why did they call him? Was it her friend who had told Jolene that Trevor was on the bus?

Stepping way out of character, he even bought a local newspaper on his only grocery store visit, just to read the article about Trevor's death and the obituary, which was very kind, probably written by Terry and Jolene. It was good she could say some nice things. "Good provider, hard worker, enjoyed hunting and other outdoor sports." No mention of wife beating as a hobby.

On Tuesday, he figured she would likely be back in Bismarck, and maybe even back at work. He wondered if he'd hear from her. Even if she didn't want to move back in or even see him again, she did have some clothes and stuff at his condo. Maybe she'd send Terry or Terry's husband to pick them up.

He kept himself sober all day, partly to dry out, and partly because he was holding out hope that she would call. He had to wait all day before she called, just before dark.

"Hi."

"Hi."

That brutally brief conversation was followed by a moment of silence. Then Jolene continued.

"I hear you make really good scrambled eggs. Is that true?"

"I like to think so."

"Any chance of a dinner invitation? Or are you playing hard to get now?"

"I would love to scramble some eggs for you. Right now?"

"Give me an hour. I completely collapsed after yesterday and need to clean up a bit. No need to hide my car anymore. I'll park out front, and you can buzz me in, just like a regular visitor."

C4 smiled to himself and said,

"Why don't we meet at the back, as usual, and you can park inside. No need to start the gossip now."

"That makes sense. Usual spot. One hour."

What he actually did for the next hour was clean himself up. His first shower in days. He shaved and put on clean clothes. Then he cleaned up the condo and took out the garbage, much of it empty scotch bottles. It took the full hour to make himself and his home presentable.

C4 stood by the man door looking out the window and was ready with his garage door opener when he saw Jolene's car.

She drove straight in and to spot number seven. He walked over, not sure what to do. A hug, a kiss? Just a hello? This again, was new territory.

Jolene stepped out of her car and opened her arms. He was happy to give her a hug. Still not sure if was a romantic hug or a condolences hug, but at least they were together. Despite their previous intimacy, this seemed different. Like there was a ghost in the room and yet no barriers to their relationship.

Jolene whispered into his ear,

"Can we go upstairs?"

C4 laughed.

"Of course."

They held hands to the elevator, in the elevator and into the condo. There they hugged again. Jolene took off her coat and hung it on the coat tree by the door. Like it belonged there. She then walked to the kitchen.

"I'll scramble the eggs. You make some toast."

C4 just nodded. This was the oddest mix of familiarity and strangeness he'd ever felt. He really was not sure what to say next, so making toast gave him something to do.

Several times they both started talking and then stopped. Jolene looked at C4 and said,

"Why don't you talk? Ask me questions, whatever? Just don't ask me how I've been. That might make me cry. Ok?"

"Ok. I am so glad you have a good friend like Terry. I am thinking that she was a great help."

"She was. Couldn't have made it without her. Even when I just laid around her house today deciding when and how to restart my life."

C4 nodded.

"The eggs are great. How's the toast."

"Never better."

C4 decided to try one specific line of questioning.

"And how are things with your family? Mom, dad, ok?"

"They were very supportive. Came to the visitation and the funeral. More time than I'd spent with them since Trevor and I got married. I kind of found out by accident over the weekend that his family wasn't thrilled with our marriage either. Thought I was too young… but now that's over."

C4 studied her carefully, wondering if she was going to hold up. She did and went on.

"I knew we were headed for some kind of breakup, though with his temper it was not going to be easy. Even before I met you. His death, while horrible, is almost providential. Like I am getting a new opportunity without having to deal with the agony of a separation and divorce. I feel so bad for his family. They never saw the bad side of Trevor and I'll never say anything about that to them. Thank God I had no bruises when I had to go be with them for the funeral. And obviously, there was no mention of you, whatsoever. Though you did save me, and I will never forget that. Even Terry recognizes that. Though, since she has lived in Bismarck longer than I have, she also mentioned to me that you have quite a reputation."

"All good, I'm sure."

C4 looked Jolene directly in her eyes. She was smiling.

"More like I was not the first damsel to share your bed."

"All rumors. Very little truth. You know how these legends grow in a town like this."

"Terry just said she could name names. I declined."

"Good choice. No need to refuel old rumors."

They ate in silence for a bit. C4 decided to take a chance and probe the last few days.

"How was the visitation and funeral? Well attended? Comforting?"

"Yes, to all of that. Lots of people. Some I'd met through Trevor. Many of his family and friends from around Jamestown. My family and a number of friends from Wahpeton. Some people from the Riverview and from my school here. A few people from Trevor's work. Kind of a crush of people, but very reassuring. Lots of support. The memorial money is still coming in. I think I'll give it to the church in Jamestown."

C4's brow furrowed.

"How are you going to live? I assume Trevor made most of the money."

"Yes, he did. But his employer had both life insurance and accidental death benefit insurance, and since he died at work, there will be some worker's compensation death benefit as well. I'm not sure, but I think it will add up to almost $300,000."

"Good. That's a lot better than nothing."

"Of course, some of that will be needed to fix up our house. My house now, I guess. Which reminds me, can your dad help me through all that? Neither Trevor nor I had a will. We just figured there wasn't much to split or to leave to anyone. The house is about it. He had a bank account with some money. We had a joint account, and I still have a bank account where my paychecks go. Since he was gone so much, we only had one car. He did keep his old pickup truck from high school, and that's what he used when I was on the run."

C4 took that all in.

"I'm sure my dad can help you work through all that. It will just take some time. Hopefully his bill will be less than $300,000."

Jolene actually laughed a bit.

"If he takes all my money, I'll just have to move in with you and make you support me."

So, there it was. Some kind of overture about the two of them maybe having a future together. C4 let that soak in. Jolene smiled at him and stared at him for a bit.

"Cat got your tongue?"

"Not at all. Just wasn't sure where we were in this brave new world. Or if you're just kidding around with me."

"Let me back down a bit. Can I stay here with you while I get my house cleaned up? Just that? I think Terry and her husband have put up with me long enough. I will clean your house and scramble your eggs and keep you warm at night. How's that for an offer? Short term only, at least for now. Just for a week or two."

C4 nodded. That would be just fine. He had not enjoyed his past few days of drinking and living like a hobo in his own home. He didn't share those thoughts out loud, rather he simply said,

"That sounds great. You already have some clothes here. Just don't throw my stuff out to make room for yours"

"Mr. Tappen, your terms are acceptable."

"Then there's only one more really important step."

Jolene looked puzzled. C4 smiled.

He opened a drawer in the kitchen and dug around a bit.

"Your very own garage door opener. You need to be able to come and go whether I'm here or not."

Jolene laughed as she accepted the opener.

"This is kind of like a token that we're going steady!"

This time C4 laughed.

"I'm fine if you want to think of it as just that."

And just like that C4 had his first real roommate since college.

Chapter 15

"SHE'S WHAT?"

"Staying with me until she gets her house put back together," C4 replied.

"In your spare bedroom?"

"Not exactly."

"So, she's living with you?"

"Just temporarily."

"Even you can't believe that. She moved in. Women don't move in with men for a week or two. This isn't some old army or college buddy who needs a place to stay until they get on their feet. Women are different."

"Like you're an expert?"

"I know more than you do. Please, just listen to me. I can't tell you what to do but I just want to tell you what I know. Ok?"

C4 nodded. He knew he needed to hear his old man out, because they were soon going to launch a big business deal together and he couldn't afford to lose the deal now. At least he knew it was a big business deal that he would be part of even if his dad didn't.

"Fair enough. Go ahead."

"I understand that she's beautiful and charming and lovely and fun to be with. But there are a few other things you need to consider. One, she's extremely vulnerable right now. She was with you when her husband died. In your arms. In your bed. You gave her shelter and solace and love and support. Someday that will wear off. Just know that."

C4 nodded. He had given that some thought.

"And two, she's 21 years old. You are almost twice her age. You are the same age as her parents. I'm not sure how better to put that. In a year or two or three she will want a nice big house and some kids, who will go to school and play soccer and t-ball and take dance classes. All the things they should do. And she deserves that. Can you give her that? Will you change enough to give her that?"

C4 had to admit to himself he hadn't quite painted that picture in his mind. Right now, he was in full honeymoon mode. However, he also wanted his dad to put all his thoughts out there, so they could end this topic.

"Anything else?"

"Have you mentioned what you do for a living? Or rather don't do? Her dead husband at least had a job."

That kind of hurt. C4 had the Baker plan and then he'd be on easy street. That was surely enough to support the dream his dad had just laid out for Jolene and a family. But he couldn't tell his dad that was his sole vision for providing himself a means of support. He certainly hadn't told his dad that he expected to be on his dad's payroll forever. He would just tell Jolene that he had some business deals that supported him, or them.

Now he realized that he owed his dad some kind of response, to acknowledge that he had heard his dad's concerns.

"I hear you, dad. I do. I had not thought through all of that as well as I should. I do know she's vulnerable, and I don't ever want to hurt her. I will take this next couple of weeks and make sure we have the right conversations. I need to give some serious thought to your description of the future, and I do need to figure out how I'd support her. I appreciate your thoughts."

"Good. Looks like our food is here. By the way, where is she tonight?"

"Back at work at the Riverview."

"What if she picks some guy up and brings him home? I heard she did that before. What are you going to do then?"

"That's just mean."

"Yeah, it was, I guess. One more thing. Her living with you starting just before her husband died and continuing right after doesn't help her reputation. Are you going to keep this a secret? From her friends? Her family? Trevor's family?"

C4 looked at his plate. He couldn't look at his dad. This he had not considered, he had to admit. A secret life with a hot girl half his age. Who wouldn't want that? That's about as far as he'd gotten. And the future stuff about a family and all that, that was the future, and may never happen. This issue of their relationship was real and right now. Terry and her husband knew about their relationship. He wasn't sure anyone else did. He'd have to ask Jolene how this was going to work, and who was going to know and what if people found out. Reality sucks.

Once again, he had a huge conflict. How to have exactly what he wanted, which was Jolene in his bed every night, and not hurt her or her reputation or her relationship with her friends and family. Life was so much easier when you ignored conflicts and just did what you wanted. Kind of like 'borrowing' five gold coins from old man Baker.

"You raise another good point, dad, and one I need to talk to Jolene about sooner rather than later. How's your steak?"

"Not bad and do talk to her. I think she needs to face reality as much as you do. Let me know when she wants to talk about her late husband's estate. Shouldn't take much, but we might as well get started. And I hope you are not in this relationship because of all the death benefits coming her way. Those are hers and she needs those. Got it?"

"Absolutely."

Oddly, he had not thought of getting his hands on her newfound wealth. Maybe he was growing up. Maybe he really did care about her. That was a new thought, and he was really tired of having new thoughts.

C4 sat back in his chair. Eating the rest of their meal in silence had been a nice break.

"I suppose I'll be picking this up," asked CT.

"No, I can get it," said C4.

"You can?"

"Sure. I have a little cash. I can spring for dinner once in a while. Not too often, though."

C4 had decided that to show his dad that he had some means of his own, after the lecture on how to deal with Jolene, would let him leave their dinner with a bit of pride intact.

"Go for it. And remember you can't bring the waitress home now either. Those days are over."

"Maybe I won't pay. Maybe you should get the bill and make your play for the waitress."

"No, I don't play that game anymore. Get the check. I'll quit picking on you. For now, anyway."

The waitress approached a moment or two later.

"Can I get you anything else? Dessert? Coffee? Cappuccino? We have a nice selection of after dinner drinks."

C4 looked her way and said,

"I think we're good for the night. I'll take the check."

CT looked over at C4.

"No dessert?"

The waitress smiled. C4 shook his head and said,

"You know neither of us ever eat dessert."

"I know. Just kidding. He'll take the check."

The waitress put the check tray down on the table. C4 opened his money clip and pulled out two one hundred dollar bills. Laying them in the tray he said,

"That should do it. Nice tip also."

"Is that your Baker money? Remember you have a wife and almost kids now."

"You just can't leave my situation alone, can you?"

"I am really enjoying the entertainment value of your situation, as you called it. I just hope no one, meaning her, gets hurt."

"Thanks, and you're welcome for the meal."

His dad wasn't done, but the topic took a more positive turn.

"I almost forgot to mention. I have an update on my estate planning meeting with Baker. It went well. He spoke very highly of you. I asked him if he had you confused with someone else."

C4 rolled his eyes.

"You just can't give me any credit, can you?"

"No, I didn't say that. I told him you liked him and enjoyed his company and really enjoyed going to Minnesota with him. Positive as I could be."

"Any word on redirecting his estate management?"

"We talked about that. Making sure we have his will and the trust and all the other documents written the right way, and that the trustee takes an active interest in managing the properties well. He listened. May talk to his kids. We'll see what happens. We meet again in a couple of weeks."

"Sounds like you planted the seed."

"Yes, and I think it may take root. Just be sure you continue to take good care of him."

"I always do."

As C4 drove home, he thought about the evening's conversation with his dad. His dad had been right about just about everything. C4 was not the suburban dad role model, and at some point, Jolene would want that to be her life. Should he try to have the conversations now to set things straight between them?

On the other hand, if he and his dad could get control of the Baker fortune, he could be whatever he wanted to be. Maybe a hot 21-year-old widow wouldn't mind an older, independently wealthy sugar daddy of a husband.

He continued to drive toward home deep in thought. Then, just as the garage door opened his plan became clear. He thought about the times he'd welcomed Jolene into his home through this very door, and the good times they'd had. Scrambled eggs, other meals, but mostly their time in bed. Why would he mess that up? Let her stay until she figured things out for herself. In the meantime, he had exactly what he wanted, a regular and charming bedmate, someone to help with the cooking and cleaning and bill paying. Someone to talk to, yet, unless she brought up some future scenario conversation, no commitment. ust a day-to-day really great deal.

His dad was therefore only partly right. He'd hang on to her until she decided to move on, or if it came to that, try to force him into some kind of long-term commitment. He'd deal with the question of kids' soccer and dance classes only if it came to that. Maybe she'd ask him or maybe she'd find some other guy to create that with. In the meantime, he would enjoy her company and focus on the Baker plan. This was perfect! C4 was back!

C4 opened the door to his condo and, after taking off his coat and hanging it up on the coat tree by the door, he walked to the end of the counter and poured himself a scotch on the rocks. On the scotch bottle was a yellow sticky note.

"Should be home by midnight."

Also on the sticky note was a heart with what looked like a happy face. He was not sure what to make of that. He laughed. He'd have to keep that and show it to her if she ever brought another guy home from the Riverview.

He had finished his scotch, then another, was halfway through a third and was half asleep on the couch when Jolene came in, trying to be quiet. She hung up her coat, went to the fridge and got a bottle of water. C4 watched her as she moved about. Bottled water? Where did that come from?

She caught him watching her and smiled.

"You even watch me with all my clothes on! How adorable!"

He laughed.

"I'd watch you dressed in a snowmobile suit and a parka. No helmet though. I need to make sure it's you."

She laughed and sat down next to him on the couch.

"What's on TV?"

"I haven't been watching. Big dinner with my dad and a couple of drinks here and I've been half asleep for the last hour. How was work?"

"Good. Nice crowd. My share of the tips was not bad. People were nice. No problem drunks or loud parties. I helped at the bar a bit and made a few more tips. The three evenings a week I work at the River-view, with the tips, I make almost as much as I make in my teaching job."

"Good for you. Do you enjoy it?"

"Mostly. Sometimes we get a problem drunk or two, usually guys from out of town. All the locals tend to behave. Once in a while, we have a family squabble, or some unruly kids. I should keep a diary and someday I could write a tell-all book about the hoi polloi of Bismarck!"

C4 nodded.

"Sounds about right. How about your teaching job?"

Jolene beamed. C4 knew he'd made a mistake.

"I love it. I just love the kids, working with them, seeing them grow, seeing how excited they get when they learn something. Listening to them tell me stories about what goes on at home. That would add a chapter or two to my tell-all book!"

C4 knew he needed to cut this off.

"Can I pour you a scotch?"

"No, but right next to your scotch on the counter is a nice bottle of red wine I picked up. Would you open that for me?"

C4 wondered how he'd missed the red wine sitting right there on the counter. Guess he was just focused on the scotch.

"Absolutely."

He stood and stretched, then went over and eyed the bottle of wine. It was better than anything he'd bought in a long time.

"There's a corkscrew in the drawer right in front of you. I brought that over from my house today."

C4 opened the drawer and sure enough, there was a corkscrew. He began to wonder what other surprises awaited him. In his own home. He opened the wine and deep in a cupboard found a juice glass. No stemware. At least not yet.

She accepted the wine, took a sip and set it on the coffee table. C4 knew he had to steer any conversation from love of kids to any other topic. Jolene took care of that.

"What did you and your dad talk about?"

C4 took a drink of melted ice water with just a hint of scotch remaining, and took his time answering. He certainly wasn't going to cover any of that. Not his dad's thoughts on Jolene, certainly not the Baker deal. Not now, maybe never.

"Usual stuff. He likes you. Wants to make sure I'm being nice to you."

That brushed on the truth. Not bad, not bad. Given that success, he continued.

"He wants you to come in next week to get started on your probate process."

"We should do that. You'll come with me, won't you?"

"Absolutely. We just need to schedule a time."

Jolene nodded. Now she looked sad. This must be the vulnerability his dad was talking about. Not sure how she could be sad about losing her husband, but there probably had been some good feelings at one time.

"Should we turn in?"

"Let me finish my wine. Go ahead if you want. I won't be long."

C4 wasn't sure what to do with that info, so he just sat there, now looking at the TV. Even sitting on the couch with her was enjoyable.

"I'll wait. It's just nice to sit with you."

C4 knew the topic they needed to discuss was how they presented themselves to the people of Bismarck. Should they go to the grocery store together? Out to breakfast or dinner? Jolene broke the silence.

"My mom and dad wanted to come out to see me this weekend. I told them not to come because I was staying with a friend and couldn't live in the house just yet. Then they wanted me to come and see them. I declined, saying I didn't want to drive that far, since I only have Sunday off. Then Trevor's parents called and wanted to come out and see me and get Trevor's stuff. When I got all this straightened out, I think I made the ultimate compromise."

C4 looked at her and waited to see what that was.

"I worked out a way to meet them all in Jamestown on Sunday, and I would bring some of Trevor's stuff with me."

C4 nodded.

"That makes sense."

"So, you have Sunday free. I'll get up early, stop at the house and put whatever of Trevor's stuff I can find in some boxes in my car and then head to Jamestown."

"Are you sure you're ok to do that?"

"I think so."

"I can't imagine that I should tag along…"

"No, though maybe I'll see if Terry wants to come with me. That might help."

"I think that's a great idea."

Now C4 had another brilliant thought. There was no need to bring up any sensitive issues whatsoever. Jolene was thinking pretty clearly and rather than force what might turn into an emotional conversation, he would just broach the issues as they arose, letting Jolene take the lead as much as possible. Let things flow more naturally.

"I'll ask Terry in the morning. And how about I invite Terry and Carson over for dinner Sunday night when we get back? Kind of a couples' date with the only other couple who know we're a couple. And a thank you for all they've done for me. And to ask Carson to see if he knows who can do the repairs on my house. It's time to get that started."

"So, Carson is Terry's husband?"

"Yes, had I never mentioned that?"

"I don't think so."

"Well now you know. He's a really nice guy. You'll like him."

C4 just nodded as Jolene finished off her glass of wine.

"Mr. Tappen, will you escort me to the bedroom?"

"Of course, my dear. Walk this way."

Chapter 16

WHEN C4 AWOKE ON SATURDAY MORNING, Jolene was not in bed, but he could hear the shower running. He smiled. She was the best bedmate he'd ever had. It would be hard for him when she finally came to her senses. In the meantime, he was going to enjoy the relationship. His first, ever.

He lay in bed until she came out of the bathroom, waiting to enjoy the view. Maybe this could last. Time would tell. She had said her parents were pretty mad when she left home and married Trevor. Maybe she had daddy issues and he was the solution!

"What the heck are you thinking about? You're all smiles," said Jolene when she emerged from the bathroom.

"Just happy to be looking at you, without a parka, or anything else for that matter."

"I'm glad you are so easy to keep happy!"

"Me too."

Then his thoughts turned a little more somber. This would be the first day they were together as a couple, if that's what they were, when they would have to face a very real issue.

Yesterday she had worked both at school and the Riverview and he'd had the day to himself. Now it was the weekend. Most couples would, C4 thought, on a typical Saturday, go out for breakfast, run some errands, and go home to put away their purchases. After that maybe even a movie or some entertainment at one of the colleges, like a game of some sort. He knew his approach was to let her decide how to handle such things, and she did not disappoint him. She opened the topic.

"I've been thinking about today."

Then she paused. C4 was genuinely curious so he replied, "And?"

"I need to leave for work about 4:30. Until then, there are a few things we need to get done."

"And those are...?"

"I texted Terry this morning and she agreed to help me out tomorrow. I'll pick her up about 9:00 and go to my house, pick up whatever of Trevor's I can find, box it all up, and then the two of us will drive to Jamestown. We'll meet Trevor's parents for lunch and drop his stuff with them, then my parents will meet us about 2:00 at another restaurant for dessert and coffee. The two sets of parents never really got along and there's no need to start now. I'm just glad my parents are willing to make the drive from Wahpeton. We'll try to head for home about 4:00."

She paused, having described her Sunday, with no mention of how that affected Saturday. C4 decided he needed to prompt her.

"So, you should be home tomorrow about 5:30 or so?"

"That sounds about right. Today, one of us needs to get the stuff I need to make Sunday supper for Carson and Terry and us. Then this afternoon, I will put it all together and put it in the fridge. Tomorrow I'll call on our way back, around 5:00 or so. When I do, I'll need you to take it out of the fridge and put it in the oven. Simple as can be."

C4 vaguely remembered his mom doing things like that, a long time ago. He replied,

"I can do whatever you need me to do."

"Why don't you get some more wine? Maybe a Rose' – they're not really drinkers, but some light wine would be nice. And whatever else you need to do today."

"Absolutely."

"So we can go our separate ways this morning and have the afternoon together before I have to go to work."

"Sounds like a plan."

And then it happened.

"I feel bad having to go to work all the time. By the way, you haven't gone to work since I've been staying here, not that I've been here every day. What do you do to afford this nice place and your almost new SUV?"

Thankfully, partly thanks to his dad's questioning at Friday dinner, C4 was ready.

"I help manage some properties for a wealthy client. Mostly farm and ranch land, so there's really not much to do in the winter. I may have to run out of town once in a while, but not too often."

"And that's why you were gone that Monday and Tuesday after we first, let's just say, 'met'?"

"Yup. That was it, exactly."

"I see."

C4 needed to stop any further probing, so added,

"I was just lucky to get back to town that Tuesday night, with the winter storm that I had to drive through.

It worked. Jolene responded just as he had wished.

"Me too. I was at my wit's end. I couldn't go to work or spend too much time at friends' places, in case Trevor found my car, from that, found me."

C4 decided that hugging her was probably the right thing to do now. So, he did. It was the right thing. They stayed embraced for what seemed like a long time. Finally, Jolene said,

"I know where this usually leads, but I'm all clean and you're not, and we have things to do, so we probably both need to get dressed and started on our errands."

Despite their embrace not leading them back to bed, C4 was ecstatic. She had bought his story, which was about to be true, anyway, with the Baker Plan, and he now had a license to lounge around at home or be gone somewhere at any time, even overnight. He had just written himself the best boyfriend ticket ever.

Then Jolene brought him back to reality.

"So that brings us to today. As much as I'd like to take you by the hand and walk around the grocery store and the mall with you, I know we can't do that - at least not yet."

C4 nodded and as was becoming his role in the relationship, tried to lighten the mood a bit.

"At least not until we both put some clothes on."

She laughed. That was good.

"You are so correct. In fact, I'm getting cold."

She walked to his chest of drawers and pulled a bra and a pair of panties out of the top drawer. He had to wonder where his clothes had gone. She looked over at him and read his thoughts.

"Don't worry. Your clothes are still in here, I only took the top drawer. It was easy to get yours into the other drawers."

C4 nodded.

"Good. I didn't want to be held captive here, with no clothes."

"Don't worry. I remember the deal I made when I brought my stuff over."

C4 noted that she didn't say 'moved in'.

They both dressed, and C4 went out and started a pot of coffee. Jolene came out dressed for her errands.

"I'm going to drive to the grocery store where I used to shop rather than the one right here. I can also check the mail at my house so it doesn't look quite so abandoned."

C4 couldn't help but note how fortunate it was that Trevor had decided to trash the place. It created a perfect reason for Jolene not to live there. Although staying with friends would also make sense given her loss.

"Coffee before you go?"

"No, I'll grab one at the store and drink while I shop. See you in an hour or two."

"No hug, no kiss?"

"Of course."

Following the briefest of kisses, she was gone. C4 poured his first cup of coffee and relaxed a bit. He could walk over to the liquor store in a bit. Rose'? Really? Who were these people? Oh, well, they'd been very nice and helpful to Jolene when she needed them, so he had good reason to be nice to them.

C4 felt lonely. It was weird. On Wednesday and Thursday and Friday, when Jolene had gone to work he had been alone, and that seemed normal. Now, when she was gone, he missed her. Guess it was because he knew she was doing things they could have done together. So they weren't really a normal couple. Lost in that thought, his phone rang.

"Hello?"

"Hello, Calvin?"

"Yes. Is that you, Mr. Baker?"

"It is. Can't make secret phone calls to anybody anymore, can we?"

"I guess not. What can I do for you?"

"I heard the fish are biting. Are you up for a trip to Minnesota?"

"Could be. When?"

"Next week. I know this is short notice. So, what if we just went Tuesday through Friday, instead of Monday?"

C4 took a moment. This was going to disrupt his conjugal bliss. But he needed to work the plan.

"Sure, that would work. I have some business in town that I can get done on Monday. Pick you up at 9:00 as usual?"

"That works just fine. See you Tuesday at nine."

Now C4 was glad he'd told Jolene about his 'career.' He would have to be gone Tuesday through Friday, and Jolene would believe he was doing his job. Perfect. Except for sleeping alone in Minnesota instead of in Bismarck with Jolene. If sleeping with her every night was the new normal, he liked the new normal. One change he was quite fond of.

He took a final swig of his coffee and dressed for the short walk to the liquor store. He had to find some kind of Rose' wine and buy some scotch of course. The store owner would be highly suspicious if he didn't replenish his scotch supply.

C4 went out the back door and walked up the hill to the liquor store. He was glad Jolene had gone to a different grocery store. Bumping into her would create some sort of tension. Did they pretend they didn't know each other?

C4 went first to the wine aisle and took his time finding a midrange Rose'. He opted for one bottle. These people weren't going to spend the night. Have a drink, eat, have another drink and they would hit the road. He knew Terry and Jolene would be tired from their day in Jamestown. He had enough sense to know it would be tougher on Jolene than she thought, seeing her family and Trevor's family for the first time since the funeral.

He moved over to the much more familiar scotch section and was about to grab his usual choice when he was abruptly bumped. He looked and it was Vicki.

"How you doing, Cal? Haven't seen you in a while."

"Seen or talked to?"

"Seen, actually. I have eyes on you, just not mine."

"Why am I so interesting to you? Still in love with me? Can't be the two grand. Unless you're broke."

C4 was enjoying having the upper hand for once, despite being ambushed.

"Not in love, trust me. But I do find you interesting. Not as interesting as the widow Buchanan finds you, of course."

And just like that, Vicki had control of the conversation. That wouldn't do. C4 thought hard.

"Look. I have the money. I'll get you that and then you can quit having me followed. Save you time and money. I just need a slight discount."

"No discount, but I'll take it any time. So, you don't deny playing house with the hot young widow?"

"She seems to enjoy my company. Who am I to argue?"

"Let me get this straight. You pick her up from the Riverview. Spend the night together, and then her husband goes on a rampage. You immediately go out of town, and when you come back, you and his wife start living like an old married couple. Then he suddenly and tragically dies. How fortunate for you. If I was a murder mystery author, I'd have a lot of fun writing all kinds of stuff about what your role was in all this. And what if I was a police detective? It wouldn't take much to launch that investigation. Especially knowing what a sleazy life you normally live."

C4 had to think a bit to get his thoughts on track. Her portrayal of events was horrendous. He hoped no one else was thinking like that.

"You have quite the imagination. When she came back to me, she was terrified for her life. Like you said, Trevor was on a rampage. You know I don't deal in such things. I operate like a juvie, you said. This does not have my fingerprints on it. I just like the girl. Who wouldn't? And apparently, she likes me."

C4 looked hard at Vicki to finish making his point, once again trying to control this conversation, hopefully by ending it, and then get out the door with his purchase, and back to the sanctity of his own home.

"You said you have my money? And you want to get rid of me? Then pay up. Right now."

"I'm not carrying it around. I can get it to you tomorrow. Just say when and where."

"Archie's at 3:00."

"Let's make it Archie's at 2:00."

Vicki laughed.

"Oh, the little woman, or should I say girl, has you on a tight schedule?"

"Sure, just go with that."

"Ok. You head out. I have some shopping left to do."

C4 paid and left. It would be so nice to be done with Vicki. Forever.

Chapter 17

C4 WAS HOME WELL BEFORE JOLENE. He put the Rose' in the refrigerator, a little internet research indicating it was to be served chilled. He sat down on the couch, resisting the urge to open the scotch and start pouring it into himself. Why did Vicki hound him so? It had to be more than the $2,000 he owed her. She said she found him interesting. And then that hypothetical about him having Trevor killed? That was dangerous talk. Hopefully that never crossed Jolene's mind. Or any police officer, ever. He had to pay her off and cut her out of his life. Looking back, he could have impressed Baker with $300 as well as with $1,000. Big mistake taking that money from Vicki. Now he had to fix it, whatever it took.

By picking 2:00 p.m. instead of 3:00, he figured Archie's would be as empty as it would get on a Sunday, and since Jolene was meeting her parents at 2:00, there is no way she'd be on the road before he finished with Vicki, no matter how long it took. And even if her parents didn't or couldn't make the trip from Wahpeton, she couldn't get out of Jamestown much before 2:00.

C4 stood up, went to his bedroom in order to count out and put $2,000 into an unmarked envelope for Vicki. He absentmindedly opened his top dresser drawer to get his cash and it was full of women's underwear. Why had he not noticed this when Jolene opened the drawer this morning? Oh, yeah, she was naked and that took all his attention. His heart stopped. She had moved his clothes. What did she do with the money? What did she think when she saw the money? His phone rang. He ignored it. He opened the second drawer and looked carefully, feeling around with his hands. There it was. The envelope containing the other envelopes with the cash from each gold dealer. Thank God he'd hidden the silver in the closet. Had she found that? His phone rang again.

He went to the living room just in time to miss the call. He looked at the screen. It was his dad. He gathered himself and dialed back, simultaneously walking to the closet to check on the silver.

"Well, you are alive? Thought you might be walking your girl around town, showing her off."

"Not likely. We're trying to be quite discreet."

"Good for you. If she wants me to help her with her probate, you should get her in here. Does Monday work?"

"It does as long as it's after 3:00 p.m. That's when she gets off work."

"3:30 is just fine. Must be interesting living with someone who has a job."

C4 stuck his hand into his right cowboy boot. The silver was still there. He grabbed the boot and walked to the bedroom, dumping it out on the bed.

"Thanks dad. Always with the positive feedback."

"Sorry. If I had known she could turn you into a productive member of society so readily, I'd have done in her husband myself," CT joked.

"That's not making things better. And please, please, please don't ever say that to her, or to anyone else."

"Of course not. I'll look forward to seeing her on Monday. Are you coming along?"

"Yes, I plan to."

C4 was stacking up the silver. It was all there.

"And just so I know before we meet, is she holding up ok? I like to know just to gauge how tough this conversation may be on her, given her recent loss."

"She's doing remarkably well. And as you well know from our restraining order meeting, Trevor was abusing her. When she came back to me for protection, he'd beaten her pretty badly. No need to reference that either, ever."

"I do remember that of course, but I'm glad you reminded me, and it does explain things a bit. I will treat that with complete confidence, and of course I'll be careful not to make any casual jokes about anything related to that."

The door to the condo opened and Jolene called out,

"Are you here, Cal? I need some help carrying things up from the car."

"Absolutely, be right there."

"That's her, by the way. Just back from the grocery store. Alone. See you Monday at 3:30."

C4 dumped the silver back into the boot, put it away and walked out of the bedroom.

"What were you doing in the bedroom?"

"Nothing. Let's get the groceries."

They rode down the elevator in silence, walking to Jolene's car. She popped the hatchback and there were more groceries than C4 had ever had in his condo at one time before. He couldn't help himself.

"Is there anything left in the store?"

Jolene laughed.

"I thought you might say something like that. It's not that much. Just a lot of bags. Here, if we each take four, we're done. You get the heavy ones."

C4 took his assigned bags and had one hand just free enough to pull the hatchback down. They walked to the elevator. Jolene pushed the button, and they stepped in.

"You had empty cupboards and an empty refrigerator. I'm just helping you stock some of the essentials. And it's the stuff for tomorrow night and some other healthy choices."

Cal once again couldn't restrain his thoughts from coming out of his mouth.

"Healthy choices? We aren't kids and the last I checked we don't have any kids."

Jolene laughed.

"We can still have some healthy food around. Don't worry. I didn't buy any bibs, for us or anyone else."

"That's a relief."

C4's thoughts then turned back to the cash. While his approach with her was to leave all important discussions to her, this one he had to know. They put the bags down on the kitchen table and she began to put things away. Apparently, she knew exactly where she thought everything should go.

He unbagged and handed her things, and they worked for a bit without talking. He loved that about her. She was not addicted to needless chatter. The task completed, he worked up all the composure he could muster and asked,

"When you moved my stuff out of my top drawer, you also came across an envelope you moved down one drawer, right?"

"Yes, I did. Did I do something wrong?"

She looked genuinely concerned.

"No, I just forgot I'd left it in that drawer and had to dig a bit."

"Was it something I shouldn't have touched? I just figured it was an envelope of cash."

Well, that was interesting. Just an envelope of cash?

"It is. Thought you might find that odd."

"Not at all. I have one, too, I brought it from our, I mean my, house. Not that thick, but a couple thousand, just for emergencies and once in a while, for fun. I brought it with me here, and have it where you'll never find it."

C4 looked at her and wondered where she had stashed it. Jolene looked a bit apprehensive.

"I'll confess. Mine was so I could get away if I had to. Which I did. So, it was kind of a dark stash, and it turns out I did need it. At the old house, I had to hide it very well, for obvious reasons. I guess I shouldn't treat you the same. I'll tell you where it is if you want."

C4 was once again in uncharted territory. She was trusting him with both a very personal secret and her money. He had to think a bit.

"You don't need to show me, unless you want to. I didn't mean to open any old wounds. I know it's not in your underwear drawer."

"Did you enjoy digging through my undies?"

Jolene was laughing now. Apparently, the mood had lightened.

"Not sure how to answer that without sounding like either a curmudgeon or a pervert."

"What a vocabulary you have!"

"Yeah, I even surprised myself."

"I'll show you."

She took his hand, and they walked together into the bedroom. He wondered where this was headed. Not to the bed, apparently. She opened what was now her underwear drawer and said,

"Feel up here."

And she took his hand and guided it to an envelope taped underneath the top of the bureau. Ingenious.

"I'm sorry if I crossed some boundary with you. I didn't mean to invade your privacy. I just didn't think anything of it. Lots of people keep cash for emergencies and fun money. I know my parents always did. Once, when my youngest brother found it, they told us they kept it in case they had to run away from us kids."

"That's a good line. Were you scared?"

"I was old enough to know better, but my brothers both behaved better for a while. And my parents had to re-hide it."

That was the opening C4 was relieved to get.

"Speaking of parents, my dad called. I said we could meet with him on Monday after work, 3:30 at his office. Is that ok?"

"That's fine. Thanks for setting that up."

"No problem. And I had a call from the guy I work for. I need to go out of town Tuesday through Friday, so you'll be all alone for a few days."

"Then I'm glad I stocked up on food. I can just hibernate for a few days. I will really miss you. You are so easy to be with. No matter what we're doing. Come back early if you can!"

C4 had never felt so appreciated.

"You're easy too. Maybe I should rephrase that. You're easy to be with. In all situations."

"Thanks. I'm glad you cleared that up."

Changing gears she said,

"I see you bought some Rose'. Thanks for doing that."

Once again changing gears, she went on.

"We're in the bedroom, and you've handled all my undies. How about we fool around and maybe take a nap."

Now C4 wasn't sure which of his statements was more accurate. Easy or easy to be with. Both worked. Jolene went on.

"Normally I'd suggest we go out for a movie or something, but given our situation, this is the best substitute I can come up with."

He just nodded. Maybe they should never go public.

"It is a really good substitute!"

When he woke up, it was almost 2:00 and Jolene was getting dressed. Maybe he was too old for this lifestyle. She once again appeared to read his mind.

"Don't worry. I just woke up, too. Want a bite? In the kitchen, I mean. Food."

She smiled and winked. Could life get any better?

"I'll make a couple salads, and this time you can scramble the eggs. I bet there's some basketball on TV."

While they were not wedded, this was getting pretty close to bliss.

"Sounds great. I'll be out in a minute."

C4 laid back down in bed. That was an unbelievable exchange. He had been worried that she would wonder how he had come to have so much cash, and to her it was nothing. She expected him to have cash. Like everyone else. Now he just had to put two thousand in an envelope and get it to Vicki tomorrow and he'd be down to one woman in his life. The good one, not the evil one.

Putting those thoughts behind him he stood, dressed quickly and sat back down on the bed. He was feeling so good about his situation that he wished he could take Jolene out for a nice dinner. But that was not going to happen. She had to work, and they had to stay quiet about their life together. Only his dad, and Terry and Carson, and Vicki knew. And some number of her spies. They couldn't keep a lid on this situation forever. When they were both at his dad's office tomorrow, people might notice his car and her car both there. That was explainable. He was there often. But people around town put two and two together pretty quickly, and sometimes they got to a correct answer. At least at this point it was a matter of hurt feelings, not life or death, like when Trevor was on his last rampage.

Uncharacteristically, C4 was genuinely concerned about how the situation would reflect on Jolene. They could easily say they had met at the Riverview. No need for any further details. And that she'd turned to him for protection when Trevor had gone on his weekend rampage. Ending up as roommates this quickly, even if they made it sound like it happened after Trevor had died, was kind of hard to explain. Harder yet was the fact that the Bismarck police knew they could find her with him when they had to tell her Trevor had died. So, they knew they were together.

There were some pieces to this puzzle that really did not fit. Or C4 couldn't figure out how they fit. It was a weird coincidence that Trevor was killed right after his rampage weekend when he beat Jolene so badly. He knew he hadn't arranged it, in fact he had no idea how to do that, and yet Vicki accused him of it. The police said it was an accident. That could happen, couldn't it?

"Are you coming out here or not? I've got the eggs and the pan out and the salads are ready."

C4 stood up from the bed and dragged his thoughts back to the present.

"I'm coming, I'm coming."

By the time he said that he was in the kitchen. As promised, the eggs and pan were waiting for him. He quickly scrambled some eggs and the two of them enjoyed a midafternoon meal. The rest of the day was quite routine, except for C4's nagging thoughts about why so many people knew about Jolene living with him. When she left for work at 4:30, he had the evening alone with his thoughts. Good thoughts about his suddenly good life with Jolene, bad thoughts about Vicki and the other questions boiling over in his mind.

C4 awoke Sunday morning to the sound of Jolene in the shower. Her single glass of wine when she had gotten home as opposed to his three scotches on Saturday evening had left her better able to get up and start functioning.

He looked at the clock. 7:45 am. This was a new normal he didn't care for. He pulled on his usual sweats and went to the kitchen, finding coffee already brewing. How did she do it? Especially without waking him?

He pulled a cup from the cupboard and waited for the coffee to finish, then poured himself some of the hot black liquid. Just then, Jolene came out of the bedroom fully dressed for the day. He looked at her and did not envy the day she had in front of her. A stop at her house, a long drive, two tough family sessions, in particular the one with Trevor's family, then another long drive, then dinner with her friends.

He wondered how much she (or Terry) would reveal about her living arrangements. She'd have to lie if she said she was living with Terry. Maybe she wouldn't mention the trashed house at all. C4 wasn't looking forward to his day either, at least until Vicki walked away from him this afternoon. That would be a good moment. Highest interest rate on a loan, maybe ever, but happy to pay it to make her go away.

"You look so serious!" said Jolene.

"Sorry. You've got a tough day ahead of you. I'm glad Terry will be with you."

"Me too. Don't worry. Just behave yourself while I'm gone. I don't want to have you forget how much you care for me while I'm away for a day."

"That is impossible! I'll be here waiting for you. In fact, I may just throw a nice meal in the oven when I hear that you're on your way back."

"You'd better do that. Or we'll have a long evening waiting for our dinner to bake."

Jolene filled a travel mug with coffee. Where did the travel mug come from?

"I'm really sorry to be gone all day, but I do need to do this."

She put on her coat, walked over to him and asked,

"Do I get a goodbye kiss? I can tell this is kind of new to you."

He stood and they enjoyed a long hug and a kiss, then she picked up her mug and went out the door. He took his coffee cup, walked to the window and watched her drive away.

Alone, he enjoyed his coffee, made himself some toast and when he was done eating, he showered and shaved. No matter how the afternoon went, he could at least look decent.

Several hours later, he walked into Archie's. It was about 10 minutes before 2:00. As he had hoped, the place was almost empty. There was a booth of four on the other side, chatting, but with a few dirty dishes left on their table. About halfway down there was an elderly couple having pie and coffee. He hoped their hearing was not that good.

He walked to a far corner, careful to sit facing the door.

"Good afternoon. Here's a menu and water. Anything else to drink?" asked the waitress.

"Coffee, black. Thanks."

A moment later the waitress returned, setting down a cup of coffee.

"Do you know what you want yet?"

"Not yet. I'm meeting someone here so will just wait."

"Do you need another water and menu?"

"Just another water. We can share a menu. I'll be done reading by the time she gets here."

"Ok. I'll keep an eye out. Wave at me if you need something else."

"Will do."

As she walked away one more customer walked in, a tall, rangy cowboy who went directly to the counter at the opposite end of the restaurant from C4. As he took off his coat to hang on the rack behind him, C4 caught a glimpse of a pistol butt under his left arm. When the cowboy sat down, he was facing directly at C4, so C4 looked at his menu. The cowboy seemed to be sizing up the customers and staff just as C4 had done. The same waitress served him, walking back and forth with water and some kind of soda.

C4 sat and nursed his coffee, wishing it was a scotch, but it wasn't. Not even close. The menu was boring, it hadn't changed in years. Burgers and other standard sandwiches, fries, wings, soups and salads and then on the back page "The Best Pie in Dakota."

Not just North Dakota, but all of Dakota. There was a long list of flavors, and C4 had tried a few. He wasn't much of a pie eater. Maybe it really was the best pie in Dakota. He'd be a poor judge of that. Now, best scotch in Dakota? He'd like to try to judge that.

"Considering a piece of pie?"

Vicki slid in on the opposite side of the booth. If C4 was ever going to be a spy, he needed to get better at not letting her sneak up on him. Was she the best ninja in Dakota?

"Just looking. You're late."

"Sorry. Too many appointments today. I'm a busy girl."

"I don't doubt that."

"Coffee?"

The waitress had returned. C4 had missed that too. Vicki replied, "Sure. Black. Thanks."

The waitress walked away to get the coffee. Vicki took the menu from C4 and looked over the pie page. The waitress came back with a cup and an insulated carafe.

"Here you go. Do you know what you want? I know you just got here but thought I'd ask, just in case."

"We'll share a piece of pie. French silk. Don't worry about the small ticket. He's a big tipper."

The waitress smiled and walked away, presumably to get the pie. C4 watched her as she walked away, and also noticed the cowboy was, without being apparent, positioned to keep a close eye on Vicki and him. Vicki noticed his errant gaze.

"You dog, you. Sleeping with the cutest girl in Bismarck and watching the waitress as she walks away. You should be ashamed. And having pie in the middle of the afternoon with the most eligible divorcee in North Dakota? You live quite a life."

"I was actually watching your cowboy at the end of the counter."

C4 left it at that to see how Vicki responded. She didn't look back, just directly at C4.

"I know a few cowboys but don't see any of my friends in here. Your imagination is getting away from you. You should write murder mystery novels. You seem to have a lot of real-life experience."

"Here's your pie. Two forks. And your check. Enjoy!"

C4 wasn't sure what to enjoy. The pie or the check, or the cowboy or Vicki or getting rid of Vicki. He was careful not to watch the waitress walk away. He picked up a fork and took a bite of pie. So did Vicki, who spoke next.

"This is good. I should start eating here more often. Maybe even without you. Of course, if we met here regularly maybe Jolene would find out. Can't imagine you want that."

Where was this headed? Nowhere if C4 could control it.

"I have the envelope you're expecting. After that I really don't expect to see you anymore. Or any of your cowboys."

Vicki smiled and took another bite of pie.

"If you put the envelope next to the pie, I can slide it right into my purse. And that will be that."

"You're not going to count it?"

"You had better hope it's the right amount. Or a cowboy I do know may pay you a visit. Or to your girlfriend."

Vicki was not smiling now. This really was a disturbing woman.

"It's all there. And as lovely as this is, I hope it's the last time we meet."

"You seem kind of fixated on that. Do you not like me? You found me quite charming once. Remember that night in Dickinson? Does Jolene know about that?"

C4 ignored the question and the comment. There was just no way to stay ahead of her. He truly wanted her out of his life. Maybe he should have watched Fatal Attraction more than that one time.

"You have your money, and if you want you can have more than half the pie. And I will pay and tip. Anything else?"

"No, but I'll miss you. You really are an interesting guy. Right now, you're living like an honest, law abiding old married man and it seems like you're enjoying that. But I've known lots of guys like you. That can't last. You'll be back. I just don't know how or when or where, but you'll be back. Enjoy the pie."

Vicki stood, picked up her purse, turned to take one last swig of coffee, nodded to C4 and walked out the door.

The waitress came back.

"She seems charming. Anything else?"

"She's my sister. You can't imagine. Nothing else, thanks."

C4 pulled a 20 out of his money clip and laid on the table, on the ticket. He took another bite of pie. He looked again at the cowboy, who was putting his coat back on. No question. Yup that was a semi under his arm. And he was fine having C4 see it. If he wasn't with Vicki, that was one of the oddest coincidences ever.

The waitress came back with a tray of change and he left her most of it. Certain that Vicki and her cowboy had driven away, he stood, put on his coat, took a last swig of water and walked out the door. Not only did he dislike Vicki, she was not a cheap date. But now he was done with her. He really hoped she was done with him.

C4 enjoyed the 10-minute drive home, despite fighting the bright sunlight on the snow. He was even happier to drive into the garage and watch the door close behind him. Every block traveled, every door closed, put him further from Vicki. Jolene's unofficial parking stall was empty. Maybe he'd have to rent her another spot, before the Washburns came back from Arizona. That was quite a thought. Still living with Jolene over a month from now? He smiled to himself.

Chapter 18

C4 MOVED A LITTLE, but not much. Somewhere a phone was ringing. It stopped. Now it was ringing again. It stopped. Now it was ringing again. He moved a bit more and looked at the coffee table. It was his phone that was ringing. He picked it up and looked at it. The screen said 'JB'.

It was Jolene. He needed to answer it.

"Hello."

"Cal, what are you doing? Are you ok?"

"I'm fine."

He wasn't.

"I was just sound asleep on the couch."

"I was worried. We're almost to Steele. Can you put our dinner in the oven?"

"Of course."

He worked his way to a sitting position.

"I'll do it right now. See you in 45 minutes or so."

"Great."

"Good trip? I mean as good goes."

"It was ok. Terry was a saint."

"I'm not surprised. See you soon."

"Bye."

C4 stood up. That didn't feel good. The room spun a bit. He made it to the end of the counter and stood still. Jolene was coming back, with guests. The clock was ticking. He needed a shower and to put the casserole in the oven. But first he needed to throw up. He went to the bathroom and did the most urgent of his tasks. That felt better. He rinsed off his face and went to the kitchen, set the oven at 350° and got the casserole out of the refrigerator. He smiled a bit as he remembered to remove the plastic wrap. He put it in the oven and sat down on a kitchen chair.

He looked at the counter. No scotch bottle. He looked around. It was on the coffee table and it was almost empty. That was it. He had celebrated the end of Vicki. Scotch, lots of it. No glass. No rocks. Just him and the bottle. Now he still needed a shower, and to sober up. He started a pot of coffee and went to the shower. He knew he had maybe 35 minutes left to clean himself up.

Twenty minutes later he was out of the shower and dried off. He had thrown up a little more in the shower. It all washed down the drain. He shaved and brushed his teeth and dressed in something other than sweats. Now he needed a cup of coffee and to let his system catch up. He took a drink of water from the bathroom tap. His stomach almost rejected it but he kept it down. Now he was ready for coffee. His head hurt. Aspirin with the coffee. That would help.

Coffee in hand he sat down by the kitchen table, and took a sip, then some aspirin, then another sip, and another aspirin. He finished the coffee. What had happened to him? He used to be able to drink like that and it would have no effect. He had to feel better, and the clock was still ticking, relentlessly. What would he tell Jolene?

He laughed to himself. The truth? Was that the best he could do? She'd see the scotch bottle. He'd tell her that in order to while away the afternoon he'd had one too many scotches and fallen asleep. That might just work. He really wished he felt better. If he hadn't gone to Archie's he'd have had time to drink a lot more. That would have to do.

He felt better. Not physically yet, but now he had a story. Maybe he'd have to drink Rose' with his dinner. No more scotch, that was for sure.

He looked at his watch. They'd be here in about 10 minutes. Jolene, Terry, and Carson. He knew how to make a first impression! *Come on Cal, pull it together. For Jolene's sake. Don't screw this up. This is important to her.*

He moved slowly, but he straightened up the condo, slowly getting his legs under him, breathing a little easier. He sat down and had another cup of coffee. There was a knock at the door. Then Jolene slowly came in, followed by two other people.

"Are you decent?"

"Fairly."

She walked over and gave him a kiss.

"It's really nice to be back here. It was a long day. Terry was a saint."

C4 smiled, trying to dig deep for some of his old charm.

"That's a great summary. I'm sure she was."

"Cal, this is Carson, Terry's husband."

C4 extended his hand to Carson and said,

"It's nice to meet you. Welcome."

"Thanks. I think we've met before."

Cal studied Carson, but nothing came to mind. Carson continued.

"About five years ago, in Mandan. Upstairs at the Missouri Breaks. You and a few other guys taught me how to play poker by taking all my money."

"Oh, no. Do I owe you money?"

"No, you won fair and square, at least I think you did. It wasn't much money, and it taught me I needed to quit pretending I was a poker player. So, it all worked out for the best."

C4 laughed.

"Glad I could help. If you need to know, I'm not really all that good either. I must have just had some good cards. By the way, how old were you at the time?"

"Twenty-one. It was one of my first adult things to do after I moved here, right out of college. I'd played with the guys in college, but I wasn't ready for a real game, I guess."

C4 felt old, and figured it was time to change the subject.

"Thank you, Terry, for being such a good friend to Jolene. You have helped her with a lot, through a very tough time."

"Glad to do what I could. She's great, isn't she?"

"She sure is!"

Jolene was looking in the oven. She closed the oven and addressed the group.

"This seems to be about 10 minutes from being ready. Anybody want a drink? I know I need one."

Terry answered.

"I could use one. Do you have any Rose'?"

Jolene shot C4 a glance and said,

"Of course we do. Cal, can you pour?"

"Sure can. Carson?"

"You can skip me for now. I haven't eaten since breakfast, and I played some pickup basketball at the Y this afternoon, so I'll just take a glass of water."

C4 and Jolene shared the duty of getting drinks for their guests.

"No scotch for you?"

"No, I had a few this afternoon. You know. Instead of playing basketball. I'll just have water like Carson."

Drinks in hand, the four of them sat down at the table, like they were old friends. C4 opened the conversation.

"Tell me about the day. Both of you. How did it all go?"

Terry and Jolene looked at each other and after a moment, Terry said,

"I'll start. Jolene has talked a lot today."

C4 looked concerned, and Carson looked a bit apprehensive.

"The stop at Jolene's house was ok. We dug through Trevor's stuff. Found clothes mostly. Several guns, lots of ammo. Nothing much of interest, but we located and left some papers there that Jolene will have to go through. Then the drive to Jamestown went well. We got to the restaurant a little early."

She paused to take a sip of wine.

"Trevor's parents came in, just them. No brothers or sisters or anyone. It was awkward at first, lots of tears, but the conversation finally got flowing."

C4 looked over at Jolene, who was slowly nodding and looking at Terry, who took another sip of wine and continued.

"They really opened up. They were always worried that Trevor had a violent temper, and hoped he had never been mean to Jolene."

C4 looked hard at Jolene, so she then spoke.

"I said no, that just as any young couple, we had our arguments but that he always behaved. And he did until the last few months when he kept getting worse and worse. It was like there was something wrong with him or his life and I just took some of the abuse that he was handing out. They don't need to know that he hurt me. It just doesn't do anything for anyone. I also didn't mention what he did to the house. They feel bad that I am living there all alone."

She stopped there, unable to go on. Terry picked up the thread.

"Jolene was all class, as always. They offered several times to do anything they could to help her, including coming out and staying with her, helping her with things around the house, all the usual stuff. They were very nice, actually."

"In fact," Jolene interjected, "They said they never had anything against me, they knew Trevor was quite immature and had some anger issues and thought that getting married so young and to a high school girl was unlikely to help him grow up. They didn't dislike me. They were worried about me."

Once again Jolene had to stop talking. This time she went to the bathroom and came back with a box of tissues.

"I hope this is enough for all of us. Unless you men don't plan to cry. It gets worse, or better, depending on how you look at it."

She looked over at Terry, who took her cue and continued.

"There was a lot of reminiscing. Talking about Trevor growing up, trying to get him focused on constructive goals, getting him into the National Guard, then off to Science School in Wahpeton."

"Where he was when we met."

C4 couldn't help but ask his question.

"You mentioned that earlier, but it does make me think a bit, you may be entitled to some veteran's benefits."

Jolene looked at C4, and said,

"There were a few guys in full uniform at the visitation, and they all sat together. I was so numb it all kind of went over my head."

More tears, and Terry took over again.

"Didn't one of them talk to you at the visitation?"

Jolene composed herself and replied,

"Yes, he said how sorry he was for my loss and then handed me a business card and said to call him when I was ready."

"Do you have the card?"

"Yes, I have it with all the funeral paperwork."

"Please bring that when we talk to my dad tomorrow."

"Ok."

Terry continued.

"It gets better. They also mentioned that they had a life insurance policy on Trevor, for $100,000. They kept the premiums paid and when Trevor and Jolene got married, they changed the beneficiary to 75% for Jolene, retaining 25% for themselves, in case they had to pay for his burial, which they did. So, Jolene has more money coming from that."

Carson then spoke for the first time.

"That's a lot of insurance to put on a kid."

Jolene replied.

"Trevor's uncle was an insurance agent. Again, I knew that but never gave it any thought. Everybody needs a job, right?"

Terry nodded. C4 kind of nodded. Did they?

"And each of their four kids got those $100,000 policies when they were quite young. Mom and dad kept them funded."

C4 felt he needed to take part. But he was interrupted by the oven timer going off. So, he stood up still feeling a little woozy from his afternoon bender.

"I'll get that, " said C4.

"Thanks, honey. Just put it on top of the stove and spread the shredded cheese over it. We need to let it rest a couple of minutes."

C4 did as Jolene directed. As he spread the cheese over the top of the roaster, he was adding in his head. Employer insurance, worker's comp, military insurance, the other life insurance, this was adding up. And she owned a house that probably had some equity. She was close to rich.

Terry was talking again.

"And they offered her more financial help, until the insurance came in, they were wonderful. I wasn't sure how that whole scene was going to go, but it was perfectly nice all the way around. They are really determined to help Jolene any way they can."

Everyone looked at Jolene, who smiled a bit.

"There was the one awkward moment. And I mean awkward. For Jolene, not for me."

Jolene looked hard at Terry.

"You could leave that part out."

"No, it was out of concern that they asked, that's all."

Carson couldn't stand it any longer.

"What was the question?"

"They asked Jolene if there was any chance she was pregnant."

All eyes turned to Jolene. C4 was more than interested in her answer.

"I had to tell them no. And yes, I'm sure. I think a grandchild would have made things a little better for them."

Carson looked thoughtful.

"I can see why they would ask. It was actually good of them, assuming they meant to be supportive and involved."

Terry replied.

"That's how I took it. They seemed disappointed when Jolene said no."

Jolene picked up the thread, while she looked at her glass of wine.

"And then we went to another restaurant to meet with my family. That was much more interesting and not necessarily in a good way. But first, let's dish up. Carson, can you cut the bread? Cal would you set the table? Terry and I will dish up the chicken."

That kept them all occupied for the next few minutes. Finally, they were all seated facing their plates of food. C4 felt oddly like an outsider in this little group, despite being in his own home.

They all looked at each other.

Terry broke the silence.

"I need to pray before we eat. It's been that kind of day."

With no objections they all bowed their heads.

"Lord, thank you for getting Jolene and me safely through this day, and for this food, and for all the people who are really dedicated to helping Jolene pick up the pieces of her life and move forward. Amen."

Jolene started crying. She composed herself enough to say, "Thank you, Terry, that is just so nice."

C4 was finding himself further and further from his comfort zone, so decided to concentrate on eating. That was going to take a moment, though, as Jolene addressed him.

"Cal, can you refresh drinks for everyone? Thanks."

He was fine having something to do. Being helpful, which seemed to be the theme of the dinner. He stood and once again had to catch himself a bit. Still a bit wobbly from the scotch. He tried hard to make sure no one noticed. He moved a little more slowly than usual to the counter and brought back the Rose', then filled a pitcher with water and ice and set that on the table before sitting back down.

Just as he sat down, Carson asked the obvious follow-up question.

"Then what happened with Jolene's family?"

Both women shook their heads. Jolene spoke.

"Go ahead Terry. You were my highly paid, impartial observer."

"Highly paid?"

"Absolutely. You got an all-expenses paid round trip to Jamestown, North Dakota, complete with a nice lunch, a good dessert, and two separate venues of entertainment. What more could you want?"

"You and I shared a piece of pie, but it was really good. The entertainment was top shelf, though."

Both women laughed. C4 and Carson just looked at each other. The emotional stability of the evening was nonexistent. Terry followed Jolene's cue and began the story.

"I knew her parents from my high school years."

C4 couldn't help himself.

"You're from Wahpeton, too?"

"Yes, I was a few years ahead of Jolene in school, but we kind of knew each other. She was in my brother's class."

"And Carson, where are you from?"

"Minot. Terry and I met at UND. When I graduated, we married and moved out here. Terry finished her degree at Bismarck State."

Terry apparently decided to leave Jolene's story aside and start on her own.

"I was a hockey cheerleader at UND, and Carson never missed a game. Also, we lived in the same dorm complex, so we had no problem meeting each other. It was slow, at first because he was so shy, but we eventually became a couple."

"What brought you to Bismarck?" C4 felt compelled to ask.

"I was a civil engineering major, and the North Dakota Highway Department was hiring, so getting back closer to my family in Minot was good for me. Terry majored in elementary education and had no trouble getting a job here, at the Missouri Valley Montessori Academy. In fact, she's the one who helped Jolene get her job there as a teacher's aide."

C4 looked at Jolene. He was learning so much about her. How did he not know these things?

Chapter 19

TERRY TOOK ADVANTAGE of the silence to start the story of their afternoon meeting with Jolene's parents.

"We met at Applebee's. Lots of hugs and kisses and tears. It was like I was part of the family. When we sat down, it was a bit awkward at first. They wanted her to come back to Wahpeton, at first, we thought just for a visit. Then it became apparent that they meant permanently. They saw no reason for her to stay in Bismarck."

While C4 was still not sure about a long-term life with Jolene, he sure enjoyed the short term and with all that money coming in, the medium term looked pretty good as well. He wondered where this was headed.

Again, Jolene read his mind.

"Don't worry, Cal, I have no interest in going back to Wahpeton. My life is here now, my jobs, my friends, you. I made that clear to them. Except the part about you. You were not discussed. You were lumped into 'all my friends' in Bismarck."

Terry took over again.

"They even had a guy for her to marry. Dwight Morton."

Both women laughed. Jolene said,

"Dwight and I graduated from high school together. His family owns a pretty successful design and construction company in Wahpeton. Dwight went to NDSU and is close to finishing his degree in architecture. The plan for him is to move back to Wahpeton and take over the family business."

Terry jumped in. It was clear she was enjoying this part of the story.

"Dwight probably would have no interest in Jolene whatsoever."

C4 once again couldn't help himself.

"Why not?"

Jolene answered.

"He's quite gay. Apparently, my parents are the only ones who don't know. Of course, they haven't seen him in years. He and I went to our freshman dance together. So, my mom thought we were an item. I guess she never let go of that."

Terry couldn't help but add to the story.

"And their business is a big deal in Wahpeton. He'd be quite a catch for a farm girl like Jolene."

Again, both women laughed. C4 was having a hard time figuring out the emotional transitions. But more importantly, Jolene was a farm girl? Again, why didn't he know that?

Carson took advantage of a brief moment of silence to offer more new information.

"And his older brother, Kent works with me at the highway department. Nice guy. Not gay as far as I know."

C4 was struggling to keep up, given all this new information and the afternoon he spent with his bottle of scotch. Apparently, it was Terry's turn to talk.

"Kent graduated from high school with me. Really good golfer. Class valedictorian."

To C4 it appeared all these people knew each other, and he was an outsider. In his own home. Where would this go next? He didn't have to wait long to find out. Jolene took over the story.

"When I made it clear I wasn't going back to Wahpeton, or going to marry Dwight, my mom insisted on coming out here and staying with me for at least a month, maybe more."

Terry dove back into the conversation.

"She said she knew there was room in Jolene's house and that she would be really helpful."

Jolene leapfrogged Terry's interjection.

"I had to work to decline that, obviously not revealing that the house was trashed and where I was actually living."

Terry rolled her eyes.

"Can't imagine her living here. She is the hottest 40-year-old-woman I have ever laid eyes on. How your dad keeps her all to himself out on that farm is beyond me."

Jolene stood to get some more wine and corrected Terry.

"She just turned 41."

"She could pass for 29."

"She could. Don't want her making a play for my guy."

Terry just had to keep this going.

"He'd be going from bedroom to bedroom, wearing himself out."

Jolene reached out and put her hand on C4's.

"I'm not worried. He only has eyes for me."

"It's not his eyes I'd worry about."

"Terry! That's awful!"

Carson poured himself more water.

"Really, Terry, now I'm blushing."

But Terry wasn't done. Not by a long shot.

"Jolene, do you think you're the first girl he picked up at a bar?"

"Of course not. He was too good at it."

She smiled at C4, who was clearly not comfortable with where this was headed.

Carson looked sharply at Terry as he spoke.

"Terry, leave it alone. Don't do this."

"Sorry Carson, I want this in the open, and I want Cal and Jolene to hear it together."

"For the last time, Terry. Please don't."

"I will be quick and to the point. Then we'll drop it."

This time Carson hung his head and stared down at his plate. Jolene asked,

"Terry, are you doing this as a friend or is this some old vendetta."

Terry ignored Jolene's question and kept talking.

"A few years ago, Cal, you picked up a 'girl' at a bar and the two of you had a brief fling."

She used air quotes when she said girl. C4 was thinking as hard as he could, which was not helped by his afternoon date with a bottle of scotch, but with so little information he didn't have a clue who she was talking about.

"She was my friend, and she was married. And now she's not. Regan McCord."

That C4 remembered. He made the only reply he could.

"She was an adult, she went out with me willingly, and I certainly didn't know she was married."

Terry studied him for several long seconds.

"I believe you. But the damage was done. I'm sorry, Jolene. I know you are happy here with Cal, but we've shared a lot of your history, and I thought you should know a little about his. And Cal, I did not tell Jolene this behind your back. I'm trying to be as fair to you as I can."

Carson put his hand on Terry's.

"I know that episode really bothered you. I'm still not sure it had to be shared. But we're all adults here, so let's put it behind us. If Cal and Jolene want to discuss it further, that's none of our business."

Jolene now reached across the table and took Terry's hand.

"Terry, I know that must have hurt you to see your friend's marriage end like that. And I trust that you told us that out of your love and concern for me. And I appreciate you telling it now, so that Cal could hear it and defend himself."

Terry was now the one crying.

"Now I feel really bad. I should have kept my mouth shut. But it's been eating at me ever since I figured out who Cal is. I was trying to find a way to get it off my chest, and I guess the emotions of the day got the best of me. I apologize to both of you."

Jolene replied,

"I appreciate that. It's hard to leave emotional things like that buried."

C4 disagreed but said nothing. Jolene continued.

"Let me say this. When Cal brought me here from the Riverview that first time, I was a willing participant. I was hurting inside from the lack of loving male companionship. I was looking to find something that Trevor didn't share with me anymore and maybe had never shared with me. Cal happened to be there. It was fun getting so much attention as I went back and forth from the bar to the hostess stand, seating late-comers and delivering drinks to the people in the dining room. I was well aware that the 7-Ups he was buying me were really gin and tonics, but I didn't mind. I made a conscious decision to take off my wedding ring and put it in my pocket.

"Maybe that's how he always operated, but I enjoyed it. He was smooth and sophisticated and very, very nice to me. And he is still nice to me. Always. It was no accident that I turned to him when Trevor threatened to kill me. You saw how badly he beat me, Terry. I needed a man, and Cal helped me when I did. I didn't want to endanger you by going to your house, where Trevor would certainly find me. This was a place Trevor didn't know, and it's secured, and most importantly, Cal was here. I don't know if this is a forever kind of relationship. But right now, it's what I need. I need you to know that."

That brought a lot of silence. A speech like that is hard to follow. Jolene, however, wasn't done.

"Terry, I love you like a sister, maybe more. And I know you would never intentionally hurt me. Cal, I love all you've done for me. Let's just keep that in mind and stay on track as I sort through where I go with the rest of my life."

Then she turned.

"And I love you too, Carson, for how good you are for Terry, and for letting me borrow her this past couple of weeks."

C4 was really out of his element and had no idea what to say. Luckily Carson tried to provide some emotional stability.

"That's a lot of love. Thanks for sharing all that with us Jolene. It's the kind of emotional outlet you probably needed after today and the last week or so. Terry, let's go home and leave these people in peace."

Terry nodded. C4 half expected Jolene to go out the door with them, but after she hugged Terry again, she watched them go to the elevator and only when the elevator door closed, did she shut the condo door and turn back to him.

"I meant everything I said. You and I individually get to decide if we are together forever. I didn't move in here to trap you in any permanent relationship. I might have fibbed a bit on the 'week or two,' but you have a say in where this goes as much as I do. But I do thank you for all you have done for me, from the very start."

"Thanks for saying that, Jolene. In all honesty, I am thrilled to have you here, but I do wonder what our future holds. For the time being, I am good with us. Trust me."

Jolene somehow found a way to laugh a bit.

"I guess I may have scared you with the underwear drawer and all the groceries and the wine and the other stuff I brought with me. I suppose I just needed you and a place that felt like home. I hadn't had that in quite a while."

C4 nodded.

"I appreciate that, Jolene, and it has improved my lifestyle a great deal."

"Speaking of lifestyle. What the hell did you do this afternoon? You look half dead, and the scotch is almost gone."

"I think you just answered your own question. I just fell back into an old habit, started drinking and didn't stop. It won't happen again, I promise."

"I'll accept that."

For some reason C4 couldn't explain even to himself, more words came out of his mouth.

"So, your mom is really that good looking?"

Oh, my God. Why did I say that? Is there a way to take it back? Luckily, somehow, his muddled brain then saved him. He followed up as quickly as he could with:

"Now I see where your beauty comes from!"

"No, you are not going to meet my mom. Not anytime soon, anyway. For now, you are stuck with the junior version!"

She took his hand and led him into the bedroom and straight to bed and straight to sleep. Both were exhausted, for different reasons.

When C4 awoke it was because Jolene was kissing him all over. Apparently, she had rested enough. He opened his eyes. It was barely light out. If they were going to be together long-term, this waking up early would have to be something that got fixed.

Except for this. This was good.

The next time he woke up, she was not in bed, and he heard the shower. It must be Monday already. He laid in bed and thought. They were meeting with his dad at 3:30 that afternoon. She needed to bring all the property and insurance paperwork she could find. He'd remind her.

In the meantime, he had to pack to go to Minnesota with old man Baker on Tuesday. Before that someone had to clean up the kitchen. When they had gone to bed, they had left everything on the kitchen table-food, glasses, plates, all of it. He could take care of that. Jolene had to go to work. Even cleaning up the kitchen was more appealing than drinking all day again. He had to put that behind him.

Jolene came out of the bathroom.

"Good morning! Did you sleep ok? I bet you had a dream that we were making love, am I right?"

C4 smiled.

"Yes, oddly, I did. It's like you can read my mind. Even when I'm sleeping."

Jolene opened her underwear drawer.

"I need to get ready for work and before that I need to clean up the kitchen."

"I'll do that. Do you think the casserole is alright?"

"I got up in the night and put it in the fridge. It's fine. If you want to clean up everything else that would be great."

C4 just stared at her. She noticed.

"No touching. I really need to get ready for work."

"No, I was just looking at you and thinking how wonderful you are, not just skin deep. You are an amazing woman. Especially for someone your age, who's been through what you have."

"Now I'm blushing, and you can see all of me, so you know that."

"I'll stop if I am embarrassing you. But I mean it."

C4 rolled out of bed, pulling on his usual sweats. He could still feel the effects of his scotch binge yesterday. No more of that, certainly not today.

He then walked out to the kitchen, giving Jolene some privacy to dress.

The coffee was made and ready. He poured himself a cup, took a sip and set it down. He started putting dirty dishes next to the sink. When was the last time he'd done dishes, more than a plate and a glass? When was the last time he had hosted more than one person at his condo? More changes in his life, all thanks to Jolene.

He thought back over the evening prior. That had been quite an emotional session. Laughing, crying, personal history, some good, some bad, and lots of love and forgiveness. Again, all new. Who knew people were so complicated? No wonder he'd always kept his distance and concentrated exclusively on his own wants and needs. Was this new connected lifestyle actually better? He thought about that a while as he found the dishwashing soap and filled the sink with hot soapy water, then put the glasses and plates in to soak.

He took the dishcloth and wiped off the table, then sat down with his coffee, again rehashing the prior evening in his mind. He did remember Regan. Quite well, and he knew full well she was married. In fact, they had hooked up more than once, including a long weekend in Fargo while her husband was playing in a softball tournament right here in Bismarck. She said she had told him that she had left town to visit her sister. Yes, he knew she was married, but she was clear that it didn't matter to her. Was that his problem? In fact, she had told him that her marriage was on the rocks already. There were a lot of blurry lines in life.

The good news was that he enjoyed meeting decent people, thanks to Jolene, and he sure enjoyed being with Jolene. The bad news was that it required a lot more thinking and introspection. *Is that a word? Where did that come from?*

Jolene came into the kitchen, fully dressed and ready for work.

"Can I bother you for a cup of coffee? I tip well, though it may be later tonight if you know what I mean."

"Yes, and I do. I know very well what you mean. I guess I need to be careful about casually dropping the 'I do' phrase."

"No, you don't. I thought I covered that last night. But I would like some coffee, please."

C4 grabbed her travel mug and filled it, putting the lid on carefully.

"You did, and I apologize for trying to be funny," said C4.

She had put on her coat. He walked over to her and exchanged her coffee for a hug and a kiss.

"Have a great day. See you at 3:30 at my dad's office. I texted you the address. I thought we should arrive and depart separately."

"That makes sense. See you at 3:30. Have a good day and stay out of the scotch!"

"Will do. I'm still hurting from my last binge ever."

He wondered if she'd picked up on his 'last binge ever' statement. She didn't respond, so he wasn't sure. She went out the door. He picked up his coffee and watched out the window until he saw her drive away.

Chapter 20

HE FINISHED THE DISHES and left them in the rack to dry. Apparently, he now owned a dish drying rack. He looked in the fridge. The casserole was still in the pan with the plastic wrap back in place. Most of it remained. The evening had been too full of conversation to do much eating.

No need to do anything with that. That might be dinner!

He walked to the counter and grabbed a pen and a notepad. Also new to his home. Will wonders never cease? He looked around. Wonder of wonders, there were some small pillows on his couch, and some coasters on the coffee table. Maybe she was taking over all the space and he'd get squeezed out after all.

He topped off his coffee and sat down at the table to make some notes.

Employer life insurance

Military life insurance

Worker's Comp death benefit

Life insurance policy from his parents

Home value, less mortgage, less cost to repair

Car value, less loan

Bank accounts - Jolene, Trevor, joint

Other accounts, property?

Titles, deeds, insurance policy numbers

He jotted down some estimated numbers for each of them. Probably not much equity in the house. They couldn't have owned it for much more than a year or two. Still, with the various insurance coverages, she would have a tidy sum. Young, beautiful and rich. Now he was back in the soccer dad frame of mind. With all this money and her jobs, all he needed to do was find some token job to make him look like a productive member of society. Maybe he could be an insurance agent like Trevor's uncle. Flexible hours, commission checks, freedom to move about, not tied to a desk. This might just be the plan to focus on.

His phone interrupted his dream. He looked at the screen. It was Jolene.

"Hi! Can we move the meeting with your dad to 3:45? I need to stop at my house and pick up some paperwork. I have some of it laid out, but it may take me a little while to locate the rest of it in the mess."

"Absolutely. Just get there when you can. I know he'll want you to have as much of that with you as you have available. Also, I'm really sorry about my 'I do' comment. I was trying to be humorous, not revisit our conversation last night."

"Thank you. I should have known it was something like typical male humor, but after all of our soul searching discussions last night I was still a little tender. I really laid my heart out for you and wanted you to take what I said seriously."

"I heard you and I am very sorry. The experts say the key to humor is all about timing, and I got that dead wrong. My apologies again, and I am glad you said what you did about us. It makes me love you even more."

"Thank you. I'm parked at school now and if I sit in my car too long the other teachers will come by and ask if I'm ok and then I'll cry, and then I'll have to redo my makeup, and I don't have that much time or energy. See you at 3:45 at your dad's office."

And she hung up. Best girlfriend ever.

C4 rolled into the parking lot outside his dad's office just after 3:30. Jolene's car was not in the parking lot, as he had anticipated, since he was intentionally a little early. He parked around in the back of the building and went in through a side door, the one he generally used.

He walked to his dad's door which was standing open. As usual, his dad's assistant, Taylor, was gone for the day. She worked part time, to help manage court dates and filings and other administrative items. It was fine that she was not around, and thus able to link C4 and Jolene.

"Knock, knock."

"Oh hi, Cal, come on in. Jolene with you?"

"No, she's stopping by her house to pick up some documents she thought you'd need. She'll be here in a few minutes."

"Ok. I've got a template I use, so we can work from that. The more things she already has in hand the easier this will be."

"That's what we figured."

"So, you are still a couple?"

"Yes. And it's going quite well, thank you."

"Good. And she's holding up ok? No breakdowns?"

"She had a tough day yesterday. She and a friend drove to Jamestown to spend a little time with Trevor's parents and then with her parents. Then they drove back, and we had dinner with her friend and her husband. The emotions came out over dinner. She may be a little raw from that. I know I am."

"You are? Why?"

"Part of the unveiling of emotions included why she came to me and why she stays with me, instead of moving back with her parents or making other choices. She can't tell them she's with me, or that Trevor trashed their house, so she had to do some careful word selection, which as you know, can be tiring."

"Unless you're a highly paid professional such as a lawyer."

"Of course. That's why we're here. By the way, I'm going to Minnesota with Baker again tomorrow. Just for a few days."

"Good. Use all of your charm. Don't over imbibe. I had a good meeting with him, and we need to keep him moving in our direction. He does want to talk to his kids before we change the trustee to me. They aren't actively involved, so he is still managing everything himself and knows he has to give that up sooner rather than later. So, it comes down to having the kids or one of the kids take over or turn it over to someone else, and right now that someone is me. So, as any good coach would tell his players – don't screw this up."

Normally after such a long speech and at this time of day, they'd both have a good laugh and pour each other a scotch, but today, with Jolene on her way, they'd have to settle for the laugh. C4 wasn't sure he wanted a scotch anyway after his Sunday binge. Instead of reaching for the scotch, C4 asked the most useful question he could think of.

"How old is Baker anyway?"

CT pulled a file out of his desk drawer.

"He was born in 1936, his daughter Kelly was born in 1961, and his son Kevin in 1964."

"So, he's getting up there. And his son and daughter have no kids?"

"No."

"Interesting. So, it's just you or the kids. Wonder why they have no interest, though Baker uncovered a bit of that on our last trip. But still, it's worth a lot of money."

"Baker and I talked about that a bit. They both got good educations, developed good careers and have no interest in any element of this untamed part of the world. In short, they are financially successful and have decided to be coastal elites. The only consistent contact, according to Baker, is that the daughter, Kelly, calls him every Sunday morning to check on him. He takes that call and talks to her for a bit before he goes to church."

"Well, that's better than nothing. Kind of sad for Baker and good for us."

"You mean good for me, right?"

"Of course."

CT looked up and waved toward the open door.

"Here's Jolene. We were just talking about you. All good. And I'm serious."

Both men stood as Jolene walked in with a bundle of papers. She went directly to C4 and gave him a kiss. She turned her attention to CT.

"It's nice to see you again. In better light and with less stress than our first meeting, I can see that the two of you two really do look alike."

CT looked at C4 and said,

"Not sure if that's a compliment or an insult. I'll take it as a compliment, because you have to look younger than I do."

C4 laughed.

"I'll accept that."

"And besides," CT continued, "No one is going to notice either of us with you in the room."

"Sounds like your son takes after you in ways other than looks. He tells me stuff like that all the time."

"He's right. But he tells me you are smart and wonderful in other ways as well."

Jolene looked at C4.

"I hope you haven't shared too much about our time together."

"Absolutely not and we should turn our attention to your legal needs before this lovefest turns in some inappropriate direction."

CT nodded.

"My son is right. I see you brought some papers. Let's see what you have."

CT put the papers she handed him in a stack on the left side of his desk and his estate settlement template on the right. For a few minutes he took each piece of paper, noted it on the template, sometimes asking Jolene a clarifying question, but mostly taking notes and putting the papers in an order that matched his template.

"This is a good start, Jolene. The house was titled correctly for you to take over clear ownership. The car is in the same situation. You even brought the mortgage and car lien info. You may be underwater on the car, but the house should easily be worth more than the mortgage."

Jolene explained,

"We traded in my old beater for one decent car, so had to borrow most of it and take out a longer loan than we wanted. There is also an old pickup truck that Trevor owned before we met. That's in his name and I didn't find any paperwork in the house. And, despite the fact that Trevor's parents and mine both believed we were too young to get married, they did help us out to make a decent down payment on our house. Apparently, their aversion to rent and love of ownership overcame their lack of faith in us or our marriage. And despite his other faults, which your son may have mentioned to you, Trevor always made good money. So, with his income and my two jobs, we were doing pretty well, financially."

"So it appears. But my son also mentioned there is some damage to your house, right?"

"Yes, that's my only reason for living with him."

She playfully pointed at C4, but smiled as she spoke, and laughed after she said it, then continued.

"Just kidding. He has other good attributes, as I'm sure you're well aware."

"I sure am. We have some nice meals together and enjoy each other's company."

Jolene beamed.

"He has been a godsend for me, and I am so glad he took me in. I try to be a good roommate in exchange."

C4 decided to once again get this turned to the work she needed done.

"We do well together. We even had another couple over for dinner last night. We're adulting pretty well."

"Good for you. Jolene, it sounds like you are a positive influence on my son. And at such a tender age."

This time C4 couldn't let this go on.

"After you left this morning, I sat down and made a list of the items I thought my dad may need in order to help you."

He handed the list to Jolene. She studied it and replied.

"I did give your dad some of this. And I have the card of the guy from the National Guard."

She dug into her purse and quickly pulled out a card, which she handed to CT along with C4's list. CT gave the list a quick look and nodded, then looked at the card.

"Trevor was in the Guard?"

"Yes. As I mentioned early on to your son, he was very proud of his sharpshooter award. He could really shoot! His family lives outside Jamestown, and they are all big hunters."

C4 cringed. He really wished she had not brought that up. His dad would have way too much fun with that at their next meal together. Unfortunately, he didn't have to wait that long. His dad was ready to pick up that thread.

"Cal, you certainly are lucky to have Jolene in your life. Did you know the degree to which you risked your life to make that happen?"

"Not at first, but it has been mentioned. What else do you need from Jolene today, or have we changed the topic to picking on me?"

CT smiled.

"I'm sorry, that was just too easy to not pick up on. I apologize to you also, Jolene, because I know you were in danger as well. Let's move on."

He looked down at the paperwork on his desk, shuffling through a few sheets before he looked up.

"Well, Jolene, I have some work to do, some things to file and I need you to sign a couple of forms that allow me to represent you through this process. And given your current living situation you do get the family discount."

"Oh, good. One more reason to live with Cal. Can't have too many of those."

Again, she smiled at C4 as she spoke. She was enjoying this far too much. CT redirected the conversation.

"But in the meantime, let's add some things up."

Jolene looked serious again and said,

"Go ahead."

"Military life insurance is generally around $250,000."

Jolene interjected,

"Yes, he told me it was roughly enough to pay off the mortgage on the house."

"That sounds about right."

CT continued.

"His employer life insurance policy including the accidental death benefit adds up to another $250,000. And the life insurance policy his parents had on him will pay you $75,000. Do you have any funeral or internment expenses?"

That turned out to be the conversational touchpoint that made the situation too real for Jolene. She started to cry, and C4 instinctively stood up, moved behind her and put his hands on her shoulders. She pulled some tissue out of her purse and composed herself quickly, replying.

"No, his parents paid for whatever the Guard didn't, and he's to be buried in the cemetery at the country church where they always went. That will happen in the spring, and there will be a graveside ceremony. His mom will call and let me know when that will be."

Jolene was again wiping her eyes by the time she finished that answer. C4 remained behind her with her hands on her shoulders. Jolene reached up with her one free hand and put it on C4's.

CT was impressed by his son's compassion for his roommate. This was more than a fling. He seemed to really have some feelings for her. Or he had at least developed some level of human decency. If so, that was probably due to her anyway.

"I'm sorry if some of this is hard for you, Jolene. Don't feel bad if you break down. It's perfectly natural, and I've worked with survivors who are not nearly as composed as you are."

Jolene nodded.

"I know you know that things were not great between Trevor and me at the time he died. In some ways that helps, but in other ways it makes it worse. I wish we had been on better terms, so I don't know if I feel guilt, or shame or just feel like I should feel worse than I do. I just wish we could have made up before he left for work that night."

Now she was crying again.

"I also feel that I need to add, it wasn't bad between us because of your son. That was just a symptom. Cal has always been kind and helpful to me, and I would never blame him for the situation I was in."

She smiled up at C4 who was still standing behind her and when she did, C4 thought he may cry himself. Again, a whole new frontier of thoughts and feelings, all because he did what C4 had always done - home in on the cutest available girl in whatever bar he was in and see if he could seduce her. This time he had gotten way more than he had ever imagined.

CT the attorney came to life, saying,

"Again, I'm glad the two of you are doing so well together. I have just a couple more questions and you are free to go."

He took a moment of silence as assent to proceed, so he said,

"There will be a Worker's Comp death benefit, and it's a factor of his salary. Since he was on an hourly wage, they'll have to do some calculations, but it should be in the range of $150,000. Also, were your bank accounts joint?"

"I have a personal account, we have a joint account, and Trevor had an account in his name. We just never got around to merging every-thing."

"Are those the bank account statements you gave me? So, I have all the account numbers?"

"Yes."

"Ok, is there anything else? Both assets and liabilities. In other words, any other accounts or credit cards, properties, loans, anything else?"

"No, the only thing is that I will have to retain someone to fix up the house before I can sell it. It's a nice comfortable little home, but I just can't live there anymore."

"So, I should use Cal's address for your correspondence?"

"No, please use the house address. Neither my parents or Trevor's parents or any of our other out-of-town family or friends know that the house is unlivable, and there is no reason for them to know that. I'm keeping them away and pretending that I live there, so I need to keep that as my official address. I stop by every day or two to check on things and pick up the mail, so I will get whatever gets mailed to me fairly quickly."

"I understand, and you have the right to do that. Final hard question. Do you have a death certificate I can have?"

This time Jolene seemed to steel herself before she replied. She took a deep breath.

"Not yet. The funeral home said I should get five copies, and they should come any day now. Can I just drop some off when they come?"

"Absolutely. I think I'll need three for the filings I need to make."

Another brief period of silence followed, so CT said,

"That should do it for now. Jolene, you have been great. You are great. Keep working on my son. With you around he's a better person."

Jolene smiled over at C4.

"I do what I can. And he is good for me, too."

Turning to his son, CT said,

"And you are leaving in the morning with your client?"

"Yup, 9:00 a.m., as usual."

The senior Tappen turned to Jolene.

"If you get lonely while he's gone, give me a call. If I walk into the country club for dinner with you on my arm, I'll be the most envied man in Bismarck."

"Dad, really? You hit on her with me right here?"

Jolene laughed.

"Now boys, stop it!"

C4 said, "Jolene, you should go before this turns into hand-to-hand combat. I'll be home in a few minutes."

"I supposed I should go. Though I must say I don't mind the competition for my affection. Leftovers ok for dinner?"

"Absolutely."

Jolene stood and C4 walked her to the door, giving her a quick kiss on the forehead as she walked out. Making sure the outer office door was closed, he turned back to his dad and said,

"She's pretty impressive, isn't she?"

"In every conceivable way. I can't believe her composure for a 21-year-old woman who was suddenly and tragically widowed just over a

week ago. She's handling herself, her family, her work, you, everything!"

Chapter 21

THE NEXT MORNING, RIGHT ON SCHEDULE, C4 made the short journey from his condo garage to Mr. Baker's house, his SUV barely warming up in the process. As he drove, he thought about the past half-day. The meeting with his dad had gone well, and more than once he had found himself adding up Jolene's new wealth. Even assuming a sizeable bill to rebuild her house, it was a nice sum. Replacing the kitchen cabinets and holes in the walls were the worst of the damage. If she was moving back into the house, she would need some new furniture, unless she stayed with him…

A horn sounded behind him. Green light. *Focus, Cal.* And then there was last evening. A month ago, leftover casserole and a glass of red wine for dinner would have been unheard of, now it just seemed so normal. Again, a new normal that was pretty darned good. And of course, a wonderful night in bed, a good night's sleep, a good look at her coming out of the shower, watching her get dressed this morning as an added bonus, and then a warm goodbye as she went to work.

A horn sounded again. Green light. He looked in the mirror. It was the same car. A block later, he turned off onto Baker's street, and the other car went straight. That was a relief. A couple of blocks later, he pulled up in front of Baker's house, and his car clock said 8:58. He paused a bit and then, leaving the SUV running, he went up the walk to the front door.

Before he could ring the bell, Bella opened the door.

"Good morning, Mr. Tappen. Mr. Baker will be right down."

"Good morning, Bella."

"Hmmph."

Bella walked away, leaving C4 on the outside step. It was going to be fun to leave her homeless. An added motivation to make the Baker plan work.

Baker appeared bit by bit as he worked the way down the stairs, feet, legs, hips, torso and finally his white-haired head.

"Good morning, Mr. Baker."

"Good morning, Calvin. Are we all ready to go?"

"I am. I'll grab your bag."

C4 picked up the bag and stepped to the side, so Baker could walk in front of him. He heard Bella slam and lock the door behind them.

Baker got into the passenger seat, C4 shut the passenger door, put the bag in the back next to his, and they were off. Baker opened the conversation.

"Sometimes I think Bella may not like me. I know she doesn't like you. Her husband was severely injured in Vietnam and was never really well again. She was my wife's niece, so when Katie was still alive, we started helping them out. He lived for another couple of decades but was never able to work. When he passed away, and with Katie already gone, I took her in as my housekeeper. She runs a tight ship, so I do value what she does for me."

C4 found that explanation interesting, bordering on helpful.

"If she is helpful to you, I guess you can put up with some small differences."

Baker nodded and replied.

"She is on the Baker Company official payroll, so my accountant gives her full W-2 credit for the salary and the benefit of her lodging, so she is accruing some Social Security benefits, and I've made her the beneficiary of a deferred annuity I bought years ago. She'll be ok, when the time comes."

"Well, let's hope that isn't for a good long while yet."

C4 turned his attention to merging onto the interstate. Talking about Bella had helped him put his visions of Jolene out of his mind, which had in turn improved his driving. Three nights without Jolene. That was going to be rough. He used to enjoy these trips to Minnesota more when he was just leaving behind an empty condo.

On the road, he and Baker settled into the normal, sporadic banter. The weather, the snow coverage, the impact of the snow coverage on the pastures and crops the next year. The Bismarck basketball teams, both high school and college. The NDSU football team, which, for Baker, was a year-round topic of interest. Then Baker started reminiscing about NDSU. It was called NDAC when he was there, he and Katie. North Dakota Agricultural College. He had made the most of his education and was blessed to have met Katie there, but he had paid his tuition and had completed his studies and the constant harassment to 'give something back' (he actually used air quotes while he said that) was quite annoying. He made a small contribution from time to time but that was all they'd get.

Then he started talking about his marriage and raising a family, or rather not raising a family. Instead, he had an empire to build. Katie raised the family, alone, until she ran out of energy and everything else.

"I can't even remember what kept me so busy during the winters. I loved her and I loved the kids, I just never found any time to be at home. Maybe I was intimidated by them? The three of them were so close-knit. When I was there it was like I was an outsider, or worse, an intruder."

C4 really had nothing to say. His dad had been busy, too. Working hard took not just time but energy. Maybe that's why C4 had just opted out. He saw the payback was a big paycheck and a nice house but in the end his dad had lost all the money, the house and the family because of one foolish, egocentric decision. One last run at being young. But Baker was still talking.

"So not only do my kids not have any interest in the property empire I built, or North Dakota, but I think they actually resent it. I think they associate it with the death of their mother. That I sacrificed her, and maybe even them for my empire."

And then he was quiet. C4 felt he had to say something, even if it wasn't completely true.

"My dad worked hard too, and he worked smart, and gave us a good life, financially. College for all of us and a nice home, and my mom was great. But what died for us was their marriage. By the time he had time for his family, we kids were out of the nest, and my mom was tired of waiting."

Baker just nodded, but then said,

"Your dad is a good man. I like working with him. One of the few people I still trust after many, many years of working together. He always makes sure his is looking out for my interests. He'll do a great job managing my property and ultimately my estate. He and I just need to make sure my kids are comfortable with him at the helm. I don't think it will be a hard sell. My son will show little interest, but Kelly still has some maternal instincts that she will direct toward me. Even young women want to take care of someone, even if it's an old man."

C4 smiled. Then the horrid thought hit him. *Is that what Jolene is doing? Taking care of me?*

Lost in those thoughts, he started drifting off the road.

"You ok, Calvin?"

"Yes, I'm fine. Just a momentary lapse. I'll be more careful."

Apparently, Jolene was keeping him from driving safely. That must be what happened to Trevor. He thought so much about Jolene he just drove off the road.

His thoughts returning to his relationship with Jolene, he desperately wanted to believe that their relationship was deeper than that.

The rest of the journey was uneventful, and once at the lake home, they unpacked and had their usual first night routine. A nap, a drink, dinner at a local pub, then a little TV, then to bed. The only item of interest was the weather report, which mentioned a major winter storm forming over the Rockies. Not sure how bad, or the eventual path, but the weatherman was keeping an eye on it. That made C4 feel much better. They'd be ok as long as the weatherman kept an eye on it.

The next morning, they were at their rented fish house early and the rumors proved true. The fish were biting. They had a great morning reeling in walleye after walleye, careful to keep their daily limit under the maximum allowed until they each had the biggest fish they thought they were likely to catch.

Back at the house, C4 quickly cleaned one of the fish and cooked that with some potatoes and peppers for lunch. They enjoyed that, then a nap. C4 figured if getting old involved a lot of napping then he might just be ready to retire. He did enjoy a nap, but when he had relaxed a bit, he realized he really missed Jolene. At least that is what he thought he was feeling. He'd never missed anyone before. But if wishing she were there with him was missing her then he was definitely missing her.

He looked around the home. It was not huge, but quite comfortable. He could picture Jolene with him there, enjoying the fireplace in the winter and the lake in the summer. Jolene in a bikini. That was worth picturing. And this place was closer to Wahpeton than to Bismarck. Maybe with amends made she could reconnect with her family. C4 smiled again. Both Jolene and her mother in bikinis. This was getting interesting and a little erotic.

Maybe he wasn't as domesticated as he'd thought. Terry had all but accused him of trying to satisfy two women on Sunday evening. Might be worth a try?

No, that was too far out to be realistic at all. He'd have to dedicate himself to Jolene, with her mom as bonus eye candy. That still worked nicely. His future never looked brighter. A loving wife or whatever Jolene turned out to be, her reportedly beautiful mother, and, based on the conversation in the car the previous day, the Baker plan virtually in his lap. With these thoughts filling his mind, he fell asleep.

The rest of that day and the next were some of the happiest of C4's life, despite desperately missing Jolene. If the Baker plan was on his doorstep, why couldn't he keep her? They could marry, have a couple of kids, live in a nice house, he could tap the Baker empire by exchanging a steady stream of some easy duty or another with a nice solid income. He'd be as reputable as anyone in Bismarck. Job, family, and his checkered past would be far behind him. Even Terry would have to admit that he'd been fully reformed. People would talk about what a good guy he'd become after such a questionable past. He may have to pay off a few debts, once word of his financial success got around. That was ok. And his dad was right. It was all due to Jolene. What a catch!

A little stress intruded into his blissful thoughts on Thursday evening as he and Baker were watching the weather, as usual. This time the winter storm the meteorologist had been watching was fully formed and moving quickly to the northeast out of Colorado and into the Dakotas. It would move into South Dakota overnight and head into North Dakota and western Minnesota over the course of the day Friday.

C4 and Baker discussed the situation and made a decision. They had caught plenty of fish, had eaten plenty of fish, and could pack their limits in a cooler and take them back to Bismarck earlier than planned. C4 thought Jolene would enjoy the fruits of his honest labor, and he could show off his fish frying and baking skills. For once he'd bring home some food.

That became their plan. They'd get up in the morning, pack up and leave. Their route of I-94 through Fargo to Bismarck should be on the northern edge of the storm allowing them to get back home before the storm worked its way that far north.

The next morning started normally enough, then -

"Calvin, come in here. Quickly!" Baker was actually yelling from his bedroom.

This was odd. C4 had been sitting at the kitchen table finishing off a cup of coffee, having packed his bag and was waiting for Baker to come out of the master suite. He was calculating his day. A drive back to Bismarck, hopefully uneventful, dropping off Baker. Maybe a quick visit with his dad, then back to his condo to put the fish in the fridge, and about that time Jolene would come home from school. A quickie with her, lovingly of course, and she'd be off to the Riverview and he could continue to bask in all the glory of his future. But then the shout from Baker. Since C4 had never been invited into the master suite before, this was odd.

"Coming!"

He stood and walked to the doorway of Baker's bedroom. No Baker in sight. Was he having a health issue?

"Where are you?"

"In the closet."

He must have fallen. That was not good. He needed to be healthy and alive until his dad finished converting the estate to the Tappen coffers.

C4 walked into the closet and sure enough old man Baker was on his hands and knees on the floor. Health issue? No, he had the floor safe open and had stacked up the gold pieces next to the safe.

"Calvin, I've been robbed!"

C4 felt his knees almost buckle. This was the worst thing he could imagine. *Think, Cal, think. You need to put this fire out. How?*

"Are you sure? That's a lot of gold coins."

"I had a hundred and eight. Now there's a hundred and three."

"You mean someone got into your safe and took just five gold coins?"

"Yes, exactly."

"Are you sure?"

"Of course I'm sure. I had it written down."

"When did you last count them?"

"A year or so ago. I don't know for sure."

"That's a long time."

"I said, I had it written down. I haven't taken any out in years."

It was clear that Baker was pretty worked up, and C4 didn't want to press him anymore. Besides, he had run out of questions.

"I need to call the police!"

"No offense, Mr. Baker, but before you do, let's think about what you have to tell them."

"What do you mean, Calvin?"

C4 wondered that himself. He was thinking as hard and fast as he could. He needed to get Baker under control, to avoid having some forensics team come in and start a thorough investigation. He wasn't sure that would happen for this odd theft, but he had to make sure it didn't.

"Let me see if I can frame this up for you. Just hear me out. First, let's get you up off the floor. Sit here on the bed."

He helped Baker up and walked him to the edge of the bed. Baker sat down and stared into the closet at the gold coins stacked up around the gaping hole of the floor safe. C4 took the time to compose himself. He hoped Baker couldn't see the beads of sweat on his forehead. The bridge plan had gone so well he had all but forgotten that he'd lifted Baker's coins to make it happen. Having Baker count the coins this soon was not on his radar at all.

"Can you provide the police an exact date of the last time you counted the coins?"

"No, of course not. It was at least a year ago."

"Who knows there's a floor safe?"

"Kevin and Kelly only."

"And do they know where the combination is?"

"Yes. But they haven't been here in the past year, and they wouldn't steal from me."

"Ok. Let's change direction a bit. Who can get into the house?"

"Only me. No, wait. There's a spare key in the bin outside."

"Who knows about that?"

"A neighbor or two. We all do that around here."

"Anyone else?"

Baker was thinking hard, now, and C4 felt like he was getting the situation under control. Last thing he needed was another situation. Baker was responding to his last question.

"I guess the plumber I had to call once, and the cleaning lady who comes once a month all year round. Maybe others."

This was good. It was going exactly like C4 wanted. Baker was following C4's logic exactly as planned.

Mr. Baker continued thinking out loud. "I guess that's a bit of a problem with the police. Too many people have access, one way or an-other. But why take just five? Why not clean me out? If I'd died, no one would have known."

"Your kids don't know what's in the safe?"

"Not fully. I've always been vague when I tell them. I always say just some cash, a few ounces of gold and copies of my will and some other papers. I didn't think they needed an inventory."

"I can see that."

Now for some misdirection.

"So, the plumber, would he have come across the safe when he was working here?"

"He hasn't been here in years."

Failure. Try again.

"How about any other workers? Or the cleaning lady? She must have noticed the safe at some point."

"I suppose, if she's doing a good job. And I think she does. But would she steal from me? I pay her well and she's been with me for years. Why steal from me now?"

"There are probably all kinds of reasons. Maybe something changed in her life?"

C4 took a breath. No objection from Baker so he went on.

"Who knows why people steal? It could have been the plumber, or any of his guys, or the neighbors, or the cleaning lady, or anyone any of them may have told about the spare key."

"She was just here the other day. Let's call her and see if she noticed anything out of place. Not really accuse her, just ask some innocent questions," Mr. Baker suggested.

Now we're back off track, C4 thought Maybe she had noticed something from C4's tracks in the driveway to anything else he'd thought he'd put back correctly. This needed derailing.

"Let's not do that. Let's think some more. If you were to call the police, you would have to say that sometime over the past year or more, someone probably used the hidden key to come into your house and take a few gold pieces from a stash of over a hundred gold ounces and a pile of cash, out of a hidden floor safe using a well-hidden combination. Does that sound about right?"

Baker hung his head, then replied.

"I guess. But how did they find the combination? I had that very well hidden. And why take only five? Why not clean me out? The whole thing just makes no sense."

"Exactly. Not something the police are good at. They like clear cut crimes. Here, it's an odd theft, and a long list of unlikely suspects. It is not their forte."

"Then what should I do?"

C4 took a long look at Baker before answering. Baker had never looked older, almost defeated. Not the multimillionaire empire builder he had been for the last 60 years. C4 actually felt sorry for him. He'd always heard that the worst part of being robbed is the feeling of being violated. Probably how Jolene feels about her house. Not just a trashed house, but a violation of the home she was trying so hard to build. He wished she was with him now.

"Calvin, I'm serious. Any ideas on how to get to the bottom of this?"

"No. Not off the top of my head. And I hate to say this, but we do need to get going because of the blizzard heading our way. Why don't you close up the safe, and we can discuss this further as we drive?"

"I guess that's what we'll have to do. Why don't you roll our bags out to your car and I'll put everything back. Except for the gold someone stole from me."

C4 nodded and figured that his best bet was to follow Baker's instructions and end the conversation for now. He took Baker's bag and rolled it to the front door along with his. He grabbed the cooler with the fish and took that out first, then came back for the two bags. By then, Baker was at the door, ready to go.

"Before we go, Calvin, I want to give you something. You've been a good companion to me over the years. The reason I opened the safe was to grab a few of the gold pieces to give you, in a small show of appreciation."

He handed C4 three of the gold rounds.

"I thought I'd have a hundred and five left, but now I'll only have a hundred."

C4 almost swooned. At least that's the only word he could think of. If he hadn't stolen the five pieces from Baker, with these three, he'd have had enough to pay back Vicki, right on time, and enough to live on. Of course he couldn't have known that.

Of course, if he'd stayed in Bismarck maybe Trevor would have found and killed him. And Jolene. That's the problem with life. You can't go back and fix things. You just have to go forward.

"I can't take these, Mr. Baker. You know I enjoy these trips as much as you do. You just keep them."

"No, Calvin, my mind is made up. Think of them as a gift. I want you to have them."

C4 reluctantly took the gold pieces and put them in his pocket. The problem was that while he didn't want to take them, they would be handy. Shorter term, they really needed to get going to beat the storm.

"Thank you so much, Mr. Baker. Please do me one more favor."

"And that is?"

"Don't tell Bella. She always looks at me like she'd like to do me in as it is. If she knew I had these she'd grab a gun for sure."

Baker laughed. C4 took that as a good sign. Maybe this was over.

"I sleep with one eye open myself. That's why I come here. To get some rest." Baker winked.

Baker handed C4 the keys to the house and started down the sidewalk.

"Lock up carefully. I still want to know who took my coins."

Chapter 22

THE TWO MEN made it to Jamestown for their usual stop, with no sign of bad weather except for ominous clouds building from the southwest. But when they came back out of the convenience store, they walked into some light flurries.

"Looks like we're getting the snow we were promised," said Baker.

C4 looked straight ahead but replied.

"Yup. Let's see if we can beat it home."

They rolled back out onto I-94 and were on their way in a minute or two. The road was still good, so C4 was relieved. They should get back to Bismark and Jolene just fine. Jolene. Someone to come home to. That made the trip back to Bismarck entirely different, and in a really good way. Was Vicki right? Would he screw it up with Jolene somehow? Was his dad right? Was he not soccer dad material?

Lost in thought, he slowly became aware that Baker was talking.

"You know, I have a contact, let's say, who does some PI work. Maybe I'll call him and just ask him to poke around a bit. He's in Fargo, so it won't be far out of his way. He always has his ear to the ground. Whoever took that gold has almost certainly cashed it in. Maybe right there in Fargo. I'll call him when I get home. Send him a little retainer."

While C4 didn't want anybody poking around at all, he couldn't think of any good reason to head this off. Besides, he hadn't cashed in any coins in Fargo, so he should be safe. He offered his only plausible reply.

"That's worth a try. Keeps the police out of it and might just prove effective. Those guys often have better, meaning shadier, contacts than the cops."

Baker laughed.

"Exactly. I feel better having a plan. I'd sure like to know who took those coins."

C4 felt a need to reply.

"I don't blame you."

He just hoped none of the evidence pointed to him. It shouldn't, he had covered his tracks very well, hadn't he? An hour or so later, still early afternoon, they rolled into Bismarck.

Baker safely delivered, with no excess guff from Bella, C4 rolled into his garage spot and now, from habit, looked over at Jolene's parking spot. It was empty. She was still at school, as expected. He rode the elevator up to his floor and walked into an empty condo. Like so many times before over many years. So, the same. But not the same. There were signs of Jolene all over. Pillows on the sofa, a dish drainer. A note on the table. The place even smelled better. Like her.

He walked over and read the note.

"Getting off at 2:00. Coming straight home. Hope you are there waiting for me. Look in the fridge! J."

"J?" Was he just "C?" He'd need to ask about that. Or not. Let it happen, Cal, let it happen.

He checked his watch. 1:15. Perfect timing. Time for a scotch on the rocks? No, look in the fridge first. A nagging thought. Had he really headed off Baker's inquiry? He sure hoped so. Having Baker find out he'd taken those gold pieces would be ruinous to a lot of people. Him, his dad, Baker himself. Jolene. And it would prove Vicki right.

He opened the fridge. There was a sandwich with another note.

"Made this for you. Should go well with the Coors Light I bought. J"

C4 took the sandwich, grabbed a beer and sat down at the table. The sandwich was good, so was the beer. Was this a sign of pure love? Or an attempt to control his scotch habit, or was she just nannying him? And what was this 'J' thing? Was that some form of intimacy? Or was she just too lazy to spell out her whole first name?

Getting this close to someone was hard. You had to think a lot. The sandwich was good, though. And the beer tasted good. And when she got home, he knew, being with her was a lot better than not being with her.

And what about Baker? Would this theft situation just go away? C4 sure hoped this PI in Fargo would take the retainer, go through the motions and conclude it was just too hard to solve. Over time It would recede in Baker's memory banks and ultimately fade away as another of life's weird, random experiences. Maybe Baker would convince himself that he'd counted wrong at some point, or that his notes were wrong.

As he ate, he looked out the window. The flurries that had accompanied them to Bismarck had turned into a steady snowfall. He and Baker had made it just in time. It was good they had headed out when they did. Baker was really working himself into a frenzy over the missing gold.

He finished his lunch and went to the bedroom to unpack his bag. He put the three gold ounces in the drawer with his cash. Should he tell Jolene about the gold? She had shown him where she had stashed her cash. He almost missed the days when he drank instead of thinking.

Suddenly it went dark. Hands over his eyes. It had better be Jolene!

"Guess who?"

"It had better be my one true love!"

He turned around. He really had to get better at not letting people sneak up on him.

A long hug, a longer kiss. Yup. He had missed her. Straight to bed. This was way better than an empty condo.

"How was your trip?"

"Great. We caught tons of fish. I brought some home. How was your week?"

"Fish! I thought you were working! You went fishing instead of being with me?

"Slow down."

C4 had to think. This had to be fixable.

"The property we were checking on was in Minnesota. When we got done, the client wanted to go to his lake place and fish for a day before we came back. Remember I work for him."

"Ok. I guess."

C4 had to move this along.

"How was your week?"

"It was fine. School was good, the Riverview was pretty quiet last night. Should be quiet tonight too, with the weather. I did drop a few more documents off with your dad. I'm going to be a rich widow. Does that make me more or less attractive to you?"

"It would be hard to honestly say less attractive, but I can't think of how you could be any more attractive!"

Jolene laughed.

"You always know just the right thing to say."

"You always do the things that lead me to say the right thing."

Jolene rose up in bed and leaned over him enough to look over his head and pillow and see the clock. Their faces were inches apart. She was truly beautiful.

"Any chance you could skip work tonight? We could just stay in bed."

"I'd love to, but I already had a text asking me to come in a little early if I could. Some of my coworkers who live farther out in the country have already called in and we'll be a little short staffed. As you know, the hostess fills in all over the place. One time she even went home with a customer. You may know something about that."

"I seem to remember something about that. The customer was and is very, very happy with that extraordinary level of service."

Jolene smiled.

"Good answer. If the customers stay home too, though, I may get off early."

"That would be great. I'll be here. Unless there's something you need me to go out and get."

"No, I think I stocked up on everything while you were gone. And you brought home fish. I love fish. I can bake some on Sunday. I have a great recipe I got from my grandma. She's the one who taught me to cook. During all the busy times on the farm she showed up and took over the kitchen. I was her chief assistant. My mom worked in town, so was busy with that.

"By the way, I talked to my mom again this past week. I think things are getting back to a solid footing between us."

"That is great!"

C4 was serious. His thoughts went back to Jolene and her mom. At the lake. In bikinis.

Jolene rolled out of bed.

"I'm going to take a quick shower before I dress. You relax. You've had a full week."

If only she knew. It was actually an easy week, but a really full day. That could still blow up in his face. Their faces. For the first time in his life, there were other people depending on him. He wasn't sure he liked it. If only Baker had left the safe alone.

As Jolene showered, C4 thought back on the day. Why, oh why did Baker have to open the safe today? Even leaving it another month would be better, once the Baker Plan was signed. And now he had three ounces of gold as a gift from the man he'd stolen from. He had to believe that Baker didn't suspect him at all. Even if Cal's name showed up on some PI's suspect list, he hoped Baker would dismiss that as preposterous.

Jolene came out of the shower wearing only the towel on her head.

He returned to the present.

"Hey! I just remembered. I have something to show you," he said to Jolene.

"Seriously Cal, I need to get ready for work. Besides, I've fallen for that trick before. You need to up your game."

"Sorry to disappoint you. I really do have something else to show you."

"Now I'm curious."

C4 got out of bed quickly pulling on a pair of sweatpants. He walked to the dresser, opened the second drawer and pulled out the three gold coins.

"I got an unofficial bonus from my client. Three ounces of gold, worth about $7,500."

"Wow! Who pays like that? You work for the mafia?"

"No, he's just a wealthy guy who tries to keep some of his money out of the sight of the government."

"And he shared that with you?"

"He sure did. Said he was happy with all I did for him."

"Congratulations. Terry seems to think you don't work at all. I will have to set her straight."

"Please do."

Terry. She was almost getting to be a problem. First with the Regan McCord story, now telling Jolene he didn't work. Why did she keep sniping at him?

"How did that come up, even?"

"Oh, she didn't mean it as an attack. Before you explained to me what you did for a living, I just mentioned that you never seemed to go to work at, like a regular job. She just said, 'that fits the pattern' or something like that."

"Was that before we had our soul-cleansing Sunday night conversation?"

"I'm sure it was. She's been very supportive of our relationship since then."

"That's good to hear. She and Carson seem nice and since they're our only couples friends, and I know how close you are, I hope we can all get along."

"Yes, and they are also helpful. In fact, while you were in Minnesota, they met with me at my house and brought a friend of Carson's who would like to do the repairs. He is an engineer who has experience with homebuilding and renovations, and would like to do the job. He helped me with pictures and has started getting estimates on how much the repairs will cost."

"Great. I hope you can get that going soon."

"Me too. Funny thing, as we discussed that Sunday night with Terry and Carson, he is from Wahpeton as well. I graduated with his younger brother, Dwight, who we discussed on Sunday night. Kent was a few years ahead of me, so I never really knew him. He seems competent and he also seems like a nice guy, so he should be easy to work with."

"That is a good step. I'm glad you found someone to do the work."

"That gives me an idea. Should I invite Terry and Carson to Sunday dinner? Is there enough fish for all four of us?"

"There should be."

"Good. I can bake it on a bed of rice, with some veggies. It will be great. I'll use another of my grandma's recipes. My dad fished a lot in the winter, so I ended up learning a variety of fish recipes."

In a few more minutes, Jolene was drying her hair and C4 finished unpacking, most of the clothes going right into the washer. He went out to the living room and sat on the couch, contemplating a scotch on the rocks. He refused to rehash the events of the day anymore.

His phone rang. It was his dad, so he picked up.

"You're home?"

"Yup, been home a couple of hours."

"No problem with the weather?"

"No, we got up early and got going. Made it just fine."

"Have you had some quality time with Jolene?"

"We have had a chance to reunite, yes."

"I'll let that term speak for itself and have no further questions."

"That works for me."

"Is she going to work tonight?"

"Yeah, she is actually going in a bit early."

"Do you want to go out for dinner?"

"Sure. When and where?"

"The country club at five. We'll beat the rush and hopefully the worst of the weather."

"See you then."

"Who was that?"

Jolene came out of the bedroom fully dressed, hair wet and stringy. Like a Tahitian model, C4 thought. There was just no way for this girl to not look good. Except for the black and blue marks left by Trevor. That was bad. Glad that is behind her.

"My dad. He invited me to dinner at the country club. I accepted. I paid last time so maybe I'll get a free meal."

"Good. I'm glad you don't have to sit home alone. I will be back as soon as I can. I hope we're not too busy, though I do like the tips when we are."

"That classic tradeoff."

Jolene left for work a little before 4:00, and C4 took advantage of some alone time to clean up for his dinner date with his dad.

Chapter 23

C4 WATCHED AS HIS DAD APPROACHED the spot he held at the end of the bar. As he walked up, CT said,

"Good evening. How long have you been here?"

"About 10 minutes, still on my first drink."

"Did you get us a table?"

"I asked for a booth by the window so we can watch it snow and blow."

"Sounds good. It is February so we have some winter left, but at least January is behind us."

CT turned his attention to the bartender.

"Hi, Jerry. Scotch on the rocks."

"Yes, sir."

A moment later Jerry returned.

"Here's your drink, CT, and the hostess just indicated to me that your booth is ready."

"Thanks. Put this all on my tab."

"Will do."

Settled into their booth, watching the snow swirl by the window, CT started the conversation.

"How is Jolene?"

"You tell me. She and I are fine. Is she doing ok with you?"

"Yes, she is. I have almost all the documents I need, and it should go pretty fast. By legal standards, of course. There's the usual posting of notices and all that. But her work is almost done. New subject. I had a call from Baker this afternoon. Apparently, someone helped themselves to five ounces of gold he had in a safe at his Minnesota lake place."

C4 shook his head. The waitress approached the booth, startling C4, who was sitting with his back to the room, and who was also thinking hard about how to manage this conversation.

"Are you ready to order?"

"I am, are you?"

"I can be. Go ahead."

Once both men had ordered, C4 again silently chastised himself. He had to sit facing the door from now on no matter what. He was really tired of being surprised. He continued the conversation with his father.

"I am well aware. He was really shaken up over it. We had a lengthy conversation about what to do about it."

"And I hear you talked him out of calling the police."

"I did. I may be wrong, but he doesn't know when they were taken. It could be over a year ago, all he has are his handwritten records about the number of coins he had, and I just didn't think the police would do any more than take some pictures and file the case away. Seemed like a waste of time. Not even a valid insurance claim. Did I miss something in that analysis?"

"No, I don't think so. Then he said he thought he'd call a private investigator he knew just to poke around, and you agreed with that."

"I did. I think that holds more promise of finding some lead. The guy is at least getting paid to work on this one case. And if he finds nothing, Baker can feel that at least he tried."

"Did you also tell him he should get a security system installed?"

"I didn't think of that. Glad you did."

"He wasn't keen on the idea. Said it kind of flies in the face of that lake home being his sanctuary. Free from the cares of the outside world. He just seems kind of hurt by the whole episode."

"I'm sure he does. I feel bad for him."

Then a long pause and CT looked his son in the eye.

"You didn't take them, did you?"

"Of course not."

"Because you have to know you are on the list of people who had access and knew where the spare key to the house was. Maybe even knew about the safe."

"I know where he keeps the spare key, but so do a lot of people. He and I discussed that. I had no idea there was a safe there, in fact I'd never been in his bedroom before, where the safe was. He called me in to show me what he'd found. I found him kneeling on the closet floor. I thought he was having a heart attack or something until I saw the open safe and the gold stacked up."

"I feel bad for him. That sense of violation, he just seemed older, even over the phone."

"I saw the same thing in person."

"He also told me something I hadn't known before. He said his daughter calls him every Sunday morning at the same time, before he goes to church. Just a check in. He said he'd tell her about the gold so she was aware. I told him to ask her what she thinks about putting in a security system. He said he would."

C4 recalled that Baker had told him about the Sunday morning calls just a day or so ago. Apparently, Baker was opening up more to both C4 and CT.

"Hard to believe she won't recommend a security system. All he needs are a few cameras."

CT nodded, and added,

"I'd bet the neighbors who go away for the winter already have them."

C4 found that less than comforting, but kept from saying anything, or showing any response at all, he thought.

Both men had been careful to keep their discussion as quiet as they could, which was a good idea because just then the waitress returned with their meals.

Settled over their food, the rest of the evening revolved around the usual mundane, mid-winter, mid-Dakota topics from high school to college sports to the Wild and the Timberwolves and of course, Fighting Sioux hockey. While the UND nickname had been changed years ago, it just felt more comfortable to use the old name. When they'd covered all that thoroughly enough, the topic turned to the eternal hope in that part of the world - an early spring.

It wasn't all that late when CT signed the tab for the evening, and C4 was home by 8:00 p.m. Was he actually getting old? Or was it the wintry weather? The streets had been slick, and he was glad to be parked and inside his condo garage. He flicked on the gas fireplace and the TV, changed into sweats and relaxed on the couch. He fought off the urge to pour himself a scotch, knowing he'd just keep on until Jolene came home. He'd told her he was done with that and didn't want to let her down. He wanted nothing to come between them.

He was fully aware he'd lied to his dad about the gold, but he really had no choice. He couldn't admit that he took it and just had to trust that the PI in Fargo was routinely incompetent. If that all played out, everything would be ok. Or even great.

The door opened, and Jolene stepped in, taking off her coat and kicking off her boots.

"You're home early!"

"I am! After 8:00, people just stopped coming in and even the bar emptied out. The weather is just bad enough to make people want to be home."

She hesitated and looked around her, then continued.

"I can see a nice warm fireplace, a TV, someone special and what am I missing? Oh, yeah, maybe a glass of wine. All I'm missing is the wine. Can you help me with that?"

"Glad to."

"Great. While you do that, I'll change into sweats, too. You look cozy."

C4 walked over to the counter and poured two glasses of wine, bringing them back and placing them on coasters.

A moment later Jolene dropped down onto the couch.

"How was dinner with your dad?"

"Nice. Good visit, nothing extraordinary."

"That's it?"

"He asked how you are doing, as usual. Said you have provided him with almost all of the documents you owe him. We talked about my business trip. He has the same client, so we collaborate a bit on that work."

"Oh, that's nice. Let's talk a little about tomorrow. Same separate missions as usual? I'll get some groceries and you can hit the liquor store. Rose' goes great with fish!"

"That sounds good. No need to rush, so we can even sleep in a bit."

"I agree. Let's see if there's a decent movie somewhere on the TV. We can watch a movie and stay up late, maybe even to midnight!"

C4 nodded and handed the remote to Jolene, thinking about how many times up until a few weeks ago that his evenings began at midnight.

C4 awoke and looked at the clock. 9:00 and the sun was lighting up the room. They had slept in, and he looked over at Jolene. She was still there, sound asleep. Every morning that she was still beside him was like waking up from a dream to find himself living a better dream. He slipped out of bed and helped himself to the first shower. All cleaned up, and dressed in sweats, he headed to the kitchen and started the coffee. He opened the drapes and looked out the window. The snow had stopped, the sun was shining, and the snow was so white it was hard to look at. He could see and hear snowplows working all across the city. By the time he and Jolene started their errands the streets should be in good condition. Another reason not to rush out the door.

An hour later Jolene came out of the bedroom, dressed in sweats.

"Aren't we cute? We should go out and buy matching sweats!"

She gave him a quick kiss. C4 couldn't think of a worse idea, so said, with as little sarcasm as possible,

"Too bad we can't do that."

"You think that's silly. I can tell, and you're right."

She poured herself a coffee, and the two of them both sat at the table. Abruptly, she stood, walked over and opened the fridge. Closing it again, she said,

"Those are nice fillets. I can bake them on rice tomorrow for dinner with Terry and Carson. That's ok, isn't it?"

"Of course. Just let me know what time, and what I need to do."

Jolene looked over at C4 and said,

"I don't deserve you."

C4 just smiled. He had no response that he wanted Jolene to hear. The rest of the day turned into as normal a day as they were allowed by society. By 4:00 p.m. they had shopped, snacked, watched some TV, fooled around, and napped. C4 couldn't think of a better way to spend a Saturday, except that at 4:30, Jolene got dressed and left for work, leaving him with an evening to kill, and killing a bottle of scotch, or finding a poker game or an all-night party was no longer on his radar. He had to figure out how to live this new lifestyle. For right now, his new addiction was going to have to be college basketball. He went through the programming guide on his TV, picked out a few games, made a few notes, called an old friend and made some small bets. Everybody, even people living with a saint needed some kind of vice, right?

The door to the condo opened and closed, waking C4 from a pretty deep sleep. The TV was on mute and tuned in to Sports Center.

"I was trying to be quiet. You were sound asleep."

"Yes, I was. How was work?"

"Super busy. Everyone wanted to get out and socialize. Had a blockbuster night. They moved a new girl to the hostess stand and had me help bartend and deliver drinks. I'm rich!"

She dumped out a large pile of cash onto the coffee table. C4 looked it over.

"How much is it?"

"I don't know, I haven't even counted it yet. I'm going to go change. Be right back."

C4 put the money in stacks, and while it was quite a volume, it was almost all ones and fives, with two twenties and a fifty. All in all, just over $200.

Jolene came back wearing sweat pants and a t-shirt.

"How much is it?"

"$207. What in the world did you have to do to get a fifty as a tip?"

"Nothing evil. It was a table of ten, five couples, and they kept me busy ordering and delivering drinks. When they left, one of the guys just slipped me a fifty. He also patted me on the butt and told me I'd done a great job."

C4 thought of all the times he'd done something like that and had thought nothing of it. Now, with Jolene as the recipient, it bothered him. He said nothing. Jolene, as usual, read his mind.

"Don't worry about it. It's kind of offensive, but no harm done and it comes with the job. Especially with a butt like mine. And I know you agree."

She winked at him.

"What did you do tonight to while away the lonely hours without me? Besides sleep, of course."

She looked at the other end of the coffee table from her cash pile to see the notes he had taken earlier.

"What are the notes, if you don't mind, of course."

C4 knew he was caught, and she was so open and honest with him he knew he had to come clean.

"Since I quit pouring scotch into myself by the bottle, I needed a new vice, so I picked out a few college basketball games and made some small bets."

Jolene stared at him for way too long before she said,

"How did you do?"

"I had won2 and lost 1 when I fell asleep. Let's see if the TV will tell us."

They both looked at the TV and within a minute C4 said,

"That's my last game, I won that too, so I won three and lost one."

"Meaning???"C4 had hoped to avoid this particular question, but knew he was trapped.

"Not quite as well as you. I'm up two hundred on the night."

Jolene did not have to think long before she said,

"So, you bet $100 on each game?"

"Yes. Max I could have lost is four hundred, but that's unlikely. I could also win four hundred which is just as unlikely, unfortunately."

"Do you do this often?"

"Not really. I just did it tonight out of loneliness. My other option was to head to the Riverview and flirt with the hostess turned bartender, but I thought this was the lesser of those two evils."

"You probably made the right choice. She was really busy tonight. But she's available now. Let's turn in. By the way, as long as it's your money you're gambling with, you can do what you want. But stay out of my underwear drawer and you know what I mean."

Sunday came and went, and C4 was awestruck by how normal it seemed. He and Jolene slept in, and with no hangovers to nurse, they enjoyed their scrambled eggs and salads. About 4:00, Terry and Carson came over and the visit was, from what C4 could tell, quite normal. There was no animosity from Terry, Jolene's fish recipe was delicious and went well with the Rose', just as Jolene had predicted. The discussion about C4 catching the fish was kept to just a perk of a business trip to Minnesota. Obviously, no mention of the gold payment to C4.

Terry and Carson left about 8:00. The farewell was also new ground for C4.

"Carson, we should go. I need to get you into bed while you're still fresh and I'm still feeling my Rose's."

Turning to Jolene she stage-whispered,

"We're trying to have a baby. It's time!"

Carson shook his head and looked at C4.

"No one needs to know that, Terry, let's just go home and mind our own business, and Cal and Jolene can mind theirs."

Terry, however, was not done.

"You two should have a baby. It would be the cutest baby in Bismarck!"

Carson took Terry by the arm.

"Now we're leaving. Please strike that last comment. Thanks for a great dinner and a wonderful evening."

Jolene helped him.

"Thanks to the two of you. Glad you enjoyed the meal and the company. We will take your baby suggestion under advisement."

With that remark she opened the door and ushered their guests out, walking them to the elevator. C4 overheard her final remarks.

"Thanks again for coming over. Take care of her Carson."

She walked back into the condo and closed the door.

"That sure got interesting. Oh, and by the way, no babies for us. No matter how cute they might be. I am nowhere near ready for that."

C4 nodded.

"Me either."

Chapter 24

MONDAY MORNING, C4 awoke to the sound of the shower. He let himself wake up a bit, and a few minutes after the shower ended, Jolene came into the bedroom wearing, as usual, only the towel on her hair. This was not hard to get used to.

She looked at him and smiled.

"You are so easily entertained. I may never get you settled down."

C4 just smiled back.

"You are really easy to look at."

With her gaze now concentrated on the top drawer she replied.

"I think I look better without bruises, don't you agree?"

"Absolutely. I'm sorry you had to go through that. Do you think you should talk to a therapist?"

C4 was not sure where that had come from, but I sounded like something he should say, and it still sounded ok after he said it, so he left it there.

"Maybe. Right now, you're my therapy. Being respected and treated like an adult woman is turning out to be very good for me."

"Glad to be of service. I'm available any time."

"You've made that quite clear, and I take it as the highest form of appreciation. But now I have to go to work."

He lay in bed while she finished getting ready. She came out of the bathroom fully dressed, with her hair dried and make up applied.

"Have a great day. Stay out of trouble."

With that, and a kiss on his forehead, she was gone.

He stayed in bed a little longer and had almost dozed off when his phone rang. He looked at the screen and it was his dad.

"Good morning. What's up?"

"Just had a call from Baker."

"And…?"

"He said he talked to Kelly on Sunday morning as usual and she is coming to Bismarck as soon as she can get on a flight. She wants to check on him and see if she can help him with the stolen gold issue or anything else she feels he may need a hand with."

"Is that good or bad?"

"Good, since I didn't steal the gold and maybe we can meet and get her on board with the transition of the trust. The risk is that she will want to take it on herself. We need to use all of our charm to make sure Baker keeps it pointed toward me."

"You have no shortage of charm, so that should be easy."

"Thanks. I'll let you know if I think it will help to involve you. Baker really seems to trust you. Or he may include you himself. I think she lands sometime this afternoon, so once she's here it's game on. Are you available if needed?"

"Of course. The old ball-and-chain is off at work every day so I'm free to do whatever you and the Bakers need."

"I'd be careful with the 'old ball-and-chain' routine. If Jolene dumps you, the line to replace you would stretch from your condo to the capitol."

"You are right, as always. I will never let a smart-ass remark like that slip out again."

"I hope you stick to that. Besides, I'd be in that line. Apparently, she's not averse to older men."

"You just never let me get away without some kind of a shot. I'm a little older. You're a lot older. She certainly must have some limits. Besides, last night we discussed babies."

Then C4 hung up. That would keep his dad thinking for a while. While the statement was true, there was no need to tell him that the conclusion was no babies for now.

C4 rolled out of bed, showered, shaved, and put on sweats. He had the day in front of him. Before Jolene he'd still be sleeping, get up around noon, make his grocery and liquor store run, fix something to eat and then, somewhere around 3:00 p.m., start nursing a bottle of scotch. Then a nap, dinner, clean up, and go out to find some entertainment. Now he slept all night and was up all day. What do people do all day? Did they all go to work like Jolene? He'd have to adapt if he wanted to keep her, and he did.

Maybe he'd actually start working out at his health club. That would shock the people of Bismarck. What's next, join a church? That pastor who came to help Jolene when Trevor died was quite nice and very good to Jolene. Could C4 completely reverse his lifestyle and reputation? Not just a tune up or a minor adjustment. He'd have to become the exact opposite of his old persona. He knew he'd changed but was it enough? Could he complete the transition?

He was halfway through his tuna salad sandwich, and his phone rang again. (When did Jolene find the time to do all this domestic stuff? Did she slip out of bed when he was sleeping and make sandwiches and clean the condo?)

He answered the call. It was his dad again.

"Hello?"

"Just me again. Bella called. Kelly lands at 5:00 and Baker wants me to pick her up and take her to his house. Just thought you should know."

"Got it. I'll be around."

Finishing his lunch, C4 looked outside. It was still winter and looked cold. He washed up his lunch dishes, started a load of laundry, and got out the vacuum cleaner. He did all the carpets and sat down exhausted. This was hard work. If Jolene was doing this regularly, God bless her.

He advanced the laundry and sat down. He wondered if the liquor store would call to see if he was ok. His new lifestyle was not helping their profits. He turned on the television and found nothing of any real interest. He ended up on ESPN. They were covering college basketball. The new rankings were out. He found that interesting enough to stay engaged. He knew he was up two hundred on his sports betting account, and as he absorbed all the intel on each of the top teams, he wondered if he could make enough money betting on basketball and maybe other sports to make some real money. Maybe betting $500 or $1,000 on each game instead of $100?

He went to his desk drawer and found a note pad and pen that he hadn't used in years. He started listing teams and checking schedules. Were there any games that would give him an edge? He spent the next couple of hours looking at rankings and schedules and was still wrapped up in his analysis when Jolene came in the door.

"Hi, honey! What are you doing?"

"Nothing much. Just looking at a couple more college basketball games to bet."

He made no mention of his thoughts on increasing his bets. He changed the subject to her.

"How was your day?"

"It was fine. A boy threw up on Terry. Wonder if she still wants to have a baby?"

"That might cause some reflection on the topic. Is the kid ok?"

"We sent him home, obviously, but as soon as he threw up, he seemed much better."

"So that was the highlight of the day?"

"No, but it was the most exciting. A little girl told me her mom moved away over the weekend and wanted to know if I could be her special friend."

"And you told her?"

"I said of course I would. At that age it's hard to know how serious these things are, so I will just let it play out. Anything exciting on your end? Besides college basketball?"

"No, wait, yes. I should let you know that my client's daughter is in town from Florida to check on her dad and I may need to help my dad shepherd her and her dad around the next few days."

"How old is this daughter? Is she cute?"

C4 stared at Jolene. Was this real jealousy or was she just teasing him? C4 decided to play it straight and just answer the questions.

"I've never seen her, and I think she's in her early 60's."

"Good. I feel better now. Maybe she's at more risk of your father's charms."

"He'd better work fast. She is flying in from Florida, so I doubt she'll spend any more time in Bismarck in February than she has to."

"I'm going to go change. Be right back. Can we just order a pizza for dinner?"

"Absolutely. I'll call when you're ready."

C4 went back to his basketball analysis. He quickly decided he'd put enough thought and energy into it for now, so organized his notes and put them back on his desk.

Jolene came back dressed in sweats and sat down next to him on the couch. She snuggled up against him and put her head on his shoulder.

"This is nice. I always thought this is what married life would be like. Not every hour of the day, of course, but when time allowed. Not sex, not working, not arguing, not making plans, just being together. Was that foolish, Cal?"

C4 had to think. How would he know? He'd never given it any thought whatsoever, but figured sharing that perspective with her was not what she needed to hear. Or wanted to hear. He thought back to his parents. When he was little, and he and his sisters weren't fighting, he did remember occasionally walking into a room, usually the den, and seeing his parents just sitting together, maybe watching some TV. So, it was normal, before his dad pulled the plug on it.

"I don't think it's foolish at all. Some down time with no agenda, just relaxing. I'd say that's not only good, but necessary."

He hoped what he'd said was ok. Again, this was pretty unfamiliar territory.

"Thank you."

And that was all she said. He had no idea what to do or say next, so they just sat there, in silence. He found that it was oddly ok. Just nice to sit for a while. No need to think or drink or plan or scheme. Just sit.

C4 awoke with a start. Jolene was gone. Then he heard the toilet flush. She came back out and sat down next to him again.

"Our theory of relaxing together met two obstacles. You fell asleep and I had to go to the bathroom. It's a cold, cruel world we live in, Cal."

"We could sit some more."

"Only after you call for a pizza."

"Consider it done."

He had just rung off the pizza call when his phone rang. It was his dad.

"Hi. Just wanted to let you know that I just picked Kelly up at the airport and she had a message waiting on her cell phone when she landed. Her dad took a fall down the stairs at home and is at the hospital. We're going there now. I'll keep you posted."

C4 didn't know how to keep from turning white, but he was trying now. If Baker died, the Baker Plan was dead too. And so was his future including any future with Jolene. Even if he could make enough money betting basketball, for her he needed a job.

"Who was that?"

"My dad. He picked up our client's daughter, from the airport, but she had a message when she turned her cell phone back on after the flight telling her that her dad had fallen down the stairs at his house and was in the hospital. He'll keep me posted."

"Oh, no. I hope he's ok."

"So do I, honey, so do I."

And he meant it.

Chapter 25

C4 WAS JUST FINISHING his second slice of pizza when his phone rang. He looked and it was his dad. He took a swig of the lite beer Jolene had placed prominently in his diet and answered.

"Well?"

"He's ok. Just a slip and fall, a bump on his head and a bruise on his hip. Also, he hurt his shoulder a bit. Because of his age, they're keeping him overnight. We dropped Kelly's things at his house, and Bella was going to put them in Kelly's room. Kelly and I are headed out for dinner. Care to join us?"

"Thanks, but Jolene and I ordered a pizza and are just finishing up. You two kids have a great time. Country club?"

"Of course. We'll talk tomorrow, ok?"

"Sounds good. Enjoy your dinner."

C4 hung up. Jolene paused from her dinner, and asked.

"Everything ok?"

She must have seen the concern in his eyes.

"Absolutely. His client is ok. They're just keeping him overnight. Dad is taking Kelly, the daughter, out to dinner at the country club."

Jolene looked thoughtful, way too thoughtful. The longer she looked thoughtful, the more concerned he became. Finally she spoke, which was good because he had nothing to offer.

"Should we get dressed up and surprise them by joining them for a drink?"

C4 was overwhelmed with thoughts. Was she really ready to be seen with him in public? She was his dad's client, and he clearly knew his dad. But the two of them arriving together? And what did she mean by dressed up? Jacket-and-tie-and-little-black-dress dressed up? Did he really want the predator guys who hung out at the country club to see her? Sure, it was a Monday in the winter so likely pretty empty, but the word would get out. There was no need to flash her beauty in front of the Bismarck social world quite yet. They knew her as the hostess at the Riverview, and she was getting hit on all the time at that. If she walked into the country club as a customer, she would be fair game, and the line from his condo to the capitol would start immediately.

"Cal, you are way too deep in thought."

"Thank you, but you are right. I had to think really hard. I am sorry but I just don't think we should do that. Not yet. It's too soon, and no one knows we're together."

She looked pensive, then she smiled.

"You're right. Or maybe you are just trying to keep me hidden away in your castle tower as long as you can."

By the time she finished her last words she was laughing.

"I have to admit, it's a bit of both. Why would I share you? The world is not ready for your beauty. At least not my dad's world. Those guys are less attached to their wives than you might imagine. At least some of them."

"I respect your opinion, and I appreciate both your flattery and your concern. But don't forget, I'm with you and I will be as long as we both want that."

"I know, and I want you to continue to want that."

"Me too. Let's clean up the kitchen. Then we can go back to the couch, and I'll see if I can keep you awake until bed time."

The next morning, Jolene at work, C4 decided to catch up with his dad, so called his office. Taylor answered,

"Good morning, Tappen Law office. How can I help you?"

"Hi, Taylor, it's C4. Is my dad in?"

"No, he isn't. Can I take a message?"

"No, thanks, I'll try his cell."

C4 dialed CT's cell and after a ring or two his dad answered.

"Hello?"

His dad's voice sounded a bit groggy. C4 checked the nearest clock. 8:45. Not exactly the crack of dawn.

"You're not in the office yet this morning?"

"Not yet. It was a busy evening."

"What the heck did you do?"

"It got to be a late night. Great visit with Kelly."

C4 heard a woman's voice in the background asking something about coffee.

"Who is that?"

"It's Kelly. We had a bit of a sleepover."

C4 was dumbfounded. Had he died and gone to a parallel universe? Him with Jolene, his dad with Kelly. Sunday dinners? Everybody had an envelope with cash? Relaxing on a couch with someone you love? The list went on forever, but his thoughts were interrupted by his dad's voice.

"We really hit it off. And at our age it's not just jumping in bed like you and you-know-who, it's actually enjoying sleeping with someone. And I do mean sleeping. Not that there wasn't some other stuff as well."

"Ok Dad, stop. You are embarrassing me and probably Kelly. Try to be a bit of a gentleman."

"You're right. Just bragging, I guess. Anyway, we need to get up and out. I'll drop Kelly at her dad's's house and then head to the office. She'll get ready and go see her dad in the hospital, and hopefully spring him from the clutches of the doctors. The three of us will have lunch together, depending on his freedom."

"Sounds like a plan. Include me if you wish. I'm open. But not if you're going to sit in a booth somewhere and neck."

"We'll behave, whether you're with us or not. I'll give you a call if I need you."

And CT hung up. C4 really wasn't sure if he liked this new world of relationships and friendships and emotions and all the effort of keeping it all straight and behaving and worrying about how other people felt. But his dad was wrong. He did love just being in bed with Jolene. To wake up and see her beside him or even to hear her in the shower.

That was good. It wasn't just sex. It was more. A lot more. He thought back a few weeks. He had even enjoyed waking up next to Vicki in Dickinson. He didn't understand at that time what that was, but there was some reassurance in having someone in bed next to you.

Once again, his phone was ringing. It was an unfamiliar number, but a North Dakota area code. He picked up.

"Hello?"

"Hello, is this Calvin Tappen?"

C4 figured that was pretty public information, so he replied,

"It is, and who is this?"

"Adam Lankin. I was retained by Mr. Kendall Baker to investigate the theft of five ounces of gold from his home in Minnesota."

C4 swallowed hard. He walked to the refrigerator and grabbed a bottle of water. God bless Jolene, she thought of everything.

"Yes, I was with him when he discovered the pieces were missing."

"That's what I understand. I'm hoping you can help me. I'm just getting started, so I'm trying to begin my investigation close to Mr. Baker and work my way out. Common practice. It could be common thieves, but there was, according to my client, a lot of other gold and quite a sum of cash in the safe, which was not taken. I'm sure I don't have to tel you that's odd and also there's no sign of forced entry. I am in his lake home now, and see no disruption whatsoever. The other mystery is how they found the combination, which, when Mr. Baker got it out of its hiding place to use, seemed similarly undisturbed."

C4 decided to wait for an actual question rather than jump in uninvited. He didn't have to wait long.

"Mr. Baker gave me your name and number since he thinks of you as a trusted friend who has been to the home many times and he wanted your perspective. I want to know more bluntly, if you saw anything out of the ordinary, inside or outside the home on your last visit. Tire tracks, foot tracks, anything out of place at all."

C4 had to take a drink of water after the word 'bluntly', but relaxed a bit with the direction it took from there. It was time to speak.

"No, Adam, I didn't. I wish I could help. I know Mr. Baker feels bad about it, and I wish I could give you something to work with. All I can think of is that a lot of people know where the spare key is. You need to have one for the plumbers, and the house cleaner, and any other service people who you may need to have come in to do some work while you're gone. I know that's not all that helpful, but it is a fact."

After a brief pause, Lankin continued.

"Yeah, that is a problem with the investigation. Thanks for your time, Calvin. If you think of anything else, the number I called you on is my cell, so you can reach me anytime. I work out of Fargo, but due to my line of work, I'm on the road a lot. I may see if I can find a fingerprint or something here, but that's unlikely since you and Mr. Baker were here for a few days before the discovery. I'd likely find just find fingerprints for the two of you. I'll keep following whatever leads I can. Something will pop up. It always does. Thanks again for your time."

The call ended, C4 realized he was standing in the kitchen. He recounted the entire conversation and told himself he'd revealed nothing. But had he spoken too little? Should he have sounded more concerned, tried to be more helpful, tossed out some thought or theory? The biggest problem was that this Adam guy seemed pretty determined to solve this crime. He didn't sound like he was just going through the motions. What would he do next? Talk to neighbors? Did some of them have cameras? Would they show his SUV that day? Would he check with gold dealers, starting in Fargo and maybe Minneapolis? Was there one in St Cloud? Would he check Grand Forks or Sioux Falls? His brain was racing. He needed a scotch.

No, no daytime drinking. If he was going to lose Jolene it wasn't going to be due to that. Even this PI had to know that there was a chance that whoever took the gold hadn't even cashed it in or had cashed it in a long time ago. Maybe he should have just cashed in a couple. As far away as Rapid City, or gone on down to Minneapolis where he could have hit a few different places. He realized he was second guessing every step of his crime except the only important one. What if he hadn't taken the gold at all? If only he'd known Baker was going to hand him the three gold pieces on that last visit…

His phone rang. He hardly dared look at it. But he did. It was his dad.

"Hey dad. What's up?"

"Baker won't get out of the hospital until this afternoon, and Kelly needs to spend some time with him, so lunch is off, but Kelly and I are having a super casual Valentine's dinner at the country club. I was just able to get us in for a late seating. Please join us."

C4's brain was once again redirected and fully engaged. It was Valentine's Day? That was never a good night when he was a predator, so he never paid any attention to it. All the women had dates, or if they didn't, they certainly didn't go out alone. Now he had a girl. This again was all new. Was Jolene expecting a date? Flowers? Candy? Was he close to getting in trouble by forgetting this? Every place had to be full, and he and Jolene still had to be discreet anyway. Was he already screwed?

"Are you there?"

"Not sure. Let me check with Jolene. I'll get back to you."

"Ok."

C4 sat down. In two phone calls over less than 15 minutes he had gone from gold coin anxiety to love life anxiety without a break in between. He had to make some kind of plan. At least some flowers. Maybe he just had to throw himself on Jolene's mercy. Maybe wrap himself in red ribbon like the old cartoons.

He kept thinking while he put on some decent clothes. The least he could do was get some flowers and some wine and some candy. And a card. That was a thing, wasn't it? Between the grocery store and the liquor store he could do that. It was a nice enough winter day so he just pulled on a hoodie and was out the door in just a few minutes.

The mission was less stressful than the thoughts leading up to it, and getting out of his condo and moving around kept him from full on stressing. At least now he could prove he had remembered it was Valentine's Day.

Back in his condo he tried to get himself focused on something constructive and clear his head for a while. He reheated some coffee and sat down on the couch and turned the TV on to SportsCenter. He could immerse himself in college basketball, at least for now.

That lasted about 10 minutes, then his thoughts turned to dinner. Should he try to take her out? If so, where could they go? No place in Bismarck. Between the people she knew and the people he knew they'd see someone one of them knew. If that happened what was their story? His dad was her lawyer, did he ask me to take her out, just as a favor? To help her heal? To not have to be home alone on Valentine's Day so soon after losing her husband? That actually could be painful, C4 thought. But was he ready to have her meet Kelly? That would force him to reveal that his alleged client was Kendall Baker, who was famously wealthy as Bismarck wealthy went. If it was just him and his dad, that would be easy to pass off. But we had decided not to do that just a day or so ago. Why is it ok now? Is Valentine's Day that powerful?

Once again, he had to tell himself no. They couldn't do it. The damage to her reputation might be too great for her to deal with. They had to stay in. If so, then what for dinner? Leftover pizza? Hardly. Then it came to him. He had to trust her. She knew their situation. He had the wine, and some flowers, and the heart-shaped box of candy and a nice card signed 'Love, Cal'. That would have to do. If she wanted more, they had to figure it out together. He had never felt so vulnerable. He was dependent on Jolene to make this holiday ok in her eyes.

He called his dad back to decline the dinner invitation. CT replied,

"Sorry you can't join us, but I understand. Hope you and Jolene find some good way to celebrate."

"Me too. Have a nice time."

He spent the rest of the day agonizing over his decision. Would this be enough? Should he whisk her off to Minot or somewhere else where there was a small chance of seeing anyone who knew them? That was a lot to do without prior planning and her input.

The door opened and Jolene walked in. He stood. He couldn't help it.

"Happy Valentine's Day!"

The words came out of his mouth. She looked at him and then her eyes turned to the kitchen table with the flowers, and the wine, and the candy, and the card propped up against the wine. She covered her face and started to cry. Not just a little, but hard. He quickly walked over and hugged her. Walking her slowly to the couch, they sat down. She continued to cry. He had no idea what to do. Luckily there were some tissues on the coffee table. It took several minutes to control her sobs.

C4 had no idea what to do or what might happen next, so he just sat there with her. After another several minutes she sat up a bit and said,

"Trevor never bought me flowers, ever."

And then she started crying again. If this was Valentine's Day, C4 wasn't a fan. She cried for a long time. At least it seemed like a long time to C4. Again, a new experience and not a good one. Not at all. And certainly not what he expected. He thought she may chide him a little for lack of a better plan and a fancy dinner, but this crying was not anywhere on his list of possible outcomes.

She put her head on his shoulder and after awhile he could feel her tears soaking through his hoodie. He started to be glad they didn't have a dinner reservation. At least not soon. Finally, the sobs subsided. She continued to just sit there. Ignoring the tissues, she wiped her eyes on the shoulder of his hoodie and sat up. She stared straight ahead, able to see the kitchen table. She stared a long time. Or maybe he'd just become a bad judge of the passage of time.

"I'm so sorry. I guess I really needed that. Terry kept telling me I hadn't really cried yet and I thought I had. Or thought that I didn't need to because, well, you know. Now I have. Thank you for putting up with that. Thank you for being here with me. Thank you for being the first man to ever buy me flowers."

C4 still didn't have any idea what to say. It didn't matter.

Jolene laughed. This was hard to keep up with.

"What does a girl have to do to get a glass of wine around here?"

C4 was ecstatic to have a task. Something useful to do. Something, anything to help her. He stood up as quickly as he could without having her fall over on the couch. He walked to the table, opened the wine and poured two glasses, bringing them back to the coffee table.

Jolene laughed again. C4 couldn't remember being this confused, ever. He had made it a point to never be this confused.

"Your hoodie is all wet and has quite a bit of mascara on it. Make sure you don't wear it out anywhere."

"I wasn't planning to go anywhere, unless you want to, of course."

"No, let's just stay in. I'll change and you can take off your hoodie. Put it right in the washer. Come on. Let's go get ready for our Valentine's Day dinner."

"Which is?"

"Lasagna. In the fridge. I kind of hid it. I'll put it in the oven after we finish our wine. It takes an hour to bake and we'll need that time to celebrate the holiday in the bedroom. First some wine and some time to relax."

Finally, something he understood - alcohol and sex.

Chapter 26

C4 WOKE EARLY ON THE 15TH, on the one hand he was glad that the emotions of Valentine's Day were behind him. On the other hand, best Valentine's Day ever. He looked over. Jolene was still sleeping. He turned to his side and watched her. She was beautiful but she was a complicated animal. Crying, laughing, ok to be with him. At least so far. Hard to figure out.

He got up and used the bathroom then headed out and started the coffee. He wondered about his dad and Kelly. CT had better not have burned that bridge, or poisoned that well, whatever expression one preferred. He looked at the kitchen clock. 6:15 am. Too early to call his dad or anyone. He listened to the coffee finish up, poured himself a cup and sat down on the couch, turning the TV on, leaving it muted. It came on to ESPN, and he watched it half interested, paying some attention to last night's college basketball scores. The admittance buzzer rang. Who the hell could that be?

He pushed the button.

"Good morning, Cal. It's your old man. Can I come up? I have something to show you."

"Sure, come on up."

C4 hit the buzzer. Should he get Jolene up? No let her sleep. He went over and silently closed the bedroom door.

There was a knock on the door and before C4 could walk over, it opened and his dad walked in with a carbon copy of the woman he'd seen in the picture in Baker's bedroom. C4, as he found himself frequently experiencing these days, had no idea what to say.

"Cal, this is Kelly. Kelly, this is my son Calvin Steele Tappen the fourth."

C4 knew he had to say something.

"Nice to meet you, Kelly. Your dad is a great guy. Hope he's doing well."

CT ignored that and spoke.

"Guess what Kelly and I did last night."

"Had dinner?"

"Yes, and then we drove to South Dakota and got married!"

C4 was beyond stunned.

"What?"

"Look at the ring!"

He looked. Sure enough, there was a ring. A really nice one.

"How did you do this? Without even telling me?"

"We didn't want to bother you on such a romantic holiday. We were walking around the mall before our dinner reservation and as we walked by a jewelry store, the idea just hit both of us. We really had a connection and, we could together run the Baker business and if we were married, we didn't need all those legal documents."

C4 was, still, too overwhelmed to speak. Where did this leave him? His dad was now rich, but was there room for him at the table?

For the first time Kelly spoke.

"My dad speaks so highly of you, Calvin. Even before this latest turn of events, he wanted to make sure you had a job in the firm, so don't worry, you may need to drive around and check on some farms and ranches, but you're in the club too!"

Her voice was like velvet. Like a high-class lounge singer. At least that was C4's best frame of reference. And she was truly beautiful, especially for someone her age. As if on cue, Jolene came out of the bedroom, wearing a t-shirt and sweatpants. Rubbing her eyes. CT nodded at Jolene and spoke.

"And now we are in the company of the two most beautiful women in the world. Kelly, this is Jolene. Jolene, this is Kelly, my new wife."

Jolene looked at C4 who could only look back. Jolene found her voice.

"Congratulations! This is quite sudden. I'm going to go and put on a sweatshirt."

Jolene disappeared into the bedroom.

Kelly turned to C4.

"She is gorgeous. You lucky guy."

"I am a lucky guy. And she's the whole package, not just beautiful."

CT chimed in.

"He's right. I've been doing some legal work for her, and she is smart and strong and courageous."

"Legal work? For her?"

"Yes, I didn't mention it before. Her husband died tragically a while back, and she has put her head on Cal's shoulder since then. He has been very good for her, and she has been even better for him."

"That must be so difficult for her. I'm so sorry."

"It's been tough, but as dad said, she's holding up remarkably well."

C4 was not going to mention Jolene's complete meltdown of the prior afternoon. When her head was on his shoulder, for a long time. Not ever.

Jolene returned from the bedroom, apparently over the shock of the news, and spoke.

"I do need to go to work in an hour, but I want to hear everything. I see Cal made coffee. May I serve? Have a seat at the table, please."

Jolene poured coffee into the cups C4 brought over from the cupboard, and they all sat down.

Kelly took control of the conversation and repeated and expanded on the quick story that CT had blurted out when they came in the door.

CT added,

"And in South Dakota, we had to wait in line for a blood test and then wait in line for the results and then wait in line again to get married. Apparently, Valentine's Day is more romantic than I thought."

Kelly chimed in,

"And we just got back to town a couple of hours ago. Had breakfast at Archie's. Told everyone there about us!"

"Have you told your dad yet?" asked C4.

"Not yet. But he'll be pleased. He thinks so much of both of you. I just wasn't prepared to be quite so smitten. Your dad simply swept me off my feet!"

Jolene laughed.

"Yes, these Tappen men are quite good at that!"

She winked at C4, then went on.

"I'm so happy for you. Where will you live?"

CT answered:

"Good question. We've discussed that. With us running the Baker family business I'm thinking here part of the time, and in Minnesota, at the lake place, but winters will definitely be in Florida. I'm not going to turn that down."

C4 once again was overwhelmed. Just when he thought he'd gotten up to speed on this new life of his, something more changed. This time it was his dad, but it still affected him and maybe Jolene. Maybe she'd really love him now, given his dad's good fortune and his steady work. He'd have to explain to her that he was already doing a lot of what Kelly talked about, just on an ad hoc basis, rather than as an employee.

"Cal, you in there?"

His dad was looking over at him, smiling and then moving on to his next question.

"It's a lot to take in, isn't it?"

"It certainly is. I am shocked at the speed of events."

Jolene laughed and looked directly at C4.

"When I moved in here, you showed no signs of being shocked by the speed of events. You seemed quite happy about it."

The phrase 'moved in' was not lost on C4. He replied as casually as he could.

"I just didn't show my cards. I was actually quite shocked at the time. But you really needed a place to stay. I was glad to help you out."

Jolene replied.

"Kelly probably doesn't need to know any more about that."

She turned directly to CT.

"Attorney client privilege and all that, right?"

"Of course."

CT was careful to cut off any further discussion of Jolene's situation regarding when and how she and C4 met or why or how they came to be living together. It may come out over time, but only if Jolene wished. He spoke casually,

"Well, you two, Kelly and I need to be moving along, we have a lot to do, and we need to go break the news to her dad. I didn't formally ask for her hand and he's pretty old school. Wish me well!"

Kelly laughed.

"He'll be fine. He's been nagging me to get remarried for decades. If he objects to our marriage, I'll mention that."

CT and Kelly stood to leave. As they all hugged goodbye, C4 couldn't help himself. His good judgment was overwhelmed by his wicked sense of humor.

"Say hello to Bella for me."

CT laughed out loud.

"Will do, son, will do."

Kelly looked puzzled and asked,

"What is that all about."

"I'll explain in the car, Kelly. Long story."

Once CT and Kelly left, Jolene went back into the bedroom to get ready for work. C4 sat at the table staring at his coffee. The only thing wrong in his life right now was the PI in Fargo. Was there some way to shut that down?

He couldn't think of anything. Maybe he could buy the guy off? Come up with some reason to give him the three gold pieces he had and a couple thousand in cash, telling him he'd found the perpetrator himself and made him cough up the money? He'd give him the name of some vagabond he knew from his partying days and make him sweat it out. That would at least buy him some time and make Baker feel better.

Jolene came out, dressed for work. She didn't notice his pensive mood and opened her own conversation.

"Ok, now you have to fill me in. Who is Kelly's dad, and who is Bella?"

C4 figured there was no way to avoid telling Jolene the truth, or at least come as close to the truth as he could.

"Kelly's dad is Kendall Baker."

He let that soak in, waiting for a reaction. He got one.

"Your dad just married Kendall Baker's daughter?"

"Yup."

"And Kendall Baker is your mystery client, the one who gave you the three ounces of pure gold?"

"Yup."

C4 realized he was being uncharacteristically taciturn so waited to see if Jolene would call him out on that. She did.

"That's all you can say, 'yup'?"

This time C4 just nodded, and Jolene took advantage of the silence.

"So, you work for one of the richest people in North Dakota and you didn't think I should know that? Or that I might find that interesting?"

"He likes to keep a low profile. I don't mention him to pretty much anyone."

"Were you worried that people would use you to connect him to me, the poor widow of an oilfield worker?"

That was a disastrous turn of the conversation that C4 had not anticipated and needed to fix right now.

"Absolutely not. I work for him on an ad hoc basis, project by project. I am not an employee, so didn't want you to think I was that close to him. As Kelly said, he likes my dad and me and likes working with us, but I didn't want anyone, especially you, to think I was in on the business. Though now it looks like I might be."

"It sure does. I don't ever want you to be ashamed of me."

"Jolene, I could never be ashamed of you. You're the best thing that ever happened to me and that includes my work for Kendall Baker. I wish we could walk hand-in-hand all over Bismarck, but we don't because you and your family and a lot of other people aren't ready for that. I am proud of you and our relationship."

He stopped there, once again, not sure how far to take this topic. He waited and Jolene looked at him apparently deep in thought. After a few moments, she spoke.

"I know. I just don't know why your work for Baker had to be a secret. I had hoped we were past that."

"Well now we're not. I'm sorry if you thought I was purposely keeping it from you. I just didn't see a need to tell you, and I can see now that was wrong. I'm sorry."

"Thank you. Now on to more interesting stuff."

C4 was not thrilled with the thought of anything more interesting than what they had just covered, but knew he had to hear it.

"And that is?"

"Who is Bella? Yet another woman ensnared by you or your dad?"

C4 laughed.

"Far from it. She is Mr. Baker's live-in housekeeper and she can't stand me or my dad. She makes it quite clear. In fact, Baker is not even sure she likes him either."

"Why does he keep her around, then?"

C4 related to Jolene the story Baker had told him about Bella and her late husband.

"Sounds like the old guy has a soft spot for her because of his late wife. That's very generous of him."

"It is. He comes across as a crusty old guy, but he's really nice and quite human when you get to know him."

"Any idea when that might be?"

"Again, I am fine to go public with you anytime anyplace. Once we are seen with Kendall and Kelly and my dad, then we couldn't be more public."

"You're right. I'm sorry. I've just never been so close to the rich and famous."

She reheated her coffee and sat down. Now she looked pensive.

"I'm sorry I was rude to you about your relationship with Kendall Baker. It really is something you were free to keep to yourself. We are still on pretty thin ice, or new ground, or some such saying, in that we're both learning how to be with each other. I am fresh out of a bad marriage and you are trying hard to live in a domestic relationship for the first time, at least as far as I know, and we both have things to learn. We need to take this step by step. And we need to be sensitive to the feelings of Trevor's family and my family and friends. I don't want Trevor's mom and dad to ever know that you and I spent a night together before Trevor died. I appreciate your patience with me. I was pretty damaged when I got here, and you have been great for me."

C4 thought that was a great summary of the situation, so tried to think of a meaningful way to state his agreement.

"Jolene, when we first met, I had no way of foreseeing the life we would be sharing together. I'm glad you came back to me, and that I could help. You have helped me more than you will ever know. Let's just keep moving forward, and if we need to talk more about this, then let's do that."

Once again, not sure if what he said was ok, let alone whether he should add to it, C4 stopped there and waited to see what reaction he might get.

"Thanks, Cal. I'm betting we'll learn pretty quickly how this all works out for you and your dad. But don't forget, however it works out for you, it now also impacts me as well, right?"

"Absolutely, and I must say, this is all very sudden. And completely unexpected. They've known each other for a total of two days."

"How long did you and I know each other before I moved in? I mean, when I came to stay just for a week or two."

They both smiled at that. Jolene continued,

"At their age, I think they can get to know each other faster than younger people and they have a bit of a sense of urgency. Why be engaged for a year when you don't know how many you have left?"

C4 nodded. That made sense. She always did.

"You're right. We should be happy for them. I hope they don't plan on having any kids!"

Jolene laughed.

"Let's hope not. That would be a miracle. I need to run. Have a great day!"

"You, too. Take care not to make too many special friends. I want room for me in your life."

"Oh, you're in my life. The first man to ever give me flowers. And other stuff, of course."

A quick hug and a kiss and she was gone.

Chapter 27

WITH JOLENE OUT THE DOOR, C4's thoughts turned back to the Fargo PI. No matter how hard he thought, he couldn't come up with a way to head that off. If he jumped in, as he had thought earlier, he was going to look guilty no matter how he played it. For the first time in his life, everything was in order, except for this. He was done with Vicki and the partying, poker playing lifestyle. He had what he assumed would be a well-paying job, with little to do. He was set for life. And he would have a respected position in society, so he at least had a shot at keeping Jolene.

And his dad was set. A couple of weeks ago they had embarked on the Baker Plan out of sheer desperation. They needed to create an income stream, and the Baker Plan would do it. They were desperate men. Now that was all fixed, except for the gold.

He spun these thoughts in his head until he couldn't think of any way to spin them any differently. He had no idea how long he'd been enmeshed in his own private world when his phone rang. He looked at the screen. It was his dad. He wondered why he would call again so soon, so asked the only question he could think of.

"Hello there. Still married?"

"Absolutely. Still happily married. Kelly is asleep. I think I had too much coffee, so I can't settle down. I'm sorry we sprung it on you that way, but I just couldn't wait."

"I understand. Are you sure this is the real thing?"

"I am, at least for now. This is not a replay of Susie Floosie. Kelly is the real deal and we really connected. Not just physically. At our age, you get past that quickly."

"And you've told Mr. Baker by now?"

"We have and he seemed surprised, but also happy for us. More Kelly than me."

"And where does this leave Kevin?"

"Good question. We all talked about that. When Baker's kids went east, they both did well for themselves. Kelly is comfortable all on her own. Kevin did even better, working on Wall Street, and apparently would scoff at the kind of money Baker has. I have been directed to rewrite Baker's will leaving a cool one million to Kevin and all the rest to Kelly, as a reward for taking over the operation of the empire. We had a quick call with Kevin to share the news of our marriage and to propose that disposition of assets and he at least verbally was in full agreement. In fact, he said he didn't even really need the million."

C4 shook his head, not that his dad knew that. He had to ask his dad the one remaining nagging question.

"One more question. What if she dumps you?"

"I have quietly thought of that. We have no prenup, obviously, so I am hoping if she decides she doesn't want me around, I will push for the same deal Kevin got. Just a million to go away. Right now, we're both so happy, I really don't picture that happening."

C4 laughed out loud. His dad had to ask,

"Why are you laughing?"

"What does Bella think?"

"As you know, Bella doesn't like me, or Mr. Baker all that much for that matter. She does seem to really like Kelly. Not sure what to make of that, or what it means now that we're married."

"She makes it clear that she doesn't like me either. You get some sleep. I have some errands to run. We can talk again later."

But the conversation wasn't over.

"Cal, I have given this a bit of thought, and I want to run this by you. Now that Kelly and I are married, I feel like I probably should tell her more about how you and Jolene came to be living together. I can sanitize it a bit, but if I don't say anything and it comes out bit by bit, it will look like I'm hiding something. Your thoughts on that?"

"I hear what you're saying. You're probably right, but let me think about it. I may run it by Jolene to make sure she's ok."

"Ok. We'll catch up later."

The call ended. C4 knew he'd lied, he had no errands to run. He just couldn't take any more of his dad's glee. He returned to his own situation. Maybe the PI would drop the case, or just hit dead ends. That was his only hope.

Desperate for something to do, C4 took advantage of a nice winter day and took a drive. He drove out past Jolene's house. You couldn't tell from the outside how badly it was destroyed inside. He drove past Jolene's school, just to see where she worked. Her car was parked there, and he fought off the urge to walk in, just to see her. He drove by the Riverview Supper Club, where he had first met her. He even drove over to Mandan and had lunch at the Missouri Breaks. Burger and fries and a Coors Light. Just like the night this whole chapter of his life had started. When he embarked on the plan to get some money of his own, after his dad had all but cut him off. He had another Coors Light, paid, tipping nicely, and headed for home.

He was asleep when Jolene came home. The beer had just tipped the scales for him. As he awoke to her presence, he hoped that no news from the Fargo PI on the investigation was good news. Maybe this would all settle down and he could fully engage in his new life as a respected citizen with a real job and a hot young wife. He and his dad would have made the fastest transition ever from destitute to wealthy men. Better than winning the lottery because it came with wonderful women. Can't win that from the Powerball.

"Hi! Were you sleeping? Sorry to wake you."

"Just napping. Went out for lunch and had a couple of light beers, which must have made me drowsy. How was your day?"

He was careful to say light beers so she wouldn't think he'd been day drinking again.

"I saw you drive by the school today. Were you checking up on me?"

"I certainly was. It occurred to me that for all I know you might be spending your days with another man."

He smiled as broadly as he could to make it clear that he was kidding.

"I am. A whole bunch of men. The oldest is no more than seven so I'm playing the long game."

She laughed, then continued,

"Really, why?"

"I was just driving around a bit. It was a nice day, so thought I'd drive by your school just to see it. Kind of made a tour of Bismarck. It's been a while since I've been out and about."

"Fighting a dose of cabin fever? I hadn't thought of that. I've been back and forth to work and all the way to Jamestown a couple of times and except for a few meals with your dad, you've been more or less hibernating. Glad you got out."

"Thanks. I did get to Minnesota once, so that helped."

"Speaking of which, how is Mr. Baker?"

"He's home resting, doing well. My dad called earlier. Kelly was resting too. He was too wound up. Hopefully he got some sleep today. He had a busy night."

"He sure did. That is amazing. I hope it works out for the two of them. It was pretty sudden."

"It sure was."

He was willing to let it all drop but Jolene wasn't.

"And this job you now have. Weren't you already doing that?"

"I more or less was. In bits and pieces, getting paid ad hoc. Apparently, Mr. Baker wants to make it a salaried position now."

"I see. But it was enough to live on?"

"It was, along with some side work for my dad, some courier work and some investigations, and some odds and ends for other clients, though this will be much better. I'm hoping I'll even have health insurance now."

"That would be great. Mine isn't so good."

C4 wondered what the implication of that was. He fought off his curiosity because he wanted to keep the conversation pointed where he wanted it to go.

"I thought I'd let them all rest today and start following up tomorrow. It's been a busy couple of days."

"That makes sense. Let me change, and you can pour some wine, ok? The little terrors must have all been high on Valentine's Day candy today."

As he poured the wine it became clear to him that just having her back in the condo was a bigger comfort than she could imagine. How could she, at half his age, be so mature? She was the most grounded person he knew, and until he met her, he didn't even know what that was.

He found it amazing. In fact, he was finding lots of things amazing lately, like how comfortable he was here with her. Drinking wine instead of scotch and eating leftovers of home cooked meals instead of bar food. Staying in for the evening instead of planning some misbegotten all-night adventure or another.

A few minutes later Jolene's phone rang. She looked at the screen and said,

"It's your dad. Wonder what he wants?"

"He didn't mention any thing to me."

She put it on speaker.

"Hello?" said Jolene tentatively.

"Hi, Jolene. I am so sorry but in the excitement of getting married and everything else I forgot to tell you. A couple of your checks have come into my office. The employer life insurance, and the $75,000 from the policy Trevor's parents took out."

"Oh, great. I can go ahead and start getting my house fixed up. And how big is the other one?"

"$265,000. Not a bad piece of change. I can recommend a broker who can help you invest that for the long term, you don't want to just leave that much in a bank."

"I'd appreciate that. Thank you so much."

Jolene hung up her phone and said,

"Your dad has been so helpful to me through all this. I am so glad you recommended he help me with the insurance claims and all the other estate stuff. He's been great."

"I'm glad. It's what he does, and I'm happy he could help you."

"Now I can call Kent and get him started on rebuilding my house."

"Kent?"

"Yes, I told you about him. He's a friend of Carson's. He said to call him as soon as I had some money from the insurance claims, and he'd order a roll-off dumpster to start the demolition. Removing all the stuff that was damaged and can't be fixed."

C4 did recall that conversation.

"Doesn't he work with Carson at the highway department?"

"Yes, so he'll do this as a side job. He'll work evenings and weekends. I can stay out of his way until it's time to start selecting cabinets and backsplash and paint or whatever else I need to pick out."

"Can he do this by himself?"

"Mostly, yes, and Carson has said he'd help with any of the work that requires another set of hands. In fact, they've already measured for the new kitchen cabinets. I just need to pick out the style I want. Knowing engineers is coming in handy! And I will have Terry help me with the decorating. She's already done their house so has more experience than I have."

C4 figured he didn't want to hear any more about the four of them working evening after evening on Jolene's house, so he tried to move the conversation along.

"Do you still plan to sell the house when it's fixed up?"

"I think I do. There are just too many bad memories there. I'll try to pick neutral colors and standard cabinets and stuff in order to make it easy to sell. Hopefully I can get it on the market by spring."

"That would be great. And before we get too drunk on all this wine, I have another perhaps touchy topic."

Jolene peered at him over her wine glass.

"Drunk, really?"

"Just kidding. My dad called me earlier today and he had a thought I said I'd ask you about."

"And that is…?"

"When they popped in this morning, we cut off the conversation about how you and I came to be a couple. My dad thinks he should share some version of events with Kelly, so it doesn't come out bit by bit and have it look like we were all hiding something from her. I said I'd check with you."

Jolene once again peered at C4 over her wine glass.

"How brutal a version is necessary? I don't want to look too pathetic, getting picked up in a bar and then having my husband beat me for it."

"I would sure hope we could make it sound better than that. Maybe more like you were in a really bad marriage and I was hopelessly adrift in life, and you and I met and connected and found comfort in each other's company, and that quickly grew into a solid relationship."

Jolene had to smile.

"You should run for office. That's pretty smooth. And essentially true. And, I like the word 'connected.' Only you and I would appreciate the full interpretation of that."

Chapter 28

THURSDAY FEBRUARY 16TH started like many other days for Calvin Steele Tappen IV. He awoke to the sound of Jolene in the shower and smiled at the good fortune of having her in his life. He was going to be a new man. He could feel it.

His dad was happily married, at least for the time being, and thus wealthy. C4 himself had an actual job that met all his personal requirements, namely, very little work for what he hoped was a healthy paycheck. Even if that fell short, his dad would and now could fill in any gaps in the money he needed. If all went well, he'd even be in a two-income household. Jolene's job at the Riverview had to go.

The last part was thanks to the fantastic woman he now had in his life, as did his father. It had all worked out. The past few weeks had been a bit of a blur, but it was all going to work out.

There were still a couple of burrs under his saddle, but hopefully those could be removed easily and soon. One potentially troubling item, from a legal standpoint was Vicki's absurd accusation that C4 had somehow had a hand in Trevor's death. While no one, except for Jolene, had enjoyed more benefit from Trevor's untimely demise than he had, he knew he was completely innocent. The fact that two different insurance companies had signed off on Jolene's benefit payment had to be a good sign, didn't it? OSHA and worker's comp and any other investigations had to be done or close to done, so hopefully that was behind him.

The more troubling problem was the case of the five gold coins. If he had had any idea that he and his dad would be on easy street this soon, he would have never taken them. He could have paid Vicki off from the proceeds of just one of the three gold coins Baker gave him, in full and on time. That would have left him over $5,000 to live on, and with Jolene as a roommate he was spending very little. She bought groceries and wine and thus covered a lot of their household expenses. His formerly sizeable scotch bill was now nonexistent. If only, if only.

Unfortunately, he was still at a loss on how to head off the PI's investigation. His only hope was that the investigation dead-ended. With his dad married to Kelly, even if she got mad and fired him from his Baker Empire job, his dad would be ok. By not involving his dad in any way, hopefully C4 had kept him in the good graces of old man Baker and CT's new wife.

It all came down to that investigation. If caught, he had to throw himself on the mercy of the Baker clan, claiming destitution. He didn't want to borrow money from his dad or Baker and was always going to put them back. Unfortunately, his violation was worse than the gold. He had entered Baker's home without permission, proceeded into the inner sanctum of his bedroom and worse yet, he had violated Baker's shrine to his late wife. Money or not, those were pretty unforgiveable offenses. Baker's generosity to Bella and C4 himself proved he would have helped C4 if he had known.

If he was caught, he had an untenable situation, and would lose his dad, Jolene, and his new job. And that was ignoring his newfound status as a decent, upright citizen that Jolene had helped him create. What could be worse?

His phone rang, jolting him into reality. He grabbed his phone and moved quickly into the living room.

"Hello?"

"Good morning, Mr. Tappen. It's Adam Lankin again."

C4 swallowed hard.

"Good morning. Any progress?"

Lankin went on.

"Not really. My investigation hasn't turned up much of anything, so I'm just wondering if you had any more thoughts."

C4 could hardly conceal his glee.

"No, I'm sorry. I just keep thinking about all the people who had access to the house key and that's not a long list, but you never know. Some plumber's assistant for example, after a few beers, may have mentioned it to someone who mentioned it to someone. That list can become pretty long."

"I've had the same thoughts and tried to follow those leads, but they've gotten nowhere. The bigger mystery is who could have found the floor safe and the combination. Both were well hidden."

C4 interjected,

"The housekeeper Baker retained at the lake house is the only one who I can think of who would have come across either."

This was going pretty well. C4 held his phone in his left hand and poured himself a cup of coffee. Jolene had apparently been up a while. Lankin was replying.

"I questioned her and I just can't picture her doing it. She hadn't been in the house since Mr. Baker had last asked her to clean, and she has instructions to simply dust the top of the cabinet where the combination was held, never to open it. It's not ironclad, but she sure doesn't seem the type. Besides, it would end her entire career, and she needs the money. She cleans a lot of the lake homes around there so ruining her reputation would end that.

C4 was borderline ecstatic, wondering what would come next. Would this be the end of it? Lankin went on.

"I checked the gold dealers in the Fargo area, official and unofficial, and nobody remembered any stranger bringing any gold one ounce rounds in to sell. Their customers tend to be regulars. So, another dead end."

C4 was getting happier by the moment.

"So, I've thrown out a life preserver. There are a bunch of us PIs in this part of the world who network with each other and I've asked them to ask around if anyone cashed in any gold pieces in the last week. That's cheaper than me getting in my car and driving from dealer to dealer, and once I get out of Fargo, I only know the licensed ones."

C4 felt a need to redirect.

"So, you are focused on this being a pretty recent event? This could have happened any time."

"You are right, Calvin, but I'm guessing not. We don't know how often Mr. Baker looks in his safe, or counts his gold stash, but he seems to think it hasn't been that long. If it goes back further than that, we probably are at a dead end, but if it was recent, we may still have a chance. And in that case either they cashed one or more in, or they didn't. If they didn't, we're done, if they did, we still have a thread. That's all we can work with, don't you think?"

C4 thought hard but he couldn't come up with any other options.

"I guess you're right, Adam. Seems like a long shot, though."

"It probably is, but I want to be able to tell my client I did everything I could. Wouldn't you?"

"I guess I would, Adam. I know he appreciates diligence. Good luck."

"Thanks. I'll let you know if I hear anything."

C4 hung up his phone just as Jolene came into the kitchen.

"Who was that, Cal?"

"Just another guy who works for Mr. Baker. We were kind of brainstorming and comparing notes."

"Will you be gone more now that you're a full-time employee?"

"I really don't know. I haven't had a chance to talk to Mr. Baker or Kelly, or my dad, who may turn out to be my day-to-day boss."

"Keep me posted. Isn't that what you business moguls say all the time?"

"I really don't know that either, but it seems to fit."

"And not that you need reminding, but I am working at the Riverview again tonight. So, you'll have time to see your dad or do whatever you need to do."

"I'll have to track down my dad sometime today. Be nice to the kids, honey. Have a great day."

"Will do, you too."

She extended her arms to hug him goodbye and he hung on.

"Nice hug Cal, but I do need to get going. Love you."

"You, too."

Embrace ended, she was gone.

As soon as Jolene left, C4 used the bathroom, showering, shaving, putting on decent clothes so he felt presentable. He then called his dad.

"Hello?"

"Hi, dad, are you in the office?"

"I am. I have a lot of legal documents to get ready to make the changes Baker needs to his trust and his will in order to reflect my new relationship as his son-in-law."

"Congratulations again."

"Thank you. Kelly is with her dad this morning. Hopefully resting."

"How is he doing after his fall?"

"He's fine, though he is still healing. Here's the weird thing. At the time he fell, he was doing some business with a woman Bella knows only by sight, but Bella claims this woman pushed him down the stairs and then ran away."

"That is weird. Why would anyone do that? Any idea who the woman is?"

"I sure don't, and Bella didn't, but Baker has a name so they'll be able to file charges and get the police to track her down."

"What kind of business? And why upstairs?"

"Who knows, but Bella said she'd been to the house before. And they always go upstairs to his office up there and shut the door. Apparently, whatever they work on, they don't want Bella listening in."

C4's thoughts immediately ran to Vicki, but what business could she have with Baker? Had to be someone else. As he thought that through, he realized his dad was still talking.

"We're all meeting here in my office at 5:00 today to sign everything, and would like you to join us, so we can also go over your job offer. Sorry it has to be all of us, but Kelly and I are taking over so we both need to be in on all phases of the business including your salary and benefits. In fact, drafting your offer letter is part of what I'm working on today. I think you'll be pleased. Then maybe out to dinner afterwards and of course, you're invited."

"That sounds great. I'll swing by at 5:00. Don't skimp on that offer letter."

"Don't worry. By the way, just between us, once you are on the Baker payroll, I'm going to stop making the utility, and tax, and other payments on your condo. It's paid for so that's not a problem, but I will be out of the condo support business entirely."

C4 was a bit shocked. He had not thought about that, but had no argument. As long as they paid him enough.

"That makes sense, and I thank you for covering those payments all these years."

"You're welcome. I need to get back to work. I need to get everything revised and out to Taylor for retyping so they're ready to sign by five."

"Got it. See you at five."

The call ended, C4 still faced a long day by himself. The old C4 would have made his usual liquor store run, but now he was drinking Rose', lite beer, and some decent red wines. Maybe he could still own a bottle of scotch, and just make sure he controlled the intake. He poured himself a cup of coffee and went back to his desk to get his college basketball notes. He turned on the TV and sat down at the coffee table. Maybe he could place his usual four basketball bets today, either on tonight's games or for something over the weekend.

He was glad this took his attention as fully as it did. However, he was still plagued by the gold coin theft investigation hanging over his head. And now the curious situation of some unknown woman pushing Baker down the stairs. Who could that be and why push him down the stairs? Who would have anything to gain by that? Or could it just be anger? Or some blackmail scheme? Bella was a bit mean, but why make up something like that?

Then his thoughts turned to what would happen at 5:00 p.m. How much would his salary be? What would he have to do for his job duties? He tried to think of some questions to ask this afternoon that would make him appear knowledgeable and thoughtful. And help him learn what would be expected of him. Would this be the final piece of the puzzle that would allow him to spend the rest of his life with Jolene?

This was a lot to think about. He turned his attention back to basketball. Now it could be a hobby, he didn't have to ramp up the bets.

By 11:00 a.m. he had made his four picks and phoned them in, at $100 each.

He walked over to the refrigerator. He found some sandwich meat and noticed a note on the Rose' bottle: "Almost empty. Please buy more if you get a chance. J" and of course the usual little heart.

He looked over at the red wine. That was low, too. Time for a liquor store run.

He ate his sandwich, washed down by a lite beer, cleaned that up and put on a jacket. Liquor store, here we come.

As he walked across the parking lot to the liquor store, a rangy cowboy got out of a car and stood in his way.

"Vicki wants to talk to you. Get in the car."

This was new. Why not accost him in the store as usual? He looked the cowboy over carefully. Both men remained really calm. To a passerby it would appear they were old friends who just bumped into each other. It was the same cowboy who had been at Archie's the day he had paid off Vicki. What could she possibly want now? The cowboy opened his jacket just a bit and sure enough, the butt of a semi was visible just like before. C4 got in the car as the cowboy indicated. Front passenger seat.

Vicki was in the back, in the shadows.

"You certainly have landed on your feet, Cal. How lucky can you get, your dad marrying Baker's daughter?"

C4 was no longer surprised by what Vicki knew. She clearly had sources everywhere.

"So what? How does that affect you?"

"I see it as a phenomenal business opportunity."

That didn't sound good. He had no idea where this was headed. He just waited and she spoke again.

"You playing the strong silent type now, Cal? Ok, I'll play along. I got a call from Adam Lankin, who as you well know, is a PI in Fargo, to help him track down some gold pieces stolen from Baker, your dad's new father-in-law. I started making some calls and found out something that didn't surprise me at all."

She paused, waited a moment, then went on.

"I started locally with contacts in Minot and Bismarck and worked my way east to kind of overlap Lankin's territory. Here's what I learned. A gold dealer in Grand Forks remembered that a guy matching your description, who he'd never seen before, cashed in one gold piece a couple weeks ago, on a Monday morning, just as he opened up for the day. He doesn't retain his camera footage, so that didn't help.

"So I kept working. I used a string of contacts to finally lead to a friend of a friend, a woman named Trixie, who said you were in her bar that Sunday night. Said you were a friend of one of her bartenders and that you were planning on staying overnight with him. I think his name is Steve."

C4 knew this was worse than the worst scenario he could imagine. Not Lankin, but Vicki had the goods on his gold theft. He said nothing.

"You are unusually quiet Cal. I'll take that as acknowledgment that I'm getting warm. Or that things are getting warm for you. Let me go on. We talked to someone at Steve's apartment. Said a guy named Cal burned a pizza at Steve's apartment. There's more but I think you get the picture."

Clearly this time Vicki held all the cards. He was caught. He was had. He was screwed. He was about to be broke and single. He used all his energy to try to look stoic. Finally, he spoke.

"So why are you telling me this?"

"Because I like you and I like doing business with you. I didn't go back to Lankin, or to Baker, or to your dad, nor God forbid to Jolene, who you love like you've never loved anyone before in your whole miserable life."

"I don't believe you like me, and why do you think you like doing business with me?"

"Because I lent you money once and you paid me back in full and early. You have the ability to come up with money when you need it. In fact, I'm thinking you paid me back with money you got from Baker's stolen gold."

C4 longed to say she couldn't prove anything, but he knew she could. She was talking again.

"I could work my sources in Sioux Falls and then maybe Rapid City, because if I were you, that's where I would have cashed out the rest of the gold. I bet I can place you in those cities, and maybe a motel room somewhere along the route. Oddly enough, all on the same weekend Trevor Buchanan was trying to find you and kill you. You are one lucky dog. And I like your luck as much as I like you."

C4 could only think of the most obvious question.

"So, what now?"

"I will kill this investigation, tell Lankin I have exhausted all sources and found nothing. He'll cash his check from Baker and be happy as a clam. He'll pass that along to Baker and you are free to start your new life, except for one little detail."

"And that is?"

"You and I are back in business. In exchange for my complicity, you put me on your payroll. And I'll make it simple. One gold ounce a month. Delivered in person. By you."

"I can't afford that!"

"I think you can't afford to not pay that. For reasons already cited. If you don't pay me, I will call Larkin and just give him my leads and he can figure out it was you. He'll be a hero to Baker and likely reap a nice reward. You, however, and maybe your dad, are back out of the Baker family business. And Jolene is long gone."

C4 tried hard not to hang his head or show the horrible sense of loss that was overwhelming him. He was now only thinking of how to get out of this, by any way possible. He asked the next logical question.

"Every month? For how long?"

"Until one of us dies. Everyone needs a pension plan, don't they?"

"That's crazy!"

"I don't think you can afford the lump sum payoff, so this will have to do. No checks, no envelopes of cash. Just one nice round gold ounce. One per month. And here's the real rub. Baker told me he gave you three ounces not long ago, so I know you have at least one. And your dad is rich now, so I know you can come up with more, for years and years to come."

C4 was now stunned, but decided to open a new topic.

"So, you met with Baker. You're the one who pushed him down the stairs. That's why you're hiding in the back seat of this car. I don't have to pay you. You're going to jail!"

"Wrong on all counts except I met with Baker. I help him with certain things once in a while. You don't build a real estate empire like his without some help from the dark side. I collect when the sheriff can't. I convince people to pay their back rent, and sometimes to evict themselves from rental properties. I am very useful to Mr. Baker. I'm sure he'll explain all that to your dad.

"But I didn't push him down the stairs, he slipped on a rug and fell. I ran down the stairs to try to help him and that's when Bella saw me bent over him and drew the wrong conclusion. I left because, as you might imagine, I have a real aversion to interacting with the police. And trust me, Baker wouldn't press charges, but Bella did."

C4 had to think. Maybe she was telling the truth. Unlikely but possible. And it was a plausible scenario.

"Back to our new business deal. As I said, I know you have some gold right now, so let's meet tomorrow to make the first payment. So neither of us forgets. That will get us off to a good start."

C4 knew he had to cut this off. There was no way he was going to pay her this much every month for the rest of his life. Or was it for the rest of her life? Which might not be that long. One ounce tomorrow and then not another one. That had to be the deal. Go along with this one payment and then figure out how to make it stop. No matter what it took. So, for right now, make it look like he'd comply with her ridiculous demand.

"Archie's?" asked C4.

"No, I need to stay out of sight. You pay me tomorrow somewhere more private, and then I leave town until I can get these charges dropped."

C4 thought. Hard.

"How about the boat landing on the river south of town? Nobody will be there this time of year."

Vicki shot a glance at the cowboy. He nodded.

"Ok. Tomorrow, 8:00 a.m."

"Make it 9:00."

"Again, you're trying to negotiate times for payments? What is that girl doing to you? I hope she hasn't ruined you."

"She hasn't but she goes to work at a school about 8:00 and remember, part of our agreement is keeping this from her. You offered that up."

"I did. We'll help you keep the secret from the lovely Jolene. By the way, how long do you think you can keep her? On the open market she'd have a lot of offers from guys younger and richer than you. And with no ties to bad girls like me."

"You forget how charming I can be."

"I have not forgotten and I'm always here for you. Now, get out, look back, wave at the cowboy like you were glad you had a chance to visit a bit, and then continue into the liquor store. See you tomorrow morning at 9:00."

C4 stepped out into the blinding sunlight, and as directed, turned and waved at the cowboy, who waved back and drove away. C4 walked into the liquor store and resisted the urge to uncork a scotch and just start drinking. But that was the old C4. The new one now knew he had a problem to solve and needed a clear head.

He walked around the store and made his purchases. He included a bottle of good scotch, better than his usual daily brand, because he was going to get rid of Vicki, once and for all, one way or another. Then, regardless of Jolene's liquor restrictions, he was going to celebrate. Big time. One last time, then he'd be a reformed man.

Chapter 29

A HALF-HOUR LATER, he was back in his condo, brooding about this horrendous setback. He was careful, for a lot of reasons, not to open the scotch and start self-medicating. He then came up with his plan.

He'd get to the boat ramp early, park his SUV, and then climb up the hill a little ways into the woods. From there he could ambush Vicki and her cowboy, using his own .22 pistol to disarm them and then shoot them each several times with the cowboy's semi, dumping their bodies into the river to float away. Someone would find their car, but with any luck, by the time they found the bodies, the forensics would be hard to complete and the cowboy's gun, left next to their car, would match whatever bullets and bullet holes they found. This had come to him like he was in a dream or a trance.

C4 stopped, his heart pounding. Where did this come from? This was like nothing he had ever done before. This was not the play of someone with just a juvie record, as Vicki had accused him. This was big time and he was thinking like a hit man. Why? He was desperate, more desperate than ever before, because he was on the cusp a wonderful life, one with money and love and respect. He could think of no better way out. Besides, the world was better off without Vicki and her cowboy. This was practically a community service.

His thoughts turned to a life with a steady income, eventually a huge inheritance and most of all, Jolene. She mattered more than all the rest of it put together. In fact, she was the reason for all the rest of it. He had to keep her. She was his ticket to a beautiful future. Someday, he'd have her picture on his dresser, the most beautiful woman he'd ever seen, only she'd still be alive. He would show Tommy and Connie and

Steve and Trixie and Adam Lankin and Bella and all the people he'd ever met that he could be more successful than any of them.

He'd show his dad that he was wrong. He could have a beautiful young wife, and raise a family, and go to soccer games and dance recitals and school plays. He'd show Vicki he could keep Jolene. He wouldn't screw it up like Vicki had said she would. But that didn't matter. Vicki would be dead.

He went to his desk and from deep in a drawer he pulled out his pistol. He hadn't shot it in years. He still owned it simply because he had no reason to get rid of it. He put it in his pocket and rode down the elevator to his SUV.

Having come up with his plan, he was now working like he was on autopilot. He had never been so focused in his life. He drove to the far end of town to a hardware store, and he bought a new pack of .22 long rifle hollow point bullets. No need to take a chance on old ammo, just in case he actually had to shoot his own gun. He then drove to the boat landing. He scouted carefully, looking for just the right place to stage his ambush. He would have to arrive early of course, to be in place before his intended victims drove up. He walked around the edge of the woods until he found a place behind a giant cottonwood tree from where he could observe the whole parking lot, and could then surprise Vicki and her cowboy. He noted where he would have to park his SUV, assuming they would park close to him to make the seamless handoff of the gold.

He envisioned his entire plan, how to approach her car, using his gun to get them out, walking them to the edge of the river and sending them to South Dakota and beyond, via the current of the great Missouri River. The perfect crime.

He sat in his SUV and envisioned it over and over, until he had every step memorized. Then he drove to the far end of the ramp, walked a little way into the woods and practice fired his gun, emptying one clip, getting familiar with how it felt. Making sure he would have the safety off, and a bullet already chambered. He was taking no chances. Then he reloaded it fully, so it was ready to go. Only then did he drive home, so he could be sitting calmly in his condo when Jolene walked in. He had never been calmer in his whole life. He finally had everything under control. His dad was taken care of. He, himself, had a steady job. He had Jolene and would do everything and anything to keep her.

He smiled to himself and pulled his thoughts together, just to remind himself of how important his mission tomorrow was.

For the first time in his life, he had a great future. A respectable, dignified upper class job. He had the virtual assurance of a huge inheritance. And he had, within his grasp, both literally and figuratively, the most wonderful woman he'd ever met in his life. It was all his and he was not going to lose it.

He stared at the newly purchased bottle of scotch. He looked at the dregs of the last bottle, and decided that he'd better leave both alone. He had an hour or so to spend with Jolene, and then the evening with the owners and operators of the Baker Empire. No scotch until Vicki was on her way to South Dakota.

The door opened, jarring him from his thoughts.

"Hi, honey, I'm home!"

Jolene practically bounded into the room.

"I'm rich!"

Before C4 could respond to either statement, she ran over, sat down in his lap and showed him a deposit slip for over $300,000.

"Tomorrow, I'll move $250,000 into a brokerage account with a guy at the bank, and leave $50,000 in the bank for my house renovation account. And your dad said the worker's comp check should be here early next week."

C4 gave her a hug.

"That is great! I'm so happy for you."

"Between us, we have three jobs and money pouring in the door! We are almost a power couple!"

"We sure are. And as it currently stands, I am the next heir apparent to the Baker fortune."

"That's right. I hadn't even thought of that!"

C4 stared at the beautiful young woman in his lap. How appropriate. The perfect woman was in his lap. A meeting and dinner with his new employer tonight, then one more ugly task tomorrow and everything he wanted would all be in his lap. He would go from desperate to distinguished. Not just a solid citizen, but a wealthy man. Jolene was kissing him. Then she pulled away and talked.

"Too bad I have to work tonight. Or we could really celebrate!"

C4 thought about the next 16 or so hours of his life.

"I have to meet with the Baker clan, including my dad, and have dinner with them tonight. See if you can get tomorrow or Saturday night off. Then wwe'll celebrate in style!

"I will. Let's shoot for Saturday night. In the meantime, let's go enjoy our own private celebration, before we have to head out to our evening jobs. You to your big business dinner and me to my same old work."

As usual, C4 awoke to the sound of Jolene in the shower. Comforting yet disturbing. Even she had to shower after she'd been with him. The shower stopped. He looked at the clock. Just after 4:00. He needed to get up and get ready to go to his dad's office.

He started gathering his clothes from where they'd been dropped as they had headed to bed. Luckily, they were fresh and neat enough to just put back on.

Jolene came out of the bathroom.

"I didn't ask. Why were you all dressed up when I came home? You're usually in sweats."

C4 had to think a second, then replied,

"When I got dressed this morning, I wasn't sure if my dad would need me sometime during the day, so I dressed in case I had to go out. Now I need to dress again so I can go to his office after you go to work."

Clearly there was no need to mention his errands of the day. She'd notice the liquor purchase at some point but that was all she needed to know and there was no need to highlight that.

C4 felt a strange sense of calm. Everything was under control.

As soon as Jolene left, he made one last check around the condo and then headed to CT's office, arriving about 4:45, parking around on the side as always. He took advantage of the solitude to open the glove box of his SUV to double check his .22. It was loaded and ready for tomorrow. He was glad he had taken a few practice shots. He shouldn't need to shoot his own gun if his plan went perfectly, but he also had to have some sense of how to operate the cowboy's semi.

He walked in through the back door of his dad's office as usual. Kelly and her dad were already there. Taylor was still there, which was unusual.

CT greeted him through the open doorway.

"Hi, Cal. We're about ready for you. Taylor is helping us get the paperwork in order and notarizing everything that requires that."

"Good afternoon, everyone. I trust it's all going well." C4 replied as he walked in.

"It is, Calvin. Glad to have you aboard."

It was Baker himself who spoke. Then Kelly.

"It's nice to see you again, Cal. Sorry we dropped in uninvited this morning. It was nice, though, to meet you and Jolene."

Before anyone else could speak, CT took control to get things on track.

"Cal, here's the offer letter for your new position. It's pretty simple actually. An annual salary of $120,000 payable monthly on the 25th of each month, with a $5,000 signing bonus. You can get it set up for direct deposit if you wish. You will also get the standard health benefit package including dental and vision, at no charge. You will also be eligible for an annual bonus. We wish we could tell you how much to expect, but in this business, it depends not only on your performance and how well we manage the company, but also the weather, crop prices, and all the other random items that can affect the agricultural world. The effective start date is Monday, and I'll hand you the signing bonus check as soon as you sign."

C4 was amazed. Not a get rich salary but not bad. Some cash up front. He knew there was no reason to question anything, but he did say,

"Shouldn't I have my lawyer look this over?"

CT laughed.

"You just did. Sign it before the disappearing ink takes effect."

Laughter all around, C4 signed the offer letter, and CT handed him the check. C4 put it in his shirt pocket. He'd have to stop at the bank tomorrow after his first task, the one at the boat landing.

Baker spoke next.

"Calvin, the job is not hard, but you do need to be diligent. I own a pretty wide selection of assets across North Dakota, with a few in Minnesota and South Dakota. Most of it is farm and ranch land, with a handful of commercial buildings and a couple of apartment buildings thrown in. You probably need to visit each one at least twice a year. The rents should come in automatically, but sometimes they need a little prodding. Mostly it's watching for maintenance on the buildings, any overgrazing on the ranch lands and checking the reported yields on the farmland. Pretty straightforward. It's time to send someone younger out on these missions. I had a consultant who helped me with especially tough rent situations, but she and I had a bit of a difference of opinion on how she handled a renter and it didn't end well."

C4 found that quite interesting and at least somewhat at odds with Vicki's version of events. *Hard to believe Vicki had lied. That just wasn't like her.* C4 chuckled, unfortunately, out loud. He covered that as quickly as he could by talking.

"Thank you, Mr. Baker. I'm sure I'll get the hang of it."

Baker nodded, then said,

"Great, then let's go to dinner. We can continue any conversations with drinks in hand. Kelly made us a reservation at the Riverview."

C4 shot a glance at CT who just shrugged. They'd have to play it by ear. Maybe Kelly wouldn't recognize Jolene all dressed up and in the dimmed lights of the Riverview.

The entourage arrived at the Riverview just before 5:30. As they assembled in the foyer Kelly said

"I hope that eating dinner this early is just a product of our meeting, I'm not used to this. Besides, in Florida you can't get through the walkers and wheelchairs to get in if you try to eat this early."

From the foyer they proceeded into the main dining room. C4 held the door for them all to walk in. Jolene was at her stand. She recognized Kelly who right away recognized Jolene.

"Hello, Jolene. I didn't know you worked here."

"I do. It's an enjoyable job and the tips are great. I have your table ready, in the corner with a nice view of the river. Please, follow me."

Jolene showed them to their table and once seated, Baker turned to Kelly.

"How in the world do you know her?"

"You don't know? Sorry to break the guy code. She's Calvin's girlfriend."

"Calvin, I didn't know you had a girlfriend. I thought you played the field."

"It's pretty recent. I guess I just played the right field at the right time and now we're, as the kids say, an item."

Baker winked at C4 and said,

"And a good-looking item at that."

CT cut him off.

"Perhaps we should order a drink. How about a bottle of wine?"

Kelly took the hint and dropped the Jolene conversation. Baker wasn't so ready.

"Calvin, if you'd told me, we could have brought her along to Minnesota. I didn't mean to keep you apart."

"It's ok. We're all caught up."

C4 figured some humor might extricate him and it worked. Baker replied,

"I'm sure you are."

CT tried again to refocus the conversation away from Jolene.

"Does anybody have a preference on wine, or do we each just want to order a drink?"

Kelly tried to be helpful.

"Do they have a good Malbec? I'm not a wine snob but I just generally like those."

CT quickly perused the wine list.

"They do. I'll order a bottle of their best Malbec."

C4 tried to be helpful.

"That sounds good. I'll signal the waiter."

For once, he was seated facing the restaurant, with windows to his side and to his back. No one could sneak up on him now. Or ever again. Certainly not Vicki. He had to remind himself that no matter what Baker offered up regarding his altercation with Vicki, he could not reveal that he knew her.

He waved at their server, who had disappeared after bringing water. The server did not see him, but Jolene did. She came over.

"May I get you something?"

CT spoke.

"Yes, please. A bottle of this Malbec,"

He pointed to the most expensive one. Jolene smiled and said,

"Of course. I'll get that for you. Anything else?"

"Not right now, thank you."

Jolene walked away. Baker spoke.

"She is quite stunning, Calvin. Is she really old enough to be your girlfriend?"

Kelly shook her head and jumped in.

"Dad, leave him and his girlfriend alone. It's really none of our business."

"You're right. I'm sorry, Calvin."

The rest of the evening went smoothly, with the conversation ebbing and flowing. C4 enjoyed the whole experience. Getting to know Kelly, learning a little about the business he would now be part of, having some wine and a good meal. And from his vantage point, he was able to feast his eyes on Jolene most of the time as she went about her duties. The perfect evening. The only thing was, the next time they did something like this, instead of being a server or hostess, Jolene would be at the table with them. Where she belonged.

He looked to his side out the window. A perfect view of the Missouri River, just a bit of a shimmer on the moving water from a waning, crescent moon. Tomorrow at this time, Vicki and her cowboy would be floating face down in that same river, out of his life forever. From now on it would be just him and Jolene and his new job helping run the Baker Empire. He and Jolene would be among what Jolene had referred to as 'the hoi polloi' of Bismarck, and for that matter, all of North Dakota.

He turned his gaze from the river, the one that would carry the last of his old life away and focused on Jolene, his favorite symbol of his new life. And then just looked at the faces around this small table in the corner of the Riverview. His new life was all right here. And it was good.

Chapter 30

C4 WOKE UP ON THE COUCH to see Jolene sitting in the recliner with her legs curled up underneath her, watching him. He pulled himself up into a sitting position.

"Sorry, I guess I fell asleep. The wine my dad picked was quite good and I think we were on our third bottle when we finally left."

"I know, when the busboy cleared the table, I grabbed the last bottle and had a small glass from what was left."

"Good for you."

"When I got home you were sound asleep on the couch. I let you sleep and watched you for a little while. Like you do to me sometimes. It is a pleasant thing to do. Except you snore a bit and were also drooling a little."

She laughed and followed up.

"You're still quite cute."

She continued.

"And Mr. Baker left a nice tip on his Baker Enterprises credit card and then your dad handed me another hundred in cash. I really shouldn't take that."

C4 couldn't help himself.

"Please don't tell me he patted you on the butt when he did that."

Jolene laughed. To C4 it was like the sound of angels singing.

"No, he just handed it to me and thanked me for in his words 'enhancing the dining experience.'"

"Well, you can just use it to pay your legal bill. Unless he decides to not bill you given all our changes in circumstances - you with insurance money pouring in, me with a job, and him with a new, wealthy wife. An amazing turn of events, wouldn't you say?"

"It sure is. Speaking of your new job, is your salary ok? I don't want to probe too much, since we're not married and need to respect each other's boundaries."

"It's not bad. I should be able to live comfortably on it. And all my medical, including dental and vision is paid. The plan covers Baker, my dad and Kelly, Bella, Baker's housekeeper, and another woman I haven't met who serves as Baker's secretary and bookkeeper. And now me."

"That is great. And you don't have to spend money buying drinks for cute girls in bars anymore. Though I could use a nice drink and dinner once in a while."

"And you shall have that. I do probably have to travel more. I'll be checking on all the properties a couple of times a year rather than just one or two that he asked me to look at once in a while like I was doing before."

C4 made sure he phrased the situation so that Jolene would believe his duties were nothing new, just expanded responsibilities. He didn't need to worry since Jolene had already moved on.

"Just so you know, I did ask for and got Saturday night off from work. I don't think I will need that job any more, but I may take that time and use it to start college. I could probably double my school salary by getting my degree. And I can do it all right here in Bismarck, doing some night classes and then summer school. It will take a while, but I think it's a better use of my time than the Riverview."

C4 was a bit surprised, but on second thought he shouldn't have been. He didn't like her working at the Riverview anyway. But the college degree, that had not crossed his mind. But before he could fully process that, she again moved on.

"And on Saturday morning I'm meeting with Terry and Carson and Kent at my house to get started on the demo. Then we'll all head out to see a guy Kent knows who builds custom cabinets. We can pick the color and style and handles and all that. I hope to be home by midafternoon, but probably exhausted!"

"Sounds like we'll need a nap before we go out for our special dinner."

"I think so. Where is dinner?"

"I was thinking about the country club. My dad includes me on his membership. Maybe he'll make me get my own now!"

"Are we ready to go that public?"

"I am. We can pretend it's a first date, if anyone asks."

"I like that. And with Kelly and her dad knowing about us, I think we have no choice but to admit we're together."

"I guess so."

C4 once again was lost in thought. Jolene spending more time with her friends, all young and productive, and maybe having a baby, and Kent and the house and maybe a college degree and a fulltime teaching job, she certainly was taking advantage of her opportunity to grow and change.

"Ready for bed?"

"Absolutely."

C4 awoke at the first hint of daylight. He looked over at Jolene. So often she was awake and up first, so this morning he enjoyed watching her sleep as the light grew across the room. He thought about how much his life had changed, mostly because she came home from the Riverview with him that one night in January. In a way, he had saved her from Trevor. Both of them actually, but she had also saved him from his alcohol-fueled self-destructive nocturnal lifestyle. The one that earned him the nickname C4. It was not an easy change, and he knew he had to worry about relapses. Then the Baker Plan had turned into the Kelly Plan. Cutting through all the forms and processes and red tape.

Then his thoughts flitted back to Baker himself. Had Vicki pushed him down the stairs? Or was it an accident like Vicki had said. Hard to know who to believe, between Vicki or Bella. Regardless his mission this morning was truly a public service. Vicki had to go.

He rehearsed the meeting with Vicki and her cowboy a few more times in his head. Then he decided that if he couldn't pull it off cleanly, he'd give her the gold piece and save the ultimate mission for another day. But the first goal was to get rid of her forever. And even if it didn't work today, someday he would have to make it final.

He lay on his back staring at the ceiling in the growing light and then realized Jolene was awake and looking at him.

"You're deep in thought, Cal. All about your new job?"

"Some of it yes. Just thinking how lucky I am that you came home with me that Saturday night less than a month ago. At least for me."

"Me, too. No matter where we go from here, I'll always remember how you took me in and kept me safe when I really needed it. I think we've been good for each other."

"We have. Do we have time to fool around before you go off to school?"

"I think we do. I think you're getting younger!"

C4 pulled into the boat landing parking lot about 8:40 a.m. He smiled at how quickly Jolene had had to get ready to get out the door to get to school on time. As soon as she was gone, he'd gotten dressed. While he didn't own any camo clothing, he'd picked from what he had in his closet, staying to grays and browns to match the late winter landscape, ending with a brown suede leather jacket. He completed his wardrobe with a gray stocking cap and a pair of matching gray gloves, a gift from his mother at some past Christmas or birthday.

He parked just as he had decided yesterday, carefully placed his loaded semi in his right jacket pocket and walked a little way into the woods to his selected waiting point.

He found his preselected spot, behind the big cottonwood, and got his feet firmly placed so he wouldn't slip as he made his exit from his hiding spot. That movement had to be quick and sure. He checked his watch, 8:45. He knew he had some time to wait. It was at times like these, when he was waiting for someone, he wondered why among all his other vices he didn't smoke. If he smoked this would be a good time to have one. It might help him relax. He played out his plan in his head over and over. It had to be flawless to work and he had to be perfectly prepared. He even closed his eyes for a bit. When he opened them, he checked his gun one more time. Safety off, clip firmly in place, first bullet chambered.

It was a cloudy day which he thought helped him. He didn't want to be fighting bright sunlight and glare. He waited. He reviewed his plan. He waited some more.

He checked his watch. 9:01. Vicki was late. He smiled a bit that he was so focused on the task of sending Vicki and her cowboy down the river that that he felt no remorse over his intended actions whatsoever. Was that wrong? Would Jolene be surprised at that? It didn't matter. She'd never know. Execute the plan or pull the plug. Go home and wait for the next opportunity.

He waited a few more minutes. It was now 9:05. Still no Vicki. Given she was trying to stay out of sight from the police, he wasn't even sure what car she'd be in. He figured it would be like the liquor store parking lot with the cowboy driving and her out of sight in the back seat.

9:08. He had always been glad she didn't have his phone number, or at least never called him. Now maybe it would be nice to track her down to see if she was still going to show.

9:11. A filthy dark gray Honda Accord wheeled in. It parked near his SUV but not too close. For another half a minute nothing happened. Then the cowboy got out and walked toward C4's SUV. C4 came out of his hiding spot, .22 drawn but at his side. The cowboy saw him and reached for his gun. C4 raised his .22 and said,

"Carefully pull your gun out with two fingers only and lay it on the hood of my car. Then step back and kneel. Vicki, get out. Join your friend on your knees."

C4 was using his best cop show technique. Nothing happened. He wasn't sure what exactly to do next, so he fired a shot from his .22 that deflected off the parking lot and out over the river. Vicki got out. She glared at C4.

"What the hell do you think you're doing? This is not you, Cal. Just stop. Give me the gold and go home to Jolene."

"No, this is me. I need to be done with you and your cowboy for good."

Vicki nodded toward her cowboy, who put his gun on the hood of C4's SUV.

As C4 spoke, he walked over and picked up the cowboy's larger caliber semi, placing it in his right hand and checking to make sure the safety was off, moving his own .22 to his left.

"Let's walk down by the river. I'm sure the water is nice this time of year."

"Are you nuts? I've got the cops on my tail and need to get out of town. If you don't have the gold, just say so and we will arrange another drop."

C4 fired his .22 again, between Vicki and the cowboy, again, the shot again ricocheting off the parking lot and out over the river, the singing sound echoing over the water.

"Move it. Get up, face the river and walk."

C4 had never felt so much in control in his whole life. Both his intended victims did as they were told, walking slowly toward the river, Vicki talking to the cowboy, but C4 couldn't hear what she was saying. He decided to move things along. He fired the cowboy's semi between them. The bark was much louder than that of his .22 and the kick was noticeable. The bullet left a noticeable scuffmark on the landing surface,

"Good choice, Cal. Don't want too many of your .22 shell casings to have to pick up."

At that moment the cowboy dropped his phone on the ground. C4 couldn't figure that out. What difference could that make? He was going to die and didn't want his phone to get wet? He'd have to kick it into the river after them,

Vicki turned slowly to face C4.

"Again, Cal, don't do this. I understand some anger. Let's renegotiate. I can work with less than a full ounce of gold a month. I didn't know I was squeezing you that hard. And let my guy go. He has no part of this. I'm the boss, the one you want. Don't kill both of us."

"No, I don't intend to leave any witnesses, Vicki. This has to be clean and complete."

For a short moment nothing happened. Then there was another voice. From the woods behind him.

"Put down your weapons, this is the Burleigh County Sheriff's Department. We have guns trained on you. Any sudden movement and we will shoot. And we won't miss."

C4 froze. Vicki froze and the cowboy froze. Time stood still. C4 thought he might faint. His brain was spinning. For any real gunman, hitting him over the 30 or so yards from the woods was a pretty easy shot. This was not in his perfectly rehearsed plan, and he had no idea what to do. It didn't matter because he had no recourse against a hidden shooter and a loudspeaker from the woods.

He put both guns on the ground. Vicki glared at him.

"Nice job, Cal. If you hadn't screwed this up, you'd be a couple thousand dollars poorer and we'd be on our way out of town. Now we're all going to jail. Maybe for a long time. You can kiss Jolene goodbye if you didn't get around to it this morning."

As she spoke two deputies came out of the woods and two Sheriff's Department cars simultaneously rolled into the parking lot. All three of the criminals were quickly on their knees, then cuffed. The ground was cold and wet. They all watched as the cops bagged both guns and the cowboy's cell phone, and found all three shell casings.

C4 looked at Vicki.

"Maybe you should have been on time."

He had no idea why he said that, but he sure knew he was frustrated with how this had ended. He had to be mad at somebody.

"We were late because we were dodging the cops and would have been long gone if you had just handed me the gold like I asked."

The oldest of the three deputies stood facing the three of them and read them their rights. It had been a long time since C4 had experienced that. Then he asked,

"Anything to say?"

Vicki spoke.

"I was trying to blackmail him."

She nodded her head toward C4,

"And I guess he didn't want that. It's all recorded on his phone."

This time she nodded toward the cowboy.

The deputy looked surprised.

"That's quite an admission. I think we can work with that, along with what we heard ourselves. Get up slowly and let's get going.

They were each put into a separate deputy's car, the two that rolled in together and another car that apparently had belonged to the cops in the woods.

Chapter 31

THE REST OF THE DAY WAS A BLUR. Vicki disappeared down a different hallway, and he and the cowboy were undressed, searched, and directed to dress in the standard orange coveralls with 'Property of Burleigh County' stamped in black across the back. C4 thought about how carefully he had picked out his wardrobe this morning. He had thought that with his mission accomplished he might just wear that outfit all day. Now that was done. The knees of those pants were all wet and muddy anyway.

Fingerprinted, brought into a room for questioning, and asked to write and sign a statement. C4 did the hardest thing he'd ever done in his life. He demanded a lawyer and then called his dad. When his dad showed up a half-hour later, he looked older and sadder than he'd ever seen him look.

Even the conversation with his dad was a blur. The cops made them listen to both Vicki and the cowboy's phone recordings. They weren't perfectly clear but along with the guns and the shell casings and Vicki's admission after their arrest, there was clearly enough there to charge C4 with two counts of attempted murder. It seemed to all be going in slow motion and he could only imagine what Jolene would think. He'd probably never see her again, anyway. Best month of his life. No question. He really felt bad for her. He hoped she could move on with her life, with her house, her college degree and find some guy who was better for her than he had turned out to be.

His thoughts were interrupted by his dad. He looked around, the cops were gone and they were alone.

"I can't fix this, Cal. This is way more serious than anything you've ever done before. All I can do is tell Jolene, which I don't relish, and tell Mr. Baker, which I don't relish, and scrape up the money to post bond. I will help you as much as I can, but you need to make a deal. You're going to prison."

And he stood up and walked out. They were together again a few hours later in the courtroom where his dad stood next to him at his arraignment. At his father's advice he pled not guilty, just to drag things out, and see if see if some extenuating circumstances came up, and to hope for some reasonable bail. He knew he would never admit to stealing the gold from Baker. That was the only thing left he could do for his dad. He hoped Vicki would stay quiet about that as well, but that was all he could do. Hope.

The weekend was the opposite of what he had planned, before his plan to get rid of Vicki failed so spectacularly. His dad came to see him on Saturday afternoon, and they had a brief, strained visit. He told C4 that he had told Jolene, and that she was free to stay in the condo as long as she wanted. Both Kelly and Mr. Baker were in complete shock and CT would have to do all he could to stay married and on the Baker payroll, pretty much leaving C4 twisting in the wind. At his age, he had no choice. Besides C4's actions were completely indefensible.

CT also told him he had advised Jolene to do the same. 'Just put this chapter of your life behind you and move forward,' is what he told C4 his advice to her was.

C4 had been in jail before, a couple of times even having to stay overnight, but this was different. Before, he knew he would walk out and get off with some kind of a fine, usually paid by his dad, or some community service, which he would skip out of as soon as he could, and then his life would go on.

This time there was no light at the end of the tunnel.

Jolene was gone, forever. Marriage, big comfortable home, kids and all that came with it, gone.

His Baker Empire job was gone, forever.

His Baker Empire inheritance was gone, forever.

And the only long-term relationship in his life, his dad, was also gone. It was like he was poison. His dad could not have his new life and C4, so even when he got out of prison, he'd have to move away and take some menial job or hope for some kind of welfare benefits to support him for the rest of his life.

He tried to find something positive. He did come up with a couple of things. One was that Jolene's parents knew nothing of their relationship. She would never have to admit that she was living with and maybe even in love with this now notorious murder suspect. This news would be in all the North Dakota newspapers so they'd hear of it.

The same was true of Trevor's parents. They would never know about him at all.

On the darker side, even Terry would have to admit this was worse than anything she could have told Jolene about him.

Over the course of the weekend quite a few men came and went. Mostly drunk and disorderly charges, C4's personal favorite from his past. Booked, sobered up, bonded out. Not him, he sat there. And as various versions of his former life came and went, he felt old. Every one of these kids still had a chance to straighten out and get their life on track. Not him. That ship had sailed and he was now watching the mast disappear over the horizon. He felt like standing up on a bench and preaching to them, "Repent now, before it is too late."

But he couldn't even let himself do that. He was laughed at, pushed around a bit and couldn't even eat in peace.

Friday turned into Saturday, with that short visit with his dad, then Sunday and still he sat there. Vicki's cowboy was bonded out Saturday morning. No one came for C4.

He went to sleep Sunday night wondering if this was the rest of his life, or if he'd ever get to see the outside world again.

Chapter 32

C4 STEPPED OUT OF THE BURLEIGH COUNTY JAIL into the bright sunlight. It was Monday, and another beautiful late winter day in Bismarck. The sunlight looked good after a weekend in jail. Too bad it was impossible to enjoy. He looked around for his dad's car and didn't see it. He had hoped that despite the situation he was in that his dad could at least pick him up from jail.

It was hope against hope that he'd see Jolene. Maybe she would at least want to say goodbye. He knew their future was gone. The best woman he'd ever had in his life, and he'd screwed it up, just like Vicki said he would.

He had to wonder why Jolene hadn't visited him in jail. Was she that appalled at his crime? Had Terry told her not to visit him? Had his dad told her to stay away? He thought there was something to their relationship that would make her want to see him, even if it was one last time. He could have told her that he did it for her, for them. To save them from Vicki who wanted to destroy them. Their only chance at peace and love and a life together required Vicki to be gone. He did this for Jolene. Didn't she even care?

Maybe she was in shock from losing her husband and now her savior/boyfriend/lover inside of a month. He was glad she had Terry and Carson, and he knew that his dad and Kelly would be helpful to her. C4 was glad she was on better terms with her family and even more glad that she had not mentioned him to them. Now she'd never have to reveal to them that she had been living with him when he went on his murderous rampage. Maybe it was Jolene. Maybe she drove all men crazy.

Then his thought shifted. Maybe this Kent guy could catch her as she fell this time. Would she cry on his shoulder like she had on his? He sincerely hoped she could heal from all this.

He scanned the small parking lot and then the street, sitting down on a bench for a moment, enjoying his temporary freedom. Surely his dad would come. He must just be busy with something. C4 would give him a few more minutes, then just start walking. His condo was only a 20-minute walk. Just then someone appeared from nowhere and sat down next to him, bumping him. C4 jumped up. The last 72 hours in lockup had created that as his natural reaction to any human touching him, or even getting near him. Some parts of his body were bruised from such contact.

He looked back at the bench where he had been perched. It was Vicki, or whatever her real name was.

"What are you doing here? Can't you just leave me alone?"

"Afraid not, Cal."

"Well, go away. My dad will be here to pick me up any time and he won't want to see you."

"He's busy, on a phone call he just can't seem to end. And Jolene is busy too, in case you were thinking her love was deep enough to keep you two together."

"Now you're just being mean."

"We need to talk, Cal. Get in my car."

"No."

"Do I have to stick a gun in your back?"

"You wouldn't dare."

"Seriously? How's my history with violence?"

Vicki walked toward the side street. She looked back. C4 shrugged and followed. Even if she was going to kill him, he figured that might be the best outcome he could hope for. They got into a car he didn't recognize, and she drove away very courteously, sure to follow all the requisite traffic laws.

"Where are we going?"

"For a ride, so we can talk, to start with."

"I have nothing to say to you and given I was just in jail for trying to kill you, it seems odd we have anything to discuss."

"You could say you're sorry. Trying to kill a girl who loves you like I love you is pretty mean."

He looked over at her.

"Just kidding. Let me explain why we're talking."

C4 figured silence was the only way this ride and 'talk' could ever draw to a conclusion, so why prolong it?

"You, Calvin, are going to prison. The DA has an ironclad case. Even if you were able to make a deal, which is unlikely, you would still get three to five years. Normally someone in your situation would then walk out on parole in maybe two or two and a half years."

C4 nodded. As usual, Vicki's logic was flawless.

"Good. I have your attention. Now this is where it gets much worse."

C4 stared straight ahead. He thought losing Jolene and his dad and his new Baker job and spending 3 years in prison was bad enough.

"Now, think about who is already in that prison."

C4 was a little at a loss.

Vicki gave him a moment, then said,

"Let me help you out. How many men in there have you cheated or stolen from over the past decade or two? How many of them have wives or girlfriends or daughters you've slept with? How many guys did your dad help put into that prison? Or just guys who think your dad maybe argued the opposite side of a case a little too strenuously?"

C4 hadn't thought of all that, but he should have. It did not make him feel any better.

"You have so many enemies in there that you won't walk out of prison on parole in two or three years. You'll make your exit from prison in a State of North Dakota-issued plywood box inside of a year. You will be dead in prison. You have too many enemies with grudges and homemade weapons. These are not choirboys you were screwing with."

C4 was way too shocked to talk. Why had he not thought of that? His mind spun. He needed a better deal. He needed to talk to his dad. Vicki let him think for a while.

"That's the stick part of my offer. Now the carrot."

"There's a carrot? What the hell do you mean?"

She opened a center console and pulled out a small bag and from that she produced two passports.

"Look at these and I'll explain."

He opened the first passport. It was British. It had her picture and the name Ellen Rose Wyndmere. He looked over at her. He opened the other passport, also British. It had his picture and the name Arthur Milnor Wyndmere. He looked back over at Vicki.

"Where did you get these? How?"

"Never mind, Arthur. Here's the deal. I have, over the years in the private eye business, squirreled away nice sum of money in the British parts of the Caribbean. Enough for both of us to live for say, 50 years, easily. I have a small villa. I have a nice sailboat. You do know how to sail, don't you? Never mind, I can teach you."

"This is absurd, Vicki. We can't do this. I can't do this. What about Jolene, what about my dad? He posted my bail!"

"Slow down, Arthur. One thing at a time.

First, your dad. He will be reimbursed for your bail money via some legal work a friend of mine needs done. Not much work, but lots of money. Besides, he has Kelly and the Baker fortune. He also has, unless Jolene beats him to it, the cash from the gold you stole from Baker. He'll be fine. And to wrap it up, you left him a letter, apologizing for everything you've done and explaining that you have no choice but to go away. Can't tell him where, but you'll be fine, and you know he'll be fine. You end by thanking him for all he's ever done for you."

Vicki paused to let that soak in. C4 had to admit it was a decent solution for his dad. He'd no longer be a burden, like he had been for all his life. Vicki continued.

"And you know, deep down, that you can't have Jolene. You really never could. You adore her. Hell, I adore her. She's like a poster girl for the perfect young woman. And she almost turned you into a model citizen. But she needs a better life than you can give her, even if she loves you and visits you in prison and waits for you to get out. But you won't. For reasons we've already covered. Besides, Terry already has her next husband picked out, and she'll be just fine. And if that fails, I doubt she'll have any trouble attracting a top-notch mate."

C4 hung his head. He knew she was right. It was a great relationship, but everyone had told him it could not last and by trying to kill Vicki and going to jail he had ended all hope. He felt like crying. But that did raise an interesting question in his mind. Before he could speak, Vicki said,

"Let's wrap up Jolene. You left her a letter also, very loving, very thoughtful, full of how much you care about her. In fact, you went to jail trying to protect her, and you are now, again, doing what is best for her. You wish her all the happiness she deserves in life. You will always treasure your time together. I've never seen her without clothes like you have, but I'm guessing that's a big part of what you treasured. I know you also saw her with the full effect of Trevor's last beating. That couldn't have been quite so much fun to look at. You go on to say that you know she'll find someone who can give her the life she deserves. You also know your dad will help her with anything she needs. You really laid it on. I almost cried at how kind and loving you were in that letter."

C4 was actually touched by the tone of the letter that had been written on his behalf. It was about as good as Jolene could get from him. But he still had the same bee stuck in his bonnet.

"But I tried to kill you."

"Yes, but with good reason. I tried to blackmail you. Lucky for me, murder is not your strong suit, and I always travel with protection. Besides, given the lives we've lived, these things happen."

"And you are being tried for attempting to kill Baker."

"That was actually an accident. He was angry and tried to grab me when I was trying to leave. I tried to push him away and he slipped and fell down the stairs. I was actually arraigned for assault of a senior citizen under some elder protection law or another. They also found some other old warrants, besides the blackmail charges that I volunteered on the phone recording. Regardless, that is why I need to go away, too. Try to keep up. I do have friends in prison, but also a lot of enemies."

By this time, they were on I-94 headed east. This was too much to process, so Cal had to leave their whereabouts aside for a bit.

"When and how will my dad and Jolene get these letters?"

"They'll be mailed from California in a few days. We'll be long gone by then."

"Where are we going?"

"The Caribbean, like I said. We'll drive to Fargo, dump the car, catch the ride to Minneapolis I've arranged, fly on a pre-booked charter to Miami, then take a private boat over to the Bahamas. After that, we are on our own."

"And you arranged all this?"

"Sadly, I've been working on this for a long time. I knew it was my only viable retirement plan. I just pulled it together once I got out of jail Friday afternoon, while your dad let you sit there for a couple more days."

"And why are you taking me with you and not killing me?"

Vicki laughed.

"Be sure to call me Ellen from now on, Arthur, though I know you've grown to love me as Vicki. As I said when we first met at the Oilpatch, I find you interesting, and as I get to know you more and more, you are now bordering on intriguing. I like you. There I said it."

"But I tried to kill you."

"You need to get over that. I have. Things like that happen in my line of work."

"Your line of work?"

"Let me give you some history."

C4 looked over at his companion and said,

"That might be helpful, though there are things I may not want to know."

"We are in bed together now, Art, long term. There are some things you need to know."

She continued.

"When we first met at the Oilpatch, I knew you weren't from Montana because I am. I grew up there and started my adult life as a deputy in the Yellowstone County Sheriff's Department. I quickly learned there is a lot more money to be made on the other side of the badge. So I resigned, got my PI license and worked both sides, maximizing my income and influence. Need a search without a warrant? I can do that. Need some justice when the court system failed? I can do that. Need somebody watched for a while? I can do that. Need somebody removed from a situation? I did that too. As things warmed up in Montana I migrated my business into western North Dakota.

When I came to your hotel room in Dickinson, I wasn't running from anyone. The first cowboy you bluffed out of that poker game was a hothead who was sure you had cheated and he was going to kill you. I cut him off, telling him I'd take care of it. I came to your room and stayed, and with a phone call, had him urgently reassigned by his employer from Dickinson to an oilfield north of Williston. He had to leave town. Saved you and him at the same time. But I did enjoy your company, until you stole that money from my purse. That's when the relationship started. I had to track you down, see who you were and how you lived. And, of course, take a shot at getting my money back."

She paused to sip her coffee. C4 said the only thing he could think of.

"Relationship?"

"Sure, what else is it? We met in grocery stores, diners, and liquor stores and eventually collided when you stole from old man Baker."

She continued.

"But there's a wrinkle I hadn't expected. I hadn't figured on Jolene moving in with you. That's where it got sticky. I had Trevor taken out, let's say, but not so you could shack up with his adorable little wife. There were many other reasons. He was fighting with everybody, and bordering on getting fired in an industry that has an unbelievable tolerance for bad behavior. He owed money to everybody under the sun, more than he could ever pay back. He actually bragged to his coworkers about roughing Jolene up. He simply had to go. He could never pay off his debts and was a threat to world order. Or at least our part of the world. Freeing Jolene was a great side benefit. Her keeping his employer and worker's comp benefits was a key part of the plan.

"How in the world did you arrange his death?"

"I didn't say I did. I just said it might have happened."

C4 shook his head. Semantics were not one of his strong suits. Vicki continued.

"Lonely country road, narrow little bridge crossing a deep ravine. A sudden set of headlights aimed right at him, an old seatbelt with some aging assistance. One guy who checked on him at the bottom of the ravine to make sure he was dead and then the suspicious headlights and any tracks all disappeared."

C4 was somewhere beyond astounded. Vicki continued,

"Settle down, Art. If anything, this proves that if I wanted you dead, you'd be dead. I like you enough to keep you alive. And I need a partner. I'd get lonely in the islands. Jolene moving in with you caused me some concern, but I knew you'd end it via some shenanigan or another and I was right. Damn, she is the whole package though, and I do admire your ability to keep her as long as you did. But then I'm the total package, too. Just a little different package. Like an aged scotch, enhanced by time and experience."

C4 looked at Vicki for a while, just trying to take it all in. He replayed all she had said and had to admit it was the best possible solution to their joint dilemma. If she had taken out Trevor, had she done others? And saving Jolene was an added goal? She had set Jolene up for a good life and now she was doing the same thing for him.

C4 thought for what seemed to be a long time before he spoke again. Vicki seemed to be willing to accommodate that.

"I think I'm getting the picture, Ellen. But I do have a couple of loose ends I'd like to get tied up."

"Go ahead, Art. Shoot."

Vicki smiled a bit without taking her eyes off the road.

"Sorry, that was just too easy. I've got a wicked sense of humor."

"I figured you might. Here's the first one. More of a puzzle than anything. Did you tell the Bismarck Police they'd find Jolene with me? And why the heads-up call to me?"

"I may have been behind that. I actually try to help the police when it works out for me. I figured why have them running all over Bismarck to find her, and I wanted to make sure you were decently enough dressed to let them in. Just common courtesy all around."

C4 nodded. Seemed to make sense. He processed that then moved on.

"For my dad's sake, him and his new wife. Did you kill the gold theft investigation?"

"I did. Told Lankin I had found nothing at all and to let it drop. It had to have been stolen long ago, if at all. Maybe Baker just had bad records or memory. You'll meet him in a bit. Nice guy."

"Meet him? How? Why?"

"He's our ride to Minneapolis, then he'll come back and arrange for this car go to California and be ditched there. Near the town where your dad and Jolene's letters will be mailed. That ties up another loose end you hadn't questioned."

"Why include him?"

Vicki laughed out loud.

"Seriously, Art, I thought you'd be better at this than you are. This makes him complicit, if he ever wakes up and figures out you took the gold. He would then have to admit or at least acknowledge that he helped you get away. Besides, he's not doing these tasks for free."

C4 had to smile at that. Vicki really was good at this. She went on.

"Don't worry Art, the letters are being handled by someone different, so no connection, except by inference. And by the way, I told Jolene to keep the cash and please, not mention it to anyone. It's the least you could do for her. No need to cause your dad to wonder how you came by all that cash. She's to offer to return the three gold coins Baker gave you."

It took more time for C4 to let this all soak in. He couldn't think of a flaw in this plan or any more questions, so offered the one thing he could think of.

"Let me know if you want me to drive a while, Ellen."

"I can handle it. But first one more thing. There's a little pouch in the bottom of that same bag. We need the contents of that pouch."

C4 did as she instructed. He opened the pouch and there were two beautiful wedding rings, one plain gold band and one with a nice diamond in a beautiful setting. He looked over at Vicki, now Ellen, who reached her left hand partway across her body to toward him as she drove.

"Ring me, Art."

He slid the diamond ring onto her finger. She smiled at him.

"And without even copping a feel. What did that girl do to you? We need to work on getting the old C4 back. Now put yours on."

He slid the ring onto his own left ring finger. It was a little big, but not too bad.

She smiled at him again and said,

"I now pronounce us the Wyndmeres."